SO

No family celebra[...] [...] Texas. Every year [...] [...]tion and gifts (always homemade) from the rest of the family. But the twentieth birthday of a Daltry child is a special event. When a Daltry turns twenty years old, Grandmother Minerva (a great fan of classical mythology) assigns the young one a "labor," in the tradition of the twelve labors of Hercules. Only three aspects of Minerva's challenges are predictable: the labor will last one year, it will help to build her grandchild's character, and it will not be easy . . .

The Ladies' Man by Lorraine Heath
Oldest son Hercules must quit ranching and be the town schoolmarm for a year . . .

The Wallflower by Linda Francis Lee
Shy daughter Persephone must spend a year in New York as a debutante . . .
Available in August 1995

The Matchmaker by Debra S. Cowan
Lovesick Cupid has one year to find a husband for a comely girl . . .
Available in October 1995

The Flirt by Rachelle Nelson
Flirtatious Venus must spend a year in the company of a blind man . . .
Available in January 1996

The Tomboy by Mary Lou Rich
Atalanta has to learn to cook, dance, and be a lady . . .
Available in February 1996

The Perfect Gentleman by Elaine Crawford
Atlas must put away his lists and take out a popular widow . . .
Available in April 1996

The Ladies' Man

Lorraine Heath

J

JOVE BOOKS, NEW YORK

THE LADIES' MAN

A Jove Book / published by arrangement with
the author

PRINTING HISTORY
Jove edition / June 1995

ISBN: 0-515-11636-X

A JOVE BOOK®
Jove Books are published by The Berkley Publishing Group,
200 Madison Avenue, New York, New York 10016.
JOVE and the "J" design are trademarks
belonging to Jove Publications, Inc.

PRINTED IN THE UNITED STATES OF AMERICA

10 9 8 7 6 5 4 3 2 1

**To Melinda Metz,
who guided me
when I didn't realize I was lost**

The Ladies'
Man

Chapter One

August 20, 1878

Hercules Daltry needed to get away.

Away from the secretive meetings.

Away from the hushed giggles.

Away from the mounting excitement.

And most of all—away from the unknown.

Normally when he felt the need to escape, he hightailed it to his thinking place, but right now the last thing he wanted to do was think.

What he wanted—what he needed—was a distraction.

At the edge of town he passed the church at a flying gallop and circled the schoolhouse, taunting the demons of his past with the knowledge that he'd somehow managed to escape them. It was a ritual he performed every time he rode his favorite horse, Pegasus, into town.

With the expertise of a man accustomed to long hours in the saddle, he eased the white stallion into a slow walk as they neared the main street of Paradise Plains. He needed time to consider his options before he dismounted.

He couldn't stop by the Buccaneer for a meal because his sister, Persy, was preparing a feast in honor of his birthday. Lucky's Saloon offered male companionship, but he wasn't in the mood to discuss how the Texas and Pacific Railroad was going to affect the ranchers in the area as it began its push toward West Texas. What he wanted was a pleasant distraction.

Then he caught sight of a vibrant red that was almost bright orange emerging from beneath the delicate branches of a weeping willow tree beside the boardinghouse. The color reminded him of a sun setting beyond the horizon just before a storm swept across the land.

And it belonged to a woman—the most pleasant kind of distraction a man could find.

She'd pulled her hair back and tied it in place with a black ribbon, but it was still her most striking feature. She was delightfully small. If he wrapped his arms around her, the top of her head would probably come no higher than the center of his chest. Her slim hips barely swayed and her feet didn't stir the dust as she strolled across the wide main street.

Either he'd spent too much of the summer tending his cattle or the woman was a recluse because he'd remember if he'd seen hair that shade before—and he hadn't. Then another possibility slowly took shape in his mind. She might be new in town, in which case he felt obligated to welcome her. She was just the sort of distraction he was looking for.

She entered one of several clapboard buildings that lined Main Street. He drew his horse to a halt before the storefront that proudly proclaimed "Hank and Maybelle's Mercantile." He dismounted, not bothering to tether Pegasus. When he tamed a horse, he tamed him completely. Only his whistle would cause the stallion to move from his spot.

Confidently he ambled onto the boardwalk and opened

the door to the mercantile. A cluster of assorted bells jangled above his head just before the owner greeted him. "Howdy, Lee."

Closing the door, he nodded toward the portly man standing behind the counter. "Hank." He gave his eyes a minute to adjust to the gloom of the store. He'd tell Hank to build more windows, but the man had already stacked boxes of merchandise in front of the existing windows so they barely let in the sunlight.

"Is there something in particular you're looking for?" Hank asked.

Yep, he was looking for something in particular, and he spotted her at the far end of the counter, running her fingers over some hair ribbons. "Nah, just lookin'."

"I could show you some new things I got in just this—"

"No, thanks, Hank. I'm just gonna look over here." Lee pointed toward a far corner.

"You sure? 'Cuz I ordered—"

"I'm sure." To prove his point, he lumbered to the back of the store. He'd forgotten how nosy Hank was. He'd have to wait for the little lady to move away from the counter, or Hank would stick his balding head between them so he could hear every word they said.

Carefully he eased his way between the shelves that were laden with items no one ever bought because no one but Hank could figure out what they were used for. It took some maneuvering, but he was finally able to see the woman without Hank seeing him.

Only her back was visible. Her white bodice billowed out slightly until it met her black skirt at her tiny waist. Her hair was long enough to dip a little farther and touch her backside. He wondered if that backside carried one or two dimples. He heard her soft voice as she said something to Hank, but all the contraptions displayed between them muffled her words.

She walked toward the side of the store away from the door. He could barely see the top of her head over the merchandise. He crept toward her and peered around the shelving.

Damn! She was looking at books, actually turning the cover back on one as though she was interested in the words. She slipped two fingers beneath one lens of her spectacles and nudged them farther up the bridge of her tiny nose. Then she turned the page of the book. Surely she couldn't read that fast! She hadn't lifted her gaze from the book so she was either staring or reading, and he knew from experience staring at a book wasn't any fun.

If he was smart, he'd turn around and walk out of the mercantile, but more than one teacher had proven he was dumber than a fence post so leaving wasn't an option.

He waited another minute to make certain Hank wasn't going to come over and show her some newfangled gadget, then he made his move. "Afternoon."

She spun around, her palm pressed just below her throat, and he gazed into big brown eyes. The thick lenses of her spectacles magnified her eyes way out of proportion to the rest of her face. Blinking rapidly, she reminded him of a baby barn owl he'd once nursed back to health after he found it with a broken wing.

"You new in town?" he asked in a low voice, hoping Hank was busy with something else and wouldn't wander over to investigate the whispering.

Meredith Lewis had been so engrossed in the prose of Louisa May Alcott that she hadn't heard the man approach, but she was certain he wasn't addressing her. Men, particularly men with deep blue eyes that resembled a Texas sky at dawn, simply did not approach her nor did they engage her in conversation.

She glanced over her shoulder. The only thing visible was the cluttered counter. Had someone walked away?

Surely, the man would strive to reach the person who'd been there. Taking an uneven breath, she dared to glance back in the man's direction. He was still standing there, apparently waiting for an answer . . . an answer from her.

She shifted her gaze to the broad expanse of his chest and followed the lines to his shoulders. The tan shirt he wore did nothing to disguise the fact that he'd been shaped by the land, molded into brawn, tempered into steel. Yet he somehow gave the appearance of being apart from the cowboys she'd previously seen. She intertwined her fingers, wishing her heart palpitations would slow. "Yes, I arrived a few days ago."

His curling brown hair touched the collar of his shirt and became more visible as he swept off his broad-brimmed hat, angled his head, and bestowed upon her a smile that caused tiny dimples to form on either side of his full lips. "Then welcome to Paradise Plains. The friendliest town this side of Fort Worth."

In spite of her education and thorough acquaintance with all sorts of books, fact and fiction, she had no idea how one responded to this sort of welcome. The only response she could think of sounded trite and inane, but she decided it was better than no response at all. "Thank you."

"Got family here?"

"No."

Lee wished he had a lantern he could hold over her face. He thought he'd seen sadness touch her brown eyes and wondered at its cause. Hank really needed to do something about the light in this store. He'd probably sell all his gadgets if people could see them more clearly. "You staying at the boardinghouse?"

"Yes, Mrs. Bennett had a room available."

His smile softened. "Ah, she's a sweetheart. Have you met Simon yet?"

Meredith pursed her lips. "Indeed, I have made his acquaintance."

He laughed, a deep, rich rumble that vibrated off the merchandise surrounding them and reached out to caress her soul.

Leaning close, he confided in a low voice, "I know she loves her grandson dearly and spoils him rotten, but I'll tell you the honest to gosh truth. I can only take about five minutes with the little holy terror before I'm ready to toss him out the window."

Her lips quivered as she fought back her smile. "He does seem to be a bit of a discipline problem," she admitted.

"He's as rambunctious as a newborn colt, but then I guess most young'uns are which is why I try and steer clear of them."

"Don't you like children?"

"I got nothing against them. It's just that I've learned they move fast, fear nothing, and get into everything. I figure all children should be named Pan until they're at least sixteen years old."

Meredith couldn't believe her ears. The last thing she'd expected to discover in the developing West was an educated man. Excitement swelled within her breast at the opportunity to engage in a conversation that was comprised of more than a few grunted yeps and nopes. "Are you familiar with the classics?"

"The classics?"

"Homer?"

He furrowed his brow. "We had a Homer working for us once during roundup, but I don't recall his last name being Classic. Think it was Smith or something like that."

Then he smiled again, and Meredith almost believed he was teasing her. It was a devastating smile, the kind that could take away a woman's breath and fill her head with all manner of fanciful dreams.

Convinced his smile could not be intended for her, she looked to see who was behind her. No one. She wondered if perhaps someone had strolled by, catching his attention and bringing forth his smile, but when she again looked in his direction, his smile was still in place, his blue gaze focused on her.

Her heart went into a crazy waltz that caused hope to blossom within her chest. She'd heard that women were a rarity in this part of Texas, but even so she'd not dared entertain the idea that a man would be desperate enough to give her his attention, to overlook her plain features in order to appreciate her fine mind. Her journey west had been hinged on a dream that revolved around children, but not the prospect of a family.

The door to the mercantile opened, setting off the jangling of bells, just before it slammed shut.

"Hank, you seen a red-haired lady in here?"

"Yep, she's over there looking at books."

Worry creasing her brow, she diverted her attention away from her imaginative musings and the man standing before her. Slowly she turned around as a barrel-shaped man rounded the corner and came to an abrupt halt. "Miss Lewis?"

"Yes."

The man jerked his hat off his head. What remained of his white hair stuck out in all directions. "Miss Lewis, I'm Sheriff Sampson. I need to have a word with you." He spoke with a slow drawl, his white mustache barely following the movement of his lips.

"Is there a problem?" the man behind her asked.

The sheriff's gaze snapped away from Meredith, and he scowled. "I just make you one of my deputies, Lee?"

"You don't have any deputies."

"Exactly, so this here ain't none of your business."

"Isn't," Meredith said. The sheriff's gaze snapped back

to her. "It isn't any of his business. Ain't is not a word."

"Well, now, little lady, I been saying ain't for nigh on forty-five years, and if it ain't a word, it sure as hell ought to be." He held up a hand before she could continue. "Now, what I got to say to you is best said in private so why don't you come over to the office with me?"

"Want me to come with you?"

Meredith felt the warm, comforting hand on her shoulder and lifted her gaze to the man the sheriff called Lee. She'd spent her life longing for a touch such as the one he seemed to give without thinking. It was the kind of touch most people took for granted. Unfortunately, she didn't know this man well enough to impose upon his kindness. Shaking her head, she offered him a small smile. "Thank you, but I'm certain I can handle the situation."

"I don't mind."

"Hell, Lee," the sheriff growled. "I already told you it ain't none of your business."

"She's new in town, Tommy. She might not know your growl is worse than your bite."

"I ain't gonna growl at her, and I ain't gonna bite her. I just gotta talk to her, and if it concerned you, I'd invite you, too, but it don't, so head on home. Ain't you got something you need to be doing today?"

Reluctantly Lee removed his hand from her slender shoulder and placed his hat on his head. "You treat her kindly, Tommy, or you'll answer to me." Then tipping his hat, he bestowed upon Miss Lewis the most charming smile he possessed. "It's been a pleasure, ma'am."

Then he damned the dim light because he couldn't tell if she was blushing. He watched Tommy escort her from the mercantile. She walked with precise movements, no exaggerated swaying of her hips, no swinging of her arms. She was all prim and proper. He wished she'd talked a little more. He liked the gentle lilt of her voice and the way she talked ten times faster than anyone around these parts would ever think about talking.

He heaved a deep sigh. The distraction hadn't lasted long enough, but it was probably for the best. He'd given the wrong answer about Homer—he'd seen it in her eyes, which was why he'd given her the smile. He'd learned early on how to tell when he sounded dumb, and he'd learned to cover the wrong answers with a smile that would make females forget they'd even asked a question. Unfortunately, the tactic seldom worked on teachers, and he had the scars to prove it.

He walked out of the mercantile, mounted Pegasus, and prodded his stallion into a gallop toward home. After meeting Miss Lewis, he wasn't in the mood to seek out another distraction.

Of course, he wasn't in the mood to face what lay before him either.

Chapter Two

For twenty years this day had been coming, its arrival anticipated, imagined . . . dreaded.

Lee wondered if those who had come before him had been as apprehensive about their twentieth birthday as he was.

Probably not.

He blamed his grandfather. A cattle baron, the man had loved Lee's grandmother too much and indulged her every whim, including her infatuation with mythology.

He should have put his foot down when his wife had given their firstborn child a year-long labor to perform on his twentieth birthday.

Instead, he'd encouraged her. When his grandfather had passed away, he'd left Lee's grandmother enough wealth that she could enjoy her winter years and bestow upon her grandchildren a great prize when they completed the labor she assigned them.

Lee would have preferred a pair of socks.

He released a shuddering breath, removed his hat, and wiped his sleeve across his sweating brow.

Nature's warm fingers passed through his curling brown hair, scattering some of his tension on the wind as he rode toward home. At his back, the sun elongated the shadow of horse and rider until it appeared that a centaur traversed the gently rolling Texas plains.

As the eldest grandchild, he was haunted by the prospect of not living up to the challenge his grandmother would place before him this evening.

Although his own labor was enshrouded in mystery, he knew in minute detail the labors she'd assigned to those who had come before him. Over the years, he'd listened to the embellished tales that circled on the wind like a siren's song, drawing him toward adulthood, toward his own labor. The passage of time had lent a magical, almost mythical quality to the labors performed by his aunts and uncles— and his father, Odysseus.

Not one had failed to complete the assigned task; each had received a grand prize worthy of his or her accomplishment.

But Lee didn't care about the prize. His only concern was that he didn't fail, didn't disappoint his family. Although his parents never admitted it, he knew he'd disappointed them once before, and he was determined not to disappoint them again.

As the barn and corral came into view, he eased Pegasus into a slower lope, sensing his steed's reluctance to diminish his speed as though he, too, were anxious to take a gander at the unfamiliar mare prancing around the corral. Her coat was as white as virgin snow. She tilted her head at a haughty angle as though she knew neither man nor beast would find her lacking.

Dismounting, Lee folded his arms over the top railing of the corral as Pegasus sidled up beside him and nudged his shoulder. He would have sworn he heard his horse release a sigh of longing. Affectionately he patted his prized stallion. "I'd introduce you if I knew her name."

"Her name's Cassiopeia."

Lee snapped his head around, his gaze falling on his twelve-year-old sister. Allie was leaning so far over the railing it was a wonder she didn't fall into the corral, and a wonder he hadn't noticed her. Dust covered her pants, and bits of straw clung to her short curling brown hair.

"Where'd she come from?" he asked.

With exaggeration, she rolled her gray eyes toward the clear azure sky. "From another mare, of course! Honestly, Lee, sometimes you're not the brightest bunny in the burrow."

Despite the teasing tone in her voice, the innocence of her years, he felt the tiny jabs to his pride as though she'd used a pickax instead of words. "I meant why's she here?"

Swinging a leg over the railing, she straddled the fence. "I guess 'cuz Grandma bought her."

"Who'd she buy her for?"

"For herself I reckon."

"But she's not tamed, is she?"

"Nope. That's why I gotta stay on this side of the fence." She hopped down. "I'd best go find Bub. I was supposed—" Guiltily she stopped and glanced around.

"Supposed to what?"

"You'll see!" she called out over her shoulder as she ran off.

He watched her disappear into the barn, then turned his attention back to the mare. No one on this ranch was better at breaking a horse than he was. The tension that had been building within him all day melted away. Coincidence hadn't brought this untamed thoroughbred to the ranch on his birthday. Her presence could only mean one thing—the waiting was finally over.

After all these years of speculating, he knew at last what his labor would be. He had little doubt his grandmother wanted the horse trained for a particular purpose, but he knew horses as well as he knew the palm of his hand. Whatever his grandmother required of him and the mare, he was up to the task.

The mare stopped prancing and watched him through deep brown eyes. He was reminded of Miss Lewis and her huge, round eyes. He hoped the sheriff hadn't given her upsetting news. Tomorrow, he'd pay her a visit at the boardinghouse. It was the neighborly thing to do. Besides, for all the smiles he'd given her, she hadn't given him one. He'd seen a tiny one or two struggling to break free, but those hardly counted. He wanted to see those soft lips tilt up until the corners of her eyes crinkled.

He reached into his pocket, dug out some sugar, and held his cupped palm toward the mare.

Tentatively she approached and nudged his hand before greedily claiming the offering.

"So, Cassiopeia, you like sweets. I'll be sure and remember that." He rubbed the velvety smoothness of her muzzle. "Grandma's waited twenty years for this day. I sure don't intend to disappoint her."

Releasing a deep, cleansing breath, he felt ready to embrace the evening and all that awaited him. He swaggered toward the stables, Pegasus reluctantly following.

Lee saw the rapidly moving blur just before it rammed into him. Even though he'd been caught unawares, he had the advantage of a large, brawny build while the blur was little more than gangling arms and legs. He released an "Oomph!" but remained standing while the blur bounced off him and ended up sprawled on the ground. "What in Hades are you doing, Bub?"

His brother's gray eyes widened. "Nothin'." Atlas scrambled to a sitting position and began gathering the straw and twigs he'd dropped in the fall.

"What's that?" Lee asked.

"Nothin'." His gaze danced around the area, never lighting long enough to really take note of anything. "You seen Allie?"

"She was headed for the barn."

Atlas darted around Lee and disappeared around the side of the stables. At eleven, he was a year younger than Allie. Like a yawning abyss, too many years separated them both from Lee. He'd never attempted to bridge the years.

When they were babies, he felt like a giant hovering over their cribs. An awkward giant with clumsy hands that seemed disproportionate to the rest of his body and a brain that couldn't think of an interesting thing to say. The one time he tried to talk to Allie, she started bawling like a newborn calf when its mother runs out of milk. Her wide open mouth and tears had scared the living daylights out of him.

Shaking his head, Lee ambled into the building where the thoroughbred horses they used for pleasure riding were housed. The work horses and cow ponies were kept near the herd where they were most needed. He settled Pegasus into his stall. Taking the time to groom him, he tried to ignore the whispers in the adjoining barn that were increasing in volume with each passing moment. He knew he should finish with Pegasus and leave before he heard what he was certain he wasn't supposed to hear, but the whispering turned into arguing that the walls could no longer hold at bay.

"I like it, Bub," Allie whispered harshly.

"But it ain't on the list."

"So?" she asked in a singsong voice that had a ripple of teasing floating through it.

"We made a list of everything that was gonna go on Lee's gift, and dog ain't on the list."

"Then add dog to your list."

"You can't add to a list once it's done," Atlas explained slowly as though she were dense.

"Why not?"

"Because there'd be no point in having a list if you could change it anytime you wanted."

"Why do we have to use a list? Why can't we just put anything we want on this little herd of cattle we're making Lee for his birthday?"

Grimacing, Lee wished he hadn't heard exactly what they were working on. He'd have to act doubly surprised when he opened the gift, and he was afraid the squabble he'd just overheard would come to his mind and betray his knowledge.

He gave Pegasus extra oats before quietly walking through the stables and wandering toward the house. For weeks, he'd heard the hushed whispers behind closed doors. He would have taken offense if he hadn't known his birthday was approaching and understood his family's deep love of birthday surprises.

As he neared the back of the house, an abundance of cinnamon floated out the open kitchen window and teased his nostrils. If he was lucky, Persy might have set a pie or a batch of cookies on the sill to cool. On more than one occasion he'd snitched her goodies while they were cooling.

She was a year younger than Lee, and they'd spent many a night sitting in the gazebo, gazing at the stars, and dreaming. Often their discussion drifted to what they each thought their labor might be, what they each hoped it would be, and they always wondered if it would change their lives as much as their father's labor had changed his.

The wind whisked the blue gingham curtains outside and flicked them against the wall. Lee peered around the fluttering cloth, but the windowsill was bare. Cautiously he glanced into the kitchen. With his long reach, he could sometimes snitch something off the sideboard—but only if Persy was occupied with something else. She was timid about most things, but she took her cooking seriously and didn't hesitate to slap wandering fingers that were trying to take her creations before she was ready to present them.

He could see Persy, her blond hair braided, sprinkling flour on the oaken table. C.J. sat with his lean, sinewy body hunched over the table while he drew hearts in the flour.

Persy set a large earthenware bowl on the table, shooed C.J.'s hand away, and plopped the dough onto the floured surface. She punched the dough, then picked up her wooden roller.

"Are you sure you don't want to talk about it?" she asked tenderly.

C.J. lolled his blond head from side to side.

"Might help," she prodded as she flicked some flour toward his face.

He failed to notice, sighed, and drew arrows through the hearts she hadn't yet covered with the dough. "I just can't decide which one to give up."

"Which one of what?"

"My girlfriends."

Persy stopped flattening the dough. "I thought you were worried about Lee's birthday present."

"I am. Since we can't give presents that are bought, I figured to let him court one of my girlfriends since I've got so many."

She laughed lightly. "Lee doesn't have a problem finding women to keep him company."

"But he's never been serious about any of them, and I thought maybe it was because I've got all the good ones. I mean, he's never even brought one home."

"He will when he meets the right one."

He lifted his head, relief clearly reflected in his blue eyes.

"So you don't think he'll mind if I keep my girlfriends to myself?"

"I'm sure he won't mind," Persy assured him.

"Great!" He hopped off the tall chair their father had built for Persy when she was a child so she could reach the table and make her tiny cakes. He walked to the back of the kitchen and lifted something off another table.

Persy spun around and stalked after him. "Give me that!"

He laughed. "Ah, Persy, let me have it."

All Lee could see was Persy hopping up and down reaching for something C.J. was holding high above her head.

"That's for Lee's birthday," she said curtly.

"But I've got a powerful hunger. I'm seventeen, a growing boy. This summer, I've almost grown as tall as Lee, but if you don't feed me, I'll shrink down till I'm as tiny as you."

"Dinner will be in an hour. You can wait."

"Ah, come on, Persy. My mouth's been watering for this thing ever since I walked into the kitchen."

"So has mine, but I've put off tasting it. Now put it down. I don't want Lee's surprise ruined. I set a bowl of cinnamon before the window so if he came snooping around he'd only smell cinnamon, and I don't need you messing up my careful plans."

C.J. edged around the kitchen, and Persy lunged for him. He slung his arm out the window and almost hit Lee in the eye. The aroma of warm blueberries assailed Lee's nostrils, and his mouth started watering. He could snatch that blueberry tart out of C.J.'s hand and run like Hermes. With any luck, they'd think Atlas took it.

But if luck wasn't with him, and Persy saw him, she'd be disappointed that her surprise was ruined, especially after going to so much trouble to hide it. C.J. drew his hand into the kitchen, his laughter and teasing dancing around Persy.

Quickly Lee stepped away from the window, wishing he could wait to see who won. As he walked around to the front of the house, he put his money on Persy.

In the late afternoon shadows, his mother was kneeling before her flower garden, her blond head bowed over her sketch pad as she drew a likeness of one of her flowers. She loved her flowers almost as much as she loved her children, and like her children, each flower was unique, created by her loving hand.

Removing his hat, Lee hunkered before her. She set her sketch pad and pencil aside before reaching up to tousle his hair as though he were no more than four years old.

"You've been spying on your brothers and sisters, haven't you?" she asked, a challenge forming in her clear blue eyes.

He flashed a smile, and she wagged her finger at him. "That smile may work its wiles on the ladies of Paradise Plains, but I assure you, Hercules Daltry, it won't work on me."

He ducked his head, but his smile didn't fade away. "Ah, Ma, I didn't mean to spy on anybody. It's just that there's so many people in this family, a man can't hardly walk around without stepping on them."

"A man," she said wistfully as she placed her palm against his strong, square jaw. "And when did you become a man?"

His smile deepened, causing the small dimples to form on either side of his mouth. "I've been a man for a long time now."

"I find it hard to believe that today you are as old as your father was when I fell in love with him."

"Always before on my birthday, Pa would tell us about the labor Grandma gave him on his twentieth birthday, and how he met you while he was working on it. I don't guess he'll be telling us the story tonight."

Jane Daltry gave her head a small shake. "No, I don't imagine he will. Your father was the youngest, the last Daltry to be given a labor. I imagine tonight will be spent speculating about the future instead of reliving the past."

"Any notion as to what that future might involve?" Lee asked, unsuccessfully hiding his apprehension, his smile slipping into something smaller.

"No. Your father told me that Minerva hoards her ideas for a labor the way Midas hoarded his gold." She patted his cheek. "But whatever it is, I know you'll succeed."

His smile again became broad as he thought of the white mare. "Yes, ma'am, I'll succeed. I won't disappoint you or Grandma."

"None of my children could ever disappoint me." She picked up her sketch pad.

He watched the way her delicate hand moved the charcoal pencil to create on paper what her hands had created in the earth. Sometimes, her flowers didn't blossom the way she expected them to, but she still pointed to them with pride when neighbors came to call. If she extended that much understanding toward a plant, how much more she must extend toward her children. He wrapped his massive arms around her, knowing he hadn't turned out exactly as she'd expected, knowing she didn't hold it against him. "I love you, Ma."

She hugged him in return. "I meant what I said, Hercules. You have never disappointed me. Now run along so you won't know which of these flowers I plan to use to decorate the table for tonight's celebration."

Lee released her, unfurled his body, and strolled into the house. He heard the echo of his father's hammer as the scent of sawdust filled his nostrils. Odysseus Daltry had a love for architecture that rivaled Lee's love of the land, and he never failed to use it when any occasion arose that might require his talents. It wasn't exactly spying to glance into the family room since the door stood ajar.

Odie twisted around and smiled at the half-hidden face. "Lee, come in. Tell me what you think of your gift."

Lee pushed the door open so his large frame could enter the room. In awe, he studied his father's latest project.

Where a small window had once looked over the ranch, now a myriad of windows embraced the wall. Sunlight streamed in through the glass to touch the large oak bench his father had crafted beneath the windows. Lee would be able to sit there and look across the land he cherished. It was an enormous gift his father had given him, a reflection of his father's love, a testament to how well his father knew him.

"It just sorta brings the ranch into the room, doesn't it?" his father asked, his large hands resting on his hips as he tipped back and forth on his heels, satisfaction written across his face.

"Yes, sir, it does."

"Can you just imagine sitting on this seat in the window and reading?"

Actually, Lee couldn't imagine sitting anywhere and reading. It wasn't that he didn't like books. He did. He liked the way they looked, the way they felt in his hands, and especially the way they smelled, but reading was a slow task. It seemed his mind always wandered on to a greater adventure faster than the words on the page could take him.

"Now, go on and get out of here and pretend you haven't seen it when I give it to you tonight." Odie knelt before the bench to polish his handiwork.

Lee stopped at the door and glanced over his shoulder. Looking at his father very much resembled gazing into a magical mirror where he could see himself in later years. Of all the children sired by Odie and Jane Daltry, Lee was the one who most resembled his father. "Thanks, Pa."

His father waved a hand and went back to work. Lee walked out and closed the door quietly. Light footsteps whispering along the stairs caught his attention.

With the grace of a goddess descending from the heavens, Venus floated down the wide stairs until she reached the foyer. Batting her golden lashes, she smiled coyly at him. "What do you think of my hair, Lee? I worked on it all afternoon, wantin' it to be perfect."

Slowly she pivoted on the tips of her toes, displaying the blond curls she'd tamed as easily as she tamed the young boys who lived in the area. There were moments when he forgot his sister was only fourteen, times when he'd put his fist into a friend's face because he'd forgotten as well.

"It's right pretty, Venus."

A moment earlier she'd stood before him on the threshold of womanhood, and now she skipped across the floor like the child she was and grabbed his hand, her blue eyes alight with joy. "I'm so pleased you like it. I wanted to do somethin' special for your birthday."

"Well, you did. Now I guess I'd best clean myself up."

She crinkled her petite nose. "You do smell like horses. I guess you've been playin' with Grandma's new mare."

"Thought it would be a good idea to get to know her a little before I try and break her."

"I heard Grandma tellin' C.J. she didn't want this horse tamed."

The smile building within Lee was larger than the one he shared with the outside world. If his grandmother thought people were listening, she'd say she had no intention of breaking the mare. Otherwise, everyone would know what Lee's labor was to be, and her surprise would be ruined. He rolled his shoulders into a shrug. "We'll see."

He jaunted up the stairs two at a time and went into his

bedroom on the second floor. His father had made each piece of furniture. He shaped wood in the same manner that he shaped his sons: with a firm, but gentle hand, taking time to smooth the rough edges and whittle away the hard corners.

Squeals and laughter echoed down the hallway as everyone banged on his door when they passed by on the way to their rooms. C.J. and Atlas shared one room in the attic; Persy, Venus, and Allie another. As always, Lee was grateful he had his own room.

He loved his brothers and sisters, enjoyed their company for the most part, and couldn't imagine life without them storming through it, but there were times when he longed for solitude.

Rubbing his rough hand over his chin, he studied it from all angles in the mirror above his washstand. Then he smiled, a broad grin that created the dimples for which he was famous and left no doubt in anyone's mind that he still possessed all his teeth.

As a young boy, he spent hours before the mirror perfecting his smile so the girls would gossip about his dimples instead of the set downs he continually received in the classroom. At recess and after school, he didn't want them talking about the time he spent on the dunce stool in the corner or the way he stammered through the reading assignment.

The minute they stepped out of the schoolhouse, he was smiling at them, carrying their lunch pails, and telling them how pretty they were. He figured if he gave them enough attention, they wouldn't care if he was the dumbest boy in the school, and after a time, they didn't care.

He ignored the banging on his door as his brothers and sisters headed down to the dining room, but the soft tapping demanded attention as no shouts ever could. He walked across the room and opened the door. His grandmother smiled, and Lee bent his body to wrap his arms around her. Hugging her felt like curling around a plump pillow in the middle of the night. The years had been kind to her, aging her gracefully, only streaking her brown hair with gray.

She stepped from his embrace and patted his cheek, her eyes twinkling. "No hints," she vowed.

Lee smiled. "I wasn't gonna ask for any."

"You haven't hugged me like that since you were five years old," she said as she slipped her arm through the crook of his elbow and walked with him down the stairs.

They entered the dining room. Pulling out the chair for his grandmother, Lee helped her sit at the long table his father had made. Then his brothers and sisters gathered around him, hugging him and shaking his hand as though they hadn't seen him in years. Good-naturedly he smiled and allowed them to lead him toward the head of the table where his mother and father stood.

Smiling broadly, his father pulled out the chair in which he usually sat and stepped back. "We've waited twenty years for this day."

Lee had celebrated nineteen birthdays at this table, but the honor of sitting at the head of the table had been reserved for this singularly important day. He swallowed the lump of emotion gathering in his throat and felt it lodge in his chest. In this family, no other day was held in higher esteem. Reaching out, Lee pumped his father's large hand before sitting in his father's chair.

Applause and cheers resounded around him. Lee felt the responsibility of being the firstborn weigh down on him more heavily than it ever had before. It wasn't a pressure that anyone put on him, but he felt it all the same.

Odie helped Jane take her seat before dropping into the chair to the left of Lee. As if on cue, the children settled into their places, smiles filling their faces as food filled their plates.

Candles illuminated the large room instead of the usual lamps, and Lee knew if he took the time to count them, he'd find twenty had been placed around the room.

As usual, two to three conversations manifested themselves at once. Lee discussed the new mare with his grandmother as he listened to C.J. bemoaning his love life: the abundance of women and the shortage of time.

Allie squirmed in her seat. "Hurry up, Lee. You're taking too long to eat, and me and Bub want to show you the present we made."

"Shh, Allie," Persy scolded. "Let Lee enjoy the gift I made him."

"But you cook for us every night, so it's not like it's special."

"It is too special. I made all of Lee's favorite foods."

Lee winked at Persy, grinned mischievously, and began to eat more slowly, savoring the sweet potatoes and tender sliced beef before moving on to his other favorites. When Allie groaned, he slowed his pace even more. He glanced at Venus who was still gathering compliments on her hair the way one gathered flowers for a bouquet.

"Venus, if your hair was red, what color ribbon would you wear in it?" Lee asked.

A look of horror swept across her face. "Red?"

"Well, not red really—more like orange."

"I wouldn't wear any ribbon at all."

"You'd just leave it loose to flow around your shoulders?"

"No, I'd hide it beneath a bonnet." Her hands flew to her cheeks. "And if I had red hair, I'd have freckles. Horrible, ugly freckles." She pushed her plate away. "Oh, Lee, I do believe you've ruined my appetite."

"That just leaves more for me, doesn't it?" His face broke into a hearty grin as he reached across the table to gather his second helping. He couldn't remember seeing freckles on Miss Lewis's nose, but then it was so gloomy in the mercantile, he'd hadn't been able to tell if she'd blushed either.

A deep snore brought all conversations to a halt. Odie's head had lolled to one shoulder and his eyes were closed. Jane nudged him, and Odie snapped his head back, his eyes unfocused as he looked around the table. "Huh? What? What's Lee's labor?"

As laughter and good-hearted jibes were tossed his father's way, Lee realized just how hard his father had worked to finish the window seat in time for his birthday.

When every plate was shoved back, Persy brought out the blueberry tarts. She set one before Lee and waited, her hands clenched tightly before her. Silence hovered over the room.

Using his fork, Lee sliced off a section of the blueberry tart, brought it slowly to his lips, inhaled the sweet aroma, then plopped it into his mouth. He closed his eyes, and his approval rumbled out from deep within his throat. Opening his eyes, he took Persy's hand, drew her near, and placed a kiss on her cheek. "Thanks, Persy."

Blushing, she distributed the remaining blueberry tarts and set two more at Lee's place before taking her seat.

C.J. slapped his hand down on the table. "Hey, Persy, you forgot me."

She tilted her chin. "You had yours earlier."

Lee fought back his smile. C.J. may have won the battle, but he was about to discover he'd lost the war.

"I only ate one. You gave Lee three."

"It's his birthday."

"But you gave everyone else two so I got one coming."

"No, you don't. I made enough so everyone got two, and Lee got three."

"So there should be one left."

"There would be except I was so upset that you had

ruined my carefully planned menu that I had to eat a blueberry tart earlier to console myself, and it just happened to
be one that had your name on it.''

Lee made a great show of eating his blueberry tarts,
smacking his lips, and heaping praise on Persy for the tasty
treat. Scowling, C.J. slumped in his chair.

After finishing his dessert, Lee leaned back and rubbed
his stomach, certain a more satisfied man could not be
found in Texas.

Minerva tapped her fork against her glass, and everyone
quieted. ''A wonderful feast, Persephone.''

''Thank you, Grandma.''

''Atalanta, I think sometime during all your fidgeting, I
heard you mention that you and Atlas had a gift for Hercules.''

''Yes, ma'am!'' Allie hoisted herself out of her chair and
ran from the room. Her boots thumping across the hardwood floor, she returned carrying a big box. Lee could see
that it had no lid, but he couldn't see in it. He shoved
everything out of the way, making a place of honor for the
gift.

''Close your eyes,'' Allie said.

Lee did as instructed and heard Allie set the box down.

''Open your eyes.''

He did as she bid, surprised to discover she'd set the box
far enough back that he still couldn't see inside. He was
about to stand when she pressed her small hand against his
arm and stopped him.

''Show him what it is, Bub.''

His young face remarkably serious, Atlas slowly turned
the box until the side that was open came into view.

Genuine surprise registered on Lee's face. They'd
painted the sides of the box so they resembled the wide-
open spaces he loved. Inside the box, they'd carefully arranged a herd of cattle the likes of which he hoped to never

see in the flesh. He was certain one of the mud creatures was a dog, but he wasn't certain which one so he decided against commenting on it. They'd coated the land where the cattle grazed with hay and built a fence using sticks. Beneath some hay, Lee saw small strips of paper. He had a feeling they were the tattered remains of Atlas's list.

"I'm much obliged. I'll take this to my room when I go to bed so I can be with my cattle all the time."

"And now for my gift," Minerva said.

Lee snapped his gaze to his grandmother's. Everything in the room drifted away until all he could see was her gray eyes. Everyone grew quiet, and the tension in the room became palpable.

"Many years have passed since I assigned a labor," Minerva said as she thrummed her fingers on the table. "I think I shall announce your labor in the family room so we can all enjoy your father's latest addition."

The conversation again commenced with everyone voicing their speculations aloud as they scraped their chairs across the floor. Quickly Lee joined his grandmother and escorted her from the room.

Night had fallen. A large silver moon graced the blackened sky, visible through the windows that now stretched across the front of the family room. Lee helped his grandmother sit in her padded rocker, then walked across the room and sat on the window seat. He gazed at the stars in the heavens and the silhouettes on earth. In the distance he heard a horse neigh. Smiling, he twisted around to face his grandmother.

His brothers and sisters gathered at her feet, their hands folded in their laps, their faces anxious. Like him, they had never heard a labor as it was announced.

When bottoms stopped squirming and snickers fell into silence, Minerva lifted her gaze to her oldest grandchild. "Of all my grandchildren, you are the one whose love of mythology and legend is equal to mine. You never fell asleep when I spun my tales, and you always asked me to read the story one more time. Do you remember which story was my favorite?''

''The twelve labors of Hercules,'' Lee said without hesitation.

His grandmother smiled. ''And do you remember which labor was the most difficult for Hercules to complete?''

Lee ran the labors through his mind. ''Getting the golden apples from the Hesperides.''

''I have decided that is to be your labor.''

Lee slammed his eyes shut. Damn, she was giving him a riddle, and riddles always made him feel dumb because he could never figure them out. But this one couldn't be that hard because he already knew the answer: taming the mare, Cassiopeia. He just had to find the connection. In the legend, Hercules had carried Atlas's burden so Atlas could retrieve the golden apples. So what burden was Lee to carry?

Opening his eyes, he shook his head slightly in confusion. ''How am I to carry out the labor?''

''You'll be the schoolmarm for one year.''

Lee felt as though his grandmother had just hurled a thunderbolt through his chest. ''Schoolmarm?'' he croaked.

''Lee's gonna be our teacher, Bub!'' Allie crowed as she rolled on the floor holding her stomach.

Atlas chortled. C.J. bent over, laughing so hard Lee thought his brother might bring up his supper. He sure as hell felt like his own supper was fighting to come up.

Forgetting the hours she spent practicing the genteel laughter of a lady, Venus sounded like a honking goose.

Persy was the only one of his siblings not caught up in the hilarity of the situation. Knowing her own task was but a year away from being announced, she laid her hand on her grandmother's arm. ''But, Grandma, Lee's as good with books and children as he is with a needle and thread.''

"Is that true, Hercules?" she asked.

"You know it is," he said loudly so he could be heard above the din of laughter.

His grandmother's gray eyes met and held his, issuing a challenge. "Do you feel you're not up to completing the task?"

Into the silence that suddenly permeated the room, Lee gave the only answer a descendant of Minerva Daltry could give. "I'll complete the task."

His grandmother gave a brusque nod. "Then in one year's time, I shall grant you a prize worthy of your accomplishment.''

Chapter
Three

Lee sat in the gazebo his father had built. With its carved pillars, it resembled a Greek temple and should have housed wisdom, but it only held the warm night air and despair.

He stared at the moon as he had the past two nights, ever since his grandmother had assigned his labor as though she were a reigning monarch tossing down the gauntlet.

With five younger siblings, he should know how to act around children, but the truth was, he'd felt awkward around his brothers and sisters when they were younger. Even now, he often stumbled over himself when he was around Allie or Atlas. Sweet Lord, his labor would force him to be in their presence all day. He'd rather be in the middle of a stampede.

But there was no chance of that happening. With a teasing grin, C.J. had graciously offered to take over managing the ranch so Lee wouldn't be distracted from his labor. Then he'd promptly gone to the bunkhouse to let the ranch hands know Lee was giving up ranching to be the new schoolmarm. Their raucous laughter had caused the bunk-house walls to shake. It was a wonder the building hadn't toppled to the ground.

Tunneling his fingers through his hair, he knew matters could be worse. He could have three family members in his classroom, but Venus, who only cared about the latest fashions and resurrecting the image of the southern belle from the ashes of the Civil War, had passed the all-day comprehensive exam in the spring—the only requirement for graduation from school.

He ignored the approaching footsteps. He was fed up with his brothers and sisters tormenting him about his labor. With the exception of Persy, they all seemed to have forgotten that their own labor was taking shape in the back of their grandmother's dark and humorless mind. If his task was any indication of what awaited them, he thought they should all concentrate their efforts on softening her up, not aggravating him.

"You thought your task would be to tame my new mare."

Lee twisted around and watched his grandmother stroll slowly through the night shadows as though she were an ethereal being not of this world. The goddess of wisdom. Until his twentieth birthday, he'd always thought she'd been aptly named. She sat beside him and tilted her face toward the moon.

"Will you not acknowledge the truth of my words?" she asked softly.

"I had hoped taming a horse might be my task."

"You could tame her in a day. Where would the challenge lie?"

The goddess of wisdom had spoken, and Lee could think of no rebuttal. He bolted to his feet and crossed to the other side of the gazebo. Through the window, he saw Persy curled on the window seat, reading a book—a book filled with recipes no doubt.

"Will you admit defeat so easily?" Minerva asked quietly.

"I'm not giving up, Grandma. It's just that—" Lee plowed his strong fingers through his hair. "I've got two weeks to get my classroom ready, and all I seem to be able to do is stand in the schoolhouse and stare at the desks. I've got no earthly idea where to begin."

Smiling inwardly, Minerva studied her eldest grandchild. Whether intentional or not, he had referred to it as *his* classroom. "Perhaps Miss Lewis can help."

Remembering his pleasant little distraction in town, he turned around slowly. "Miss Lewis?"

"She only recently moved to Paradise Plains, but I've heard she earned a teaching certification."

Disappointment reeled through him. The little barn owl was a schoolteacher. He should have known. Only a teacher would walk into a mercantile filled with gadgets and look at books.

He'd meant to pay her a visit, but concern over his labor had driven all thoughts of socializing from his mind. Now, he was glad he hadn't visited her. She was probably still laughing about their discussion of Homer. She'd no doubt been referring to the poet. How could he have been so dumb as to think she was talking about ranch hands? Lord, why couldn't he have been born smart? All the charms in the world weren't going to help him find a woman willing to stay with him when he wasn't smart enough to cover up how dumb he was. He was surprised she hadn't laughed in his face. Most teachers—

He slowed down his thinking. She hadn't laughed. She hadn't laughed because she wasn't a teacher. If she was, he wouldn't have this gawd-awful labor to perform. She was certified to teach, but she wasn't teaching. He wondered what had turned her against teaching. Probably students like him.

Leaning back, he hitched up one hip so he could partially sit on the railing that ran around the gazebo. "How could Miss Lewis help me?"

His grandmother tilted her head in thought. "Perhaps you could introduce her to the area, and she could give you some hints on how to organize your classroom."

"It's all right if I ask her to help me with my labor?"

"As long as you don't explain why you're teaching school."

As a rule, according to the likes and dislikes in his life, Lee ranked teachers just below rattlesnakes, but a man could walk through a pit of vipers without getting struck if he did it slow and easy, and he'd always been good at being slow.

Dressed in his Sunday best, Lee guided Pegasus slowly down the middle of the single dusty street that ran the length of Paradise Plains. He didn't take his usual detour around the schoolhouse. This morning, he didn't feel up to taunting any demons; he felt they were all taunting him.

Few people milled along the street this time of day. He tipped his hat toward Miss Lavender as she hurried into her shop, The Hatbox. On any blustery, wind-filled Sunday, he escorted her home from church. He teased her that all her bows and ruffles were too much temptation to the wind, and it would carry her away, but they both knew it was her frail frame with its aging bones that tempted the wind.

He drew Pegasus to a halt in front of the boardinghouse. Curtains fluttered outside two of the windows on the second floor, and he wondered if either window looked into Miss Lewis's room.

He dismounted, stepped on the porch without using the

steps, swept his hat from his head, and knocked briskly on the door.

Mrs. Bennett opened the door and smiled at him. "Why, Lee Daltry, what a pleasant surprise on such a fine morning." With her blue eyes flashing and a rose petal glow on her weathered cheeks, she patted her chest as though he'd just taken air from her lungs.

"Morning, Mrs. Bennett. How are you?"

"Wonderful. How can a person not be wonderful when the sun is shining and the birds are singing? Please, do come inside."

Walking into the parlor, he glanced around. The boarding-house seemed unusually quiet. It hadn't occurred to him Miss Lewis might sleep late. "How's your grandson?" he asked.

She released a chuckle. "Land sakes, Simon reminds me so much of my dear departed husband. He's five, you know, but smart as a whip and so inquisitive. Why just the other day he asked Meredith Lewis why she had spots all over her face. Now is that not the cutest thing you ever heard?"

Lee shifted uncomfortably in his suit. The light inside the mercantile was dim, but surely he would have noticed spots unless she'd only recently acquired them. "Why *does* she have spots?" he asked hesitantly.

Mrs. Bennett's laughter floated around the room until it sounded as though it had reached up and tinkled the chandelier hanging above their heads. "He was asking about her freckles."

He smiled. So Venus was right—freckles came with red hair. "Speaking of Miss Lewis . . . is she here?"

"Why no, dear. Meredith is next door at the Buc having breakfast."

Lee thanked Mrs. Bennett with a quick kiss on her cheek that caused her face to turn a brighter pink. Then he ambled next door to the Buccaneer.

As soon as he walked into the Buc, he noticed Meredith Lewis. Even if she wasn't the only woman dining alone, she would have caught his attention. The early morning sunlight streamed in through the window behind her and illuminated her bright orange hair so it appeared she was a sunrise emerging over the stack of books on the table.

Her face was partially hidden as she read an open book resting beside her plate. She was a schoolteacher all right. Only a schoolteacher could eat and read at the same time. Only a schoolteacher would want to!

Standing in the doorway, he wondered when the spectacles perched on the end of her nose were going to fall onto her plate and become part of her breakfast. He wasn't even sure she'd notice since she was shoveling the eggs and toast into her mouth faster than any ranch hand would after a hard day of driving cattle.

Wiping his sweating palms on his trousers, he released a deep breath. He'd never before asked anyone for a handout. Long into the night, he'd tried to decide on the best way to approach her and ask for help. The words had jumbled around in his mind until every sentence sounded silly. He'd hoped when he saw her again, everything would fall into place, but it hadn't and staring at her was only making him more nervous.

He released his death grip on his hat and studied the crumpled brim. He wasn't in a schoolroom, and he wasn't a boy. Now he was the teacher, and he wanted to make sure he did it right.

Calling forth his best grin, he slowly approached her. She didn't appear to notice when he stopped beside her table. He could see the smattering of freckles that dotted her face, and they certainly didn't resemble spots. They looked as though Persy had flicked cinnamon over her nose and cheeks. As a matter of fact, they looked downright inviting.

Feeling his confidence returning, he cleared his throat. "Miss Lewis?"

She snapped her head back, her brown eyes unfocused as though she were just returning to the present. She blinked, then lifted her gaze to his. A warm glow lit her eyes as her lips softened and tipped up slightly at the corners.

Lee deepened his grin until he felt the dimples form in his cheeks, then leaned toward her. "We weren't properly introduced the other day at the mercantile. I'm Hercules Daltry—"

She bolted from the chair, staring at him with large round eyes, the softness erased from her mouth. "*You're* Hercules Daltry!"

His smile grew as he realized she'd no doubt heard about his charming sweetness. It was legendary. She'd only received a small taste of it the other day. Now, she was about to become a full-fledged recipient of it. "Yes, ma'am. I'm sure by now you've heard—"

"Oh, yes, Mr. Daltry! I've heard!" She picked up the book she'd been reading and threw it at him.

Startled, Lee hopped to the side so it only brushed his hip.

"Hercules Daltry, you must have been so disappointed when the sheriff wouldn't let you come along to share in the announcement!"

He ducked when the second book came sailing through the air. With all the tables and chairs surrounding him, he felt like a stallion trapped in a stall.

"I'm surprised you didn't stay in town to gloat! Didn't you feel the least bit guilty taking *my* teaching position?"

Stunned by her words, Lee stood immobile as the third book hit him squarely on the thigh.

"You and your wealthy family—"

The next book hit him in the chest.

"Descending from Mount Olympus and pulling strings so you can play schoolteacher!"

The last book thudded to the floor at his feet.

Her slender form took in quick, agitated breaths, her hands clenched into tight fists at her sides, her brown eyes looking for something else she could throw. Lee was afraid she was going to decide to throw the eggs, and he'd prefer the books. Bending down, he gathered her ammunition and set the books on the table. This time, he didn't need a lantern to see the sadness reflected in her eyes.

"I traveled all the way from Boston, alone, just for the opportunity to bring education and culture to these children. Did you ever stop to think how your little game might affect my life and theirs? Don't you have anything better to do with your wealth and power than disrupt lives?"

Regret rushed over him like a river overflowing its banks after a raging storm. Imploringly he reached out a hand. "Miss Lewis—"

She slapped his hand away. "You disgust me, flashing your smiles, building hope while you're secretly tearing down dreams. Fortunately, my dreams aren't so easily destroyed, Mr. Daltry. Not everyone in this town pays homage to your family. I found employment at the millinery. As soon as I've earned enough money for passage, I'll go back to Boston, but I do wonder how in God's name a man as selfish as yourself sleeps at night."

He watched her stroll from the Buc with her shoulders squared and her head held high. Now he knew why she wasn't teaching school. He wondered if it would make her feel better to know he wouldn't be sleeping tonight.

Hercules Daltry!

Meredith Lewis felt like such a fool.

After talking with the sheriff, the only thing that had saved her from despondency was the hope that she might again see the kind gentleman she'd met at the mercantile. She'd held on to the memory of his smile and his kind words of welcome. Not once had it occurred to her that Lee was Hercules Daltry.

Hercules Daltry!

It was a name she'd come to loathe, and the last thing she'd expected was for him to have the effrontery to approach her. The last thing she'd wanted was for him to be the man she'd met at the mercantile.

Like an idiot, she'd actually believed his attentions had been genuine. She'd fallen for his smile, been swayed by his charms, and the entire time, he'd been setting her up for the sheriff's visit.

Or more specifically—his grandmother's visit.

Wearing the mien of wealth and influence the way most people wore simple garments, Minerva Daltry had greeted her at the sheriff's office. Appearing benevolent with her soft gray eyes, she represented what Meredith had always longed for: a family that could trace its heritage back for generations.

As Meredith sat in the chair the sheriff pulled out for her, Minerva Daltry leaned forward. "I don't wish to cause you any sorrow, my dear, but I am afraid the teaching position you hoped to obtain here has been given to my grandson, Hercules Daltry."

Blinking, Meredith clasped her hands in her lap. "But that's impossible. I have a letter offering me this position if I could find the means to get here. I obviously found the means."

"I know, dear, and I regret any inconvenience this change in plans may cause you, but it is imperative that my grandson teach the children of Paradise Plains."

"Has he taught before?"

The older woman had smiled, mischief evident in her eyes. "No, but he enjoys a challenge."

"Is he certified to teach?"

"Allowances have been made."

"You mean you've paid someone off."

"I wouldn't be that crass—"

"But you'd be that cruel. I worked hard to obtain my certification to teach—"

"I know. I was one of the people who recommended you for this position, but that was before I realized my grandson—"

"And you wouldn't want to deny him anything, would you?"

Unwavering, the older woman met Meredith's gaze. "I wish to ensure his happiness."

"At my expense?"

"At any cost, although I assure you, Miss Lewis—"

Meredith rose to her feet. "No, don't bother to assure me of anything. I've learned life comes with no assurances, and I certainly want none from you."

Without another word, she left the sheriff's office and rushed back to the mercantile, hoping the gentleman she'd met earlier was still there, but he'd already left, and Meredith had felt a despair greater than any she'd ever known.

Until this moment.

Pacing the confines of her small, sparsely furnished room, she fought back the tears that had threatened ever since her confrontation with Minerva Daltry. She'd falsely believed Lee was providing solace when he'd offered to go with her to the sheriff's office. Now, she knew he only wished to witness her disappointment when his grandmother snatched away all her hopes and dreams. She resented Minerva Daltry for what she'd done, resented Hercules Daltry because he had someone in his life who would go to such great pains to give him what he wanted when Meredith had never had anyone.

When her agitation adequately subsided, she pulled the

fluttering curtains into the room and parted them slightly so she could gaze out. She'd chosen this corner room because it had two windows. From the back window, she could see the schoolhouse in the distance. From the side window, where she now stood, she could view the Buccaneer next door and the mercantile across the street.

She watched as Hercules Daltry, carrying her precious books, limped toward the boardinghouse. The books were her only extravagance. She'd read them until their pages were frayed and bore the marks of her fingers. She carried them with her everywhere because they were her only friends. They never turned away from her, always offered solace when no person ever had.

She heard the front door close and was grateful he had not asked to speak with her. She watched as he mounted the most beautiful white horse she'd ever seen. He looked up toward the windows, the brim of his hat casting shadows over his face. Only the knowledge that he couldn't see her kept her riveted to the spot. He tipped his hat, and she wondered if someone was looking out another window. Then he sent his horse into a gallop, and she imagined they could almost fly.

Chapter
Four

Sitting on the window seat, Lee studied the vast expanse of black heavens visible through the windows. The flame in the lamp burned low enough that it didn't reflect off the glass so nothing obstructed his view of the constellations.

When Miss Lewis tilted her chin up defiantly, her slender throat reminded him of a graceful swan. He wondered how she would have looked if he'd untied the black ribbon holding her hair captive. With her orange hair flowing around her as she threw the books, she may have resembled Medusa. But if she wasn't throwing books, if she was instead sitting in the gazebo with moonlight playing across her fair features—

"Lee?"

Startled, he glanced over his shoulder as Persy padded across the family room in her bare feet. Twisting around, he scooted to the side, giving her room to join him on the wooden bench.

"What are you doing?" she asked as she brought her

41

feet up to the seat, pulling her night wrapper down over her drawn-up knees.

Tugging on her blond braid, he gave her a small smile. ''Just thinking.''

''About your labor?''

''What else is there to think about? Hell, I could breed a new kind of cow—one with three horns—easier than I can teach school.''

''I thought you were going to ask Miss Lewis to help you.''

''I did.''

''And?''

He sighed heavily. ''Did you know she'd been hired to be the new schoolteacher?''

Persy's gray eyes widened. ''They hired her and you?''

Sadly he shook his head. ''No, they hired her. Then when she got here, they told her she no longer had the position. That it belonged to me. She holds it against me, doesn't want to help me, and I don't blame her.''

''It's not your fault.''

''But she doesn't know that. Like everyone in town, she thinks this is something I *want* to do—something I plan on doing until the day I die. If I could just explain to her it's only for one year. If she could just hold on until then, she'll get her teaching position back.''

Persy laid her hand on his arm. ''You'll forfeit your prize if you tell her anything. That's one of the rules. You can't tell anyone outside the family anything about your labor.''

''I know the damn rules. I just wish I didn't feel the need to play by them.'' He heaved a sigh, worry clearly visible in the lines around his mouth. ''And it gets worse.''

She didn't urge him to explain, but waited patiently, her eyes filled with concern. She'd never pushed him, always understood how hard some things were for him, and he loved her dearly for it.

"I lied to Grandma. I told her I'd gone into the school-house, but I haven't. I haven't been able to do anything but stand outside the door and wish this nightmare would go away." Searching for the truth, he held her gray gaze. "You never told Grandma about what happened, did you?"

She worked her hand beneath his as it gripped his thigh and tenderly rubbed the scars on his palm that only the two of them knew existed. "I gave you my word when I was six years old that I wouldn't, and I've kept my word."

He closed his fingers around hers, squeezing slightly. "I didn't mean to doubt your word. I just can't figure out why she decided to give me this particular labor, especially since it's ruined Miss Lewis's life. I'm wondering if maybe I'm supposed to be willing to give up the prize—give Miss Lewis back her teaching position. Maybe this is a test of my generosity."

"I don't think so. Grandma chose the labors she gave her children with an eye toward improving their character, and I would imagine she's doing the same for us. Since you're the most unselfish person I know, I don't think she's trying to improve your generosity."

"Then what am I gonna do, Persy? You said it yourself. I'm no good with books or children."

"I didn't say you were no good. Perhaps you can find a way to teach the lessons without relying so much on the books."

He smiled crookedly. "Think I could find a way to teach school without having children in the classroom?"

Her laughter was like a balm, soothing away his anxieties. "No, I do think children are a requirement."

"I figured as much," Lee said, feigning disgust.

"Children aren't so bad. You were one once."

"I just don't want to let them down. Do you know how much damage I could do in a year?"

"No, but I know how much good you could do."

*   *   *

With a lantern to guide him, Lee shoved the key into the lock. It turned easily. Pushing the door open, he grimaced as it squeaked in protest of his intrusion.

Cautiously he peered inside before stepping into the entryway of the schoolhouse where children would hang their coats and lunch pails on pegs secured to the wall. None of the pegs came higher than his waist. Closing the door, he wondered where he was supposed to hang his coat and lunch pail.

With two long strides, he was in the classroom. The classroom. His classroom. He groaned.

Like wolves circling an injured calf, the shadows retreated as he walked through the room, then slipped in behind him. He could feel the ghosts of his past teachers mocking him—even though as far as he knew none of them had died. He smelled the furniture polish Persy had applied to all the desks. The musty scent of the building had disappeared under her thorough cleaning.

Tomorrow morning he'd open the windows so the breeze could blow through the building. He drew comfort from the windows. As a boy, he'd spent hours gazing through the glass. Maybe that's why his grandmother had given him this labor—as punishment for all the days he sat in this room wishing he was someplace else. He sure as hell wished he was someplace else now. The black underworld of Tartarus, Hades's domain, held more appeal than this schoolhouse in Paradise.

At the back of the room loomed a large, foreboding desk. The teacher's desk. His desk. His books were stacked neatly on the corner and beside them rested his lesson plan. It was sketchy at best, but it gave him a place to begin.

Carefully he approached the desk as though he were approaching a half-crazed stallion that might rear up on its hindquarters at any time. He pressed his palms on top of the desk; it stayed in place. As did the books. The desk didn't hurl the books at him the way Miss Lewis had, didn't tell him he didn't belong here.

Slowly he shook his bowed head. It wasn't his fault his grandmother had chosen to give him this gawd-awful labor, but Miss Lewis had taken her frustration out on him. A spark of anger flitted through him, and he tried to grab on to it. He just couldn't seem to hang on to his anger where she was concerned. He continued to see her, small and spirited, heaving books at a man large enough to crush her with one hand. He wished he could mend her broken dreams as easily as he'd mended the baby owl's wing, but he couldn't do anything about her dreams when he was living in a nightmare.

He lumbered around the desk and dropped into the straight-backed chair. It protested with a loud moan. He moaned back.

Leaning forward, he studied the herd of desks. Tomorrow morning they'd be filled with skittish children ready to start a stampede at the least provocation. Well, these children were going to learn their first lesson five minutes after they were settled into their desks. Their new schoolteacher knew how to handle a stampede.

He glanced at his lesson plan. Persy had shaken her head when she'd seen what he'd written:

First Day
1. Stop stampede before it starts.
2. Put fillies on one side of room, colts on the other.
3. Brand troublemakers.

Studying it now, he understood why she'd shaken her head. He picked up a pencil and scratched through the last entry. Every child born was a troublemaker. They were always underfoot, always in the way, always asking questions that had no answers: Why does your breath look like smoke in the winter when it's cold and not in the summer when it's hot?

He'd have to find the answers to their questions, and he wouldn't make them feel stupid for asking. While Persy had cleaned, he'd shredded up the dunce cap and taken apart the dunce stool.

Then he'd worked on his lesson plan, tossing ideas off her as he'd thought about how he'd approach teaching. He didn't want to teach the way he'd been taught. He couldn't use half of what his teachers had tried to teach him so he had decided to take a more practical approach and teach these children what they needed to be good ranchers.

Standing, he lifted the lantern off the desk and walked slowly through the room, the shadows again retreating. Tomorrow, they wouldn't be here at all. Tomorrow, something worse would fill this room—children.

Stepping outside, he closed the door to the schoolhouse and locked it. Turning around, he came up short and watched the shadows of the night dance with the lantern's glow around Miss Lewis.

She stood before him with her hair pulled back, her white billowy bodice tucked snugly into place. Her fingers were intertwined, and he wondered if she kept them prisoner so they wouldn't be tempted to throw a stick at him.

"Mr. Daltry," she said in a soft, hesitant voice.

Quickly he removed his hat. "Miss Lewis."

She cleared her throat. "I can see the schoolhouse from my window. I saw your arrival. I owe you an apology."

He grinned somberly. "Considering the circumstances, I probably owe you one."

"I'm certain I reacted worse than any of my students ever would, and I just wanted to apologize. I shouldn't have thrown the books."

His grin widening, Lee tilted his head. "One book would

have been all right, maybe even two—"

"You belittle my apology, sir. I don't appreciate it."

She spun on her heel, and Lee charged after her, grabbing her arm and halting her escape. "I was just trying to make light of the incident; no harm was done."

"I saw you limping when you brought back my books."

"Oh, that. Uh . . . a horse had thrown me the day before. So, you see you didn't hurt me."

Meredith studied his face in the shadows. His expression appeared genuine. She hadn't noticed him that morning until he'd spoken her name so she didn't know if he'd limped to her table or not. She had no choice but to believe him, and with that thought no longer occupying her mind, she realized his hand had remained on her arm and was slowly moving from the crook at her elbow to just below her shoulder, so slowly, almost tenderly, again and again, calming her, warming her—terrifying her. She stepped back, and his hand dropped to his side.

"Miss Lewis, I want you to know that I honest to God didn't know you'd been hired to teach. When I went to see you at the Buc, it wasn't because I wanted to gloat."

"Then why did you come to see me?"

Lee's fingers crushed the brim of his hat. He'd had to replace the hat he'd worn to the Buc the morning he'd gone to seek her help. He hoped he wasn't going to have to buy a new hat every time he talked to her. "It's not really important now."

"But it was then?"

"I thought it was at the time." He dropped his crumpled hat on his head, working to straighten the brim as he brought it low over his brow. "I'd heard you were certified to teach so I was going to ask you to help me set up the classroom."

A small "oh" preceded her deflated sigh. "Did you manage to get everything done?"

He gave a slow nod. "My sister, Persephone, helped me."

"Persephone? And your Christian name is Hercules? It's not a nickname someone gave you because you're so—"

He took a step toward her. "So what, Miss Lewis?"

She spread her arms, one way and then the other, as though he were a piece of cloth she was trying to measure. "So large, so muscular."

By the light of the lantern, Meredith watched his grin take shape.

"Hercules is my Christian name, given to me at birth. Guess you might say I just sorta grew into it."

"Is everyone in your family named after someone from mythology?"

"Everyone but my mother."

"Doesn't that bother you?" she asked.

He studied the star-filled heavens for a moment, and Meredith wished she hadn't been so impertinent. Perhaps he'd never realized how unusual his name was.

Rubbing the back of his neck, he shook his head. "Nah, it doesn't bother me. I always call her Ma so it doesn't really matter to me what her name is."

Meredith forced her mouth not to drop open. She couldn't very well tell him she'd been inquiring about the unusual mythical names in his family, not the normal ones. "Well, I shouldn't tarry you any longer. I know you'll want to be well rested for tomorrow. The first day is always the hardest. Good night, Mr. Daltry."

"I should walk you home, Miss Lewis."

"There's no need. I walked here by myself, I can walk back to the boardinghouse by myself."

"I wouldn't be much of a gentleman if I didn't walk you."

He whistled, and Meredith was surprised to see the white horse gallop from the blackness beyond the schoolhouse, stop as he neared his master, and nudge his arm.

Lee reached into his pocket, then held his cupped hand toward the horse who claimed the offering. "This is Pegasus," he said by way of explanation.

Meredith bit back her smile. "Why am I not surprised?"

"This is Miss Lewis." He patted the horse's shoulder. "Where are your manners? I just introduced you to a lady."

In amazement, Meredith watched the horse bend down on one knee and lower his head in a mock bow. She'd never in her life had such attentions lavished on her. She was at a loss as to what she should say. As though sensing her dilemma, Lee leaned close and whispered, "Just say that you're honored."

Meredith had never heard of anything more ridiculous than carrying on a conversation with a horse, but she played along, not certain why. "I'm honored."

The stallion threw back his head, filling the night air with his neigh, before scrambling up from his kneeling position.

Lee smiled. "Now that you're properly introduced—"

He set the lantern down. Meredith shrieked as he clamped his hands around her waist and lifted her onto the saddle. She grabbed the pommel, praying she wouldn't fall from her perch. "Please, this really isn't necessary," she said, her voice quivering.

"It's the least I can do, Miss Lewis."

"I must insist you take me down."

"And I must insist you ride."

He began walking, and Pegasus fell into step beside him. Meredith was distracted from her precarious position by the sight of Hercules Daltry walking in the moonlight. He was tall. Without bending, she could have reached out and touched the brown locks peering out from beneath his hat. His shoulders were massively broad, and whenever he patted his stallion affectionately, he caused the corded brawn beneath his shirt to ripple.

"Did you put a fresh coat of black paint on the back wall?" she asked, trying to turn her thoughts away from the breadth of his shoulders. She knew teachers in rural schools painted the wall behind their desk and used it as their blackboard. "It's very important to begin the school year with new paint."

"Yes, ma'am, I did."

"And the desks are arranged so the smaller desks are in the front? You want the younger students closer to you."

"Yes, ma'am. I did that, too. And my pa sanded the tops of the desks where students had carved things they shouldn't have carved. Then Persy polished 'em up real good."

"It seems your family is very supportive of your desire to teach."

"Yeah, I reckon they are when they're not too busy laughing about me being the new schoolmarm."

"Why would they laugh?"

He was relieved she hadn't gone to school with him, didn't know anything about the boy he'd been. She only knew the man he was. He smiled. "Reckon it's because we always had women teachers before."

Briefly she wondered if she should tell the man not to smile in his classroom. It would be particularly distracting to the older female students, but it hardly disqualified him to teach. "Mr. Daltry, I hope you won't perceive my feelings as being sour grapes, but I honestly don't see how a person who is not well versed in literature can expect to instill a love for reading and learning in his students. Homer—"

"I know who Homer is."

She shook her head. "I'm not discussing your cowhand."

"I know. You're talking about the poet."

Astonishment washed over her features. "So, you were teasing me at the mercantile! You have read *The Iliad*."

"I'm familiar with the story."

"I'm so relieved to hear that. Most people don't understand what a responsibility it is to teach children. We have the power to shape their thinking."

"Yes, ma'am. A labor is what teaching is."

"A labor of love, Mr. Daltry."

"Yes, ma'am, that's what my pa keeps telling me."

The horse plodded along slowly. They neared The Hatbox, and Meredith saw a light shining through a window of the side room where Miss Lavender resided.

"Are things working out for you at the millinery?" he asked quietly.

"As well as can be expected under the circumstances. Miss Lavender is exceedingly patient with my efforts."

"I'm glad to hear that."

The horse snorted, and Meredith nearly jumped out of her skin. "I've heard that Mount Olympus is the largest ranch in this area."

Abruptly, the man stopped walking. The horse came to a halt. Hercules Daltry's eyes narrowed as he studied her. "Our ranch is the largest in the area."

"As I said, that's what I'd heard."

He nodded slowly, then began walking again. Without a word from his master, the horse followed.

"Your family seems rather fond of mythology," she said, struggling to distract her attention from a body that looked as though it had been sculpted from marble. She was certain she had seen that shape before in an art museum. Only it hadn't been clothed.

"My grandmother loves mythology," Lee said, his voice blending in with the solemn night sounds. "Greek, Roman. It doesn't matter. For as long as I can remember, every night after supper, she sat in her rocking chair and read us a story as we gathered at her feet. I remember the day she came to live with us. She brought two wagons. One contained nothing but boxes filled with books. I loved the way it smelled when she opened those boxes. My pa had to build another room onto our house just so she'd have a place to keep all her books.''

''Your house has a library?''

''Yes, ma'am.''

''You're very fortunate to have all those books at your disposal.''

''Yes, ma'am. When I was younger, after everyone else had gone to bed, I'd drag my blanket and pillow down the stairs and curl up in that room to sleep. I liked being near those books, surrounded by their smell. I used to dream about how wonderful it would be when I learned to read so I could read those books anytime I wanted, without having to wait for someone to find the time to read them to me.''

''Not everyone is as fortunate as you, Mr. Daltry. Not everyone has someone to share their books with them or to read to them.''

''Do you have someone, Miss Lewis?''

Averting her gaze from his, she turned her attention to the building emerging from the shadows, grateful to see the boardinghouse. With no more than a whisper from the man leading him, Pegasus came to a halt.

''Thank you for bringing me to the boardinghouse,'' she said, surprised by the strength, tempered with gentleness, she felt as he wrapped his hands around her waist and lowered her to the ground. ''Good night, Mr. Daltry.''

Watching her scurry up the steps, Lee dipped his hand into his pocket and distractedly handed Pegasus his reward. For long moments he stared at the door through which Meredith Lewis had disappeared. Then he pressed his face against the stallion's neck.

"Imagine living someplace you don't call home," he said quietly just before he mounted and urged the horse into a slow lope.

Chapter
Five

Meredith glanced at the small watch pinned above her left breast. It was five minutes past the hour!

Gazing out the rear window of the millinery, she could see Hercules Daltry leaning against the front of the school-house as though he had the whole day stretching before him with nothing better to do.

Just as she'd previously surmised. Like most people, he did not comprehend the responsibilities and duties for which a schoolteacher was accountable. Children needed discipline and a precise routine in order to maximize their learning capabilities. What sort of message was he sending when he didn't think school was important enough to begin at precisely eight o'clock—especially on the first day?

She drove the needle into the felt hat as diligently as she drove the tears back from her eyes. It was her misfortune to have found employment at the millinery, her misfortune to have chosen this morning to sit near the back window so she could not only see the schoolhouse, but Hercules

Daltry lounging in the early morning shade.

At an early age, she'd excelled in her studies and was soon tutoring the younger children at the orphanage. She'd found her first joy in watching a child's eyes light up when she'd correctly sounded out a word. The children surrounding her didn't care that she was unwanted—they were unwanted as well.

She jerked a ribbon off a spool, snipped it, and wound it around the hat, not paying much attention to the fact that the hat was yellow and the ribbon scarlet. The hats she worked so hard to create still sat on the shelf or adorned a window. In truth, she did not think they would ever sit on a woman's head; in truth, she did not care.

All she wanted, all she'd ever wanted was to teach. She pretended the children she helped were her children for she never expected to have children of her own. She was simply too plain. No one had wanted to take her from the orphanage and into their home. In the passing years, little about her had changed. She had no reason to believe any man would now want to take her into his home as his wife.

Her only happiness resided in teaching children, and that happiness had been snatched away by wealth and selfishness. She had little doubt that Hercules Daltry had never known anything but happiness. Otherwise, he wouldn't have a smile that encompassed half his face. A wide smile that flashed the straightest, whitest teeth she'd ever seen.

No, she was certain he'd never known misery.

The sun had barely cleared the horizon when Lee arrived at the school. He went over his lesson plan three times, moved his books from one corner of the desk to the other, opened the windows, printed his name across the blackboard behind his desk, then wrote his name in bold script beneath that.

The night before he'd snitched some of Venus's hair ribbons and painstakingly painted small honors on each ribbon: best smile, quietest, friendliest. It had taken him most of the night to come up with enough honors so every child would go home with a ribbon, but he was determined no child in his classroom would feel slighted. He set the ribbons on his desk and finally felt as though everything was in order.

He walked outside to wait for his students. Leaning against the building, his arms crossed over his chest, he took a moment to enjoy the slight breeze blowing the tall prairie grasses that stretched out in all directions around Paradise Plains. It would be a good day for working the range. He hoped C.J. appreciated it.

He smiled as Allie and Atlas came into view. They tethered their horses nearby and ran to the schoolhouse. Allie scrunched up her face. "How come you're not ringing the bell so everybody knows it's time to come to school?"

Sweet Lord! He shoved himself away from the building and rushed into the schoolhouse. He searched every nook and cranny, but couldn't find a bell. Apparently, the last teacher had taken it with her.

He ran to the mercantile. Of all the gadgets Hank had for sale, he didn't have a single cowbell, refused to part with the bells above his door, and wouldn't consider loaning them out for a day. Not even when Lee threatened to take his business elsewhere.

He finally located an old rusty cowbell at the livery. The twins who ran the Horse Hotel knew a desperate man when they saw one, and Lee hightailed it back to the schoolhouse, bell in hand, an incredible ten dollars poorer.

His spirits plummeted down to his boots when he saw Miss Lewis standing by the schoolhouse, tapping her tiny foot until the grass around her no longer sprang back to life. Out of breath, he came to a halt, hating the censure clearly written across her face.

"Mr. Daltry, do you have any idea what this is?"

She pointed to her breast, and Lee felt as though he'd suddenly jumped into the middle of a hot afternoon. He found it difficult to breathe, and it had nothing to do with the fact that he'd just run from one end of town to the other. "Yes, ma'am," he croaked.

"Do you understand its purpose?"

Did she want him to admit in front of Allie and Atlas that it was for a man's enjoyment? He glanced in their direction. Allie was slouched against the wall, and Atlas was crouched beside her. Was Atlas old enough to be aware of women? Lord, he couldn't remember when he'd first noticed women had gentle curves that men didn't. He took a couple of deep breaths and concentrated on her question. He'd learned early on to avoid trouble by answering the question with a few short words and no elaboration. "Yes, ma'am."

"Do you have one, Mr. Daltry?"

Was the woman daft? "No, ma'am."

"Would you like to borrow mine?"

The cowbell hit Lee's foot, and he hopped back, trying to ignore the pain throbbing through his big toe. How the hell did she think he was going to borrow it?

"My watch, Mr. Daltry. Would you like to borrow my watch?"

Lifting his gaze a notch to the place where she'd suddenly pressed her finger, he almost burst out laughing. He reached into his pocket and pulled out his watch, cradling it in his palm. "No, ma'am. I've got one."

"I thought you said you didn't have one."

"I, uh, I meant I didn't have one like yours, but I've got one."

She moved closer, and he could smell lavender on the breeze.

"Is it accurate?" she asked.

"Yes, ma'am."

"And what time is it?"

She lifted her round, blinking eyes to his. It was an effort, but he looked down at his watch. "Twenty past eight."

"Then why aren't you ringing your bell?"

Reaching down, he picked up the cowbell. "I had to go find one."

"Mr. Daltry, you must plan the day better than that. You have a responsibility to these children to be fully prepared." She spun on her heel and began walking back to the millinery.

He wanted to run after her and tell her he was prepared, but the bell weighed heavy in his hand, and he figured it didn't matter what he did, he'd never feel prepared. He trudged to the schoolhouse steps and clanked the old bell.

He felt ridiculous. He didn't think the sweat slithering down his neck had much to do with the warm morning. When the first child arrived, mother in tow, he felt his awkwardness evaporate like the early morning dew coating clover. He knew he could handle mothers. After all, they were female, and he saw nothing wrong with a little harmless flirtation. As more children and their mothers gathered around him, he smiled and deepened the dimples in his cheeks. With a wink, he explained that the cakes and pies they'd brought wouldn't earn their children any favors. The ladies simply smiled and left the desserts on his desk.

When the last child walked through the door of the schoolhouse, when the last mother reluctantly meandered toward home, Lee took a deep breath, squared his shoulders, and walked into what he was certain was going to be purgatory.

"Are you a man or a marm?" one of the older boys dared to shout from the back of the schoolroom as soon as Lee reached his desk.

Lee turned, leaned against the desk, crossed his arms over his chest, and laughed. His students were planning on giving him a hard time, and he couldn't blame them. He'd given a teacher or two a hard time in his lifetime. An image of flaming orange hair jumped into his mind, and he thought of a teacher he'd unwittingly given a hard time. He shook Meredith Lewis from his thoughts. Right now, he needed to concentrate on his labor.

He glanced across the sea of faces. With her hand covering her mouth, Allie was giggling. Atlas was busily scribbling something. Lee was certain he was making a list of everything that was said in this room so he could read the comments off at supper. He cleared his throat and straightened his stance. "I'm your new teacher, and together we're all gonna learn a great deal."

"How can you be a teacher if you still got learning to do?"

Lee smiled at Jimmy Stellar. A glimmer of hope seemed to dwell in the boy's brown eyes as though he thought it would be wonderful if his teacher didn't know everything. "I think we learn something every day, and we learn when we teach other people. I'll teach you how to write." He pointed over his shoulder toward the blackboard.

"Gosh darn, you got purty writing!" someone exclaimed.

Lee felt his chest swell at the praise, something he'd never before received in a classroom. "And you'll teach me patience."

The children's laughter filled the room and floated out the window. Lee gave them a moment to vent their jitters, laugh, and tease him a bit more. Then he clapped his hands together. "All right. Now that we've had a little fun teasing and getting to know each other, we need to settle into learning."

The children sitting in the schoolhouse for the first time

eagerly leaned forward, their eyes round with excitement as though they were about to witness magic. The seasoned students shuffled their books and slates around, settling in for what they were certain was going to be a boring day. Lee had settled in the same way for years, and over the years, the teachers had never disappointed him.

"Hal, why don't you begin reading from your reader?"

Hal Anderson shot his head up with such force that his sandy blond hair momentarily lifted before falling back into place low over his brows, almost obscuring his green eyes. He cast a furtive glance toward his best friend. Allie nodded brusquely before fixing her silvery gray-eyed gaze intently on Lee.

Lee rolled his eyes, wondering if she expected special treatment for her friends. She'd already told him Hal was the best reader in the class. It was the only reason he'd called on the boy. He nodded toward Hal. "Go on, Hal. Stand up and read to everybody. That's a good way to begin the day."

Hal eased out of the bench seat he shared with Atlas and opened his book, slowly turning pages. His fingers stopped, he took a deep breath and began reading in a voice that occasionally creaked with his nervousness. After he read the first sentence, he peered at Lee. Lee gave him an encouraging nod and smile before sitting at his desk, putting his hands behind his head, and leaning back to enjoy the recitation.

The Anderson ranch bordered the Daltry ranch. Hal and Allie had been friends, almost inseparable, for as long as he could remember. He figured they'd both rather be out riding horses than sitting in this classroom. He could understand that feeling. He'd rather be out working the range.

His gaze slowly drifted to the open window where the varying shades of green beckoned beyond. Scattered trees shaded the schoolhouse, then the land gave way to a wide-open field blanketed with flowers. Nothing compared to the feel of running barefoot through a field of clover and flowers.

He wondered if Miss Lewis had ever run barefoot through a meadow with her skirts hiked up, her hair hanging loose around her shoulders, the sun kissing her face. His memories of her had changed considerably since last night when he walked her home. Until then, the anger darkening her brown eyes as she flung the books at him had become his most vivid memory of her. Now, he saw the anger as passion; he'd taken her position, taken from her something that was obviously important to her. If someone took the ranch from him, he'd do a hell of a lot more than throw books.

He thought about the light smattering of freckles that graced her nose and cheeks. He'd never thought of freckles as attractive, yet on Miss Lewis they added an allure to her pale skin that made him envy the sun for having the freedom to touch her and brand her as its own whenever she stepped outside.

Last night, she'd stiffened when he'd wrapped his hands around her small waist and lifted her onto Pegasus. He wondered if she'd stiffen if he grazed the back of his hand along her cheek. His fingers were too rough from working the ranch, might scratch her cheeks, but the back of his hand—

He felt something wet hit his cheek and glanced down at the tiny wad of paper that had fallen into his lap. A ball of spit. It had come sailing from the girls' side of the room, and he knew only one girl with the skills to hit her mark. He glared at Allie, and she glared angrily back, motioning her head toward Hal.

It was only then that Lee realized the boy's voice had gone hoarse. Sweet Lord, how long had he been daydreaming? He jerked forward, listening to the scratchy voice, and filled with guilt. He cleared his throat, and Hal glanced up from his reading.

"That's very good, Hal. We're all obliged to you for reading to us. You can sit down now."

Relief washed over Hal's face as he sank onto the bench seat. Lee scraped his chair across the floor, got up, and walked to the window. Lord, but it was a beautiful morning. The sun had already gathered up the dew so the ground was dry.

"Mr. Daltry, sir, what are we gonna do now?"

He turned and studied the anxious faces studying him.

"How many of you listened, I mean really listened, to Hal while he was reading?"

Allie's hand shot up; a few other hands rose more slowly.

"Take off your shoes, boots, and socks," Lee ordered as he leaned against the sill and began to do as he'd ordered.

"What are we gonna do, Mr. Daltry?"

Smiling, Lee addressed his classroom. "We're gonna go outside."

Meredith heard the ring of excited voices, children's voices, and the deep rumble of laughter, a man's laughter. Twisting her head to glance outside, diverting her attention from her task, she jabbed the needle into her thumb. She released a small cry before shoving the thumb into her mouth, ignoring the rustic taste of her own blood.

She eased her spectacles into place and squinted against the brightness of the day. Books in their arms, the children followed Lee Daltry as though he were Pan, his laughter serving him in place of the lute.

She glanced at her watch. A few minutes past nine. Much too early for lunch, much too soon to give the children a recess.

The schoolteacher dropped to the ground and leaned

against a tree. The children gathered at his feet, their attention riveted on him. She couldn't hear his words, could only see his hands waving and creating images at which she could only guess. He wrote something on each older child's slate and handed it back. They jumped to their feet and hurried away.

He took a slate from a tiny girl and wrote something. The remaining smaller children nodded as though in understanding and then raced across the field alongside the schoolhouse.

Meredith jerked her thumb out of her mouth, clenched her jaw, and concentrated on the stupid hat resting in her lap. Lee Daltry had no concept of what it was to teach children. He'd let them play all day, and they'd learn nothing.

It had been a mistake to sit where she could see the schoolhouse, but the red clapboard building was familiar to her, was built in the shape of her dreams. She didn't want to lose sight of her dreams.

Lee watched the children scurrying over the field like so many ants at a Fourth of July picnic. A movement to the side caught his eye, and he looked toward the millinery. Miss Lewis was trudging toward him, and she looked to be a woman with a mission. Since she was by nature a teacher, it probably wouldn't work, but when she was near enough, he stood and bestowed upon her his best smile.

"Mr. Daltry, I feel compelled to point out that it is too early for the children to come outside to play."

Nope, his smile hadn't distracted her one bit. "Yes, ma'am, I figured as much."

Her gaze dropped to his feet, barely visible through the thick, tall grass and wildflowers. He didn't know it was possible for a person to turn such a deep shade of red. Her freckles nearly disappeared. She shot her gaze back up to his and thrust her chin forward.

"Then why are they outside?"

"We're having a lesson on the alphabet."

"Outside?"

"Yes, ma'am."

"Mr. Daltry, the entire reasoning behind constructing a school building is so children have a place where they can learn with no distractions. This area"—she flung her arm out in a wide circle as though to encompass the entire world—"is filled with distractions."

"It's filled with the sounds of letters, too."

The children returned with treasures bundled in their skirts or shoved into their pockets. "Now if you'll excuse me, Miss Lewis, I got a lesson to teach." He dropped to the ground, turned his attention to the youngest children, and held up the slate he'd used earlier.

"What letter is this?" he asked.

They cried in unison, "O!"

"And what sound does it make?"

They screamed the sound.

"And what did you find that begins with that sound?"

He'd sent the four youngest children out in a group together. Danny Guslock waved his hand energetically in the air, his elbow knocking the head of the little girl sitting next to him.

"What did you find, Danny?"

The towheaded boy held up an acorn. The older children snickered, then fell into silence when Lee scowled at them. He turned his attention back to the leader of the group, the pride in the boy's dark eyes mirroring that of the children who'd helped him locate his find. How did one correct a child without destroying the child's desire to learn? Lee hoped it wasn't much different from taming a horse without breaking its spirit.

"That's an acorn, Danny," he said quietly, emphasizing

the "a" in acorn as he spoke.

The members of the small group shook their heads as smiles filled their faces.

"It's an oak tree seed," Danny said, puffing his chest out. "O . . . O . . . Oak tree seed!"

Laughing, Lee whisked the acorn out of the boy's hand. "So it is! That's very good!"

With a broad smile on his face, he gazed up at Miss Lewis. Her eyes were blinking rapidly. She angled her chin defiantly, spun on her heel, and began walking back to The Hatbox. Lee wondered why the sweet victory made him feel as though he'd lost something precious.

He settled in against the trunk of the tree. "All right now, let's see." He eyed the older children. He'd written a different letter on each of their slates. "Jimmy Stellar. What letter's sound were you supposed to search for?"

The lanky boy squirmed, his skinny arms dangling out of sleeves that had become too short over the summer. "You're the schoolmarm," he mumbled. "You're supposed to remember."

"I can't remember everything, Jimmy. That's why I wrote it on your slate. What does your slate say?"

Jimmy shrugged his bony shoulders. "Don't know. It got erased by accident."

Lee studied the twelve-year-old whose eyes had never strayed from the ground. He wondered if the boy was afraid he'd see the truth if their eyes met, but more, he wondered what the truth was. "Accidents sometimes happen," he said quietly.

Jimmy's shoulders relaxed as though a burden had been lifted, and Lee wondered what the burden was. What letter had he given Jimmy? Maybe he hadn't been able to find anything that began with that letter. "Would you like me to give you another letter?"

The tenseness returned to the boy's shoulders.

"It's a stupid game. Ain't supposed to play games in school." Jimmy snapped his head up, his eyes accusatory. "Don't you know nuthin' 'bout being a schoolmarm?"

"I know that often when we teach someone, we teach ourselves at the same time."

"That don't make no sense. 'Sides, we all know our letters so we don't need to learn them again."

"The younger children don't. I was gonna let each of you share the letter I gave you with them."

"So we're doing your job. You're supposed to teach us things we don't know."

Lee raised a knee and draped his arm over it. "What's something you don't know, Jimmy?"

Jimmy's gaze darted around as though he was trying to find a way to bolt from the corner into which he'd just placed himself. Lee took pity on him. He'd had enough uncomfortable moments while in school to empathize with Jimmy, but he'd at least had the good sense to keep his mouth shut so he didn't draw attention to himself. "That's all right, Jimmy. Who wants to share their letter with the younger children?"

"Letters are stupid," Jimmy blurted out. "Who thunk 'em up anyway? Some idiot?"

"Does anyone know where letters came from?" Lee asked.

Jimmy snorted as everyone else shook their heads. "There you go again, looking to us for the answers. Bet you don't even know where they came from."

"They came from Alpha," Lee said quietly, his gaze on Jimmy, but his voice covering the remaining children like a blanket.

"Alpha was a boy king. Fifteen years old when his father died, and the golden crown was placed on his head. His kingdom was small, but his people were happy. When word of his father's death spread across the land, the mighty Lucifer decided he would conquer Alpha's kingdom. He tried time and again, but Alpha was a wise commander despite his youth and his army followed the orders he shouted.

"But the gods smiled on Lucifer, and when he asked them for help, they took away Alpha's voice so he could no longer shout orders to his men. In those days, no one had ever heard of writing."

Lee wove the tale of a courageous man who devised a way to communicate with his army using symbols painted on cloth. He described the battles in elaborate detail, the tragedy of defeat, the glory of victory.

The children sat mesmerized as he carried them to the final battle where Alpha's goodness and use of symbols triumphed over evil.

"The gods were impressed with Alpha's cunning. They gave him back his voice and turned his symbols into the alphabet so all people could communicate as Alpha had taught his soldiers."

A few words of wonder were whispered, and Lee could see an abundance of smiles. He couldn't recall ever smiling in school except for the time when a grass snake had slithered into the classroom, and the teacher had screamed and climbed on her desk. It made him feel good to see smiles on his students' faces.

"That's why we have letters. Why we learn to write and read them. Some of the stories in your reader were written by people who are no longer alive, but their words live on, are as immortal as the gods on Mount Olympus. So, Atlas, why don't you share your letter with us?"

As Atlas explained what he'd found to represent his letter, Lee looked toward the millinery and saw a flash of orange in the window. He wished Miss Lewis had stayed long enough to hear his story.

Smiling, he wondered if she was going to wear a trail between The Hatbox and the schoolhouse before the week was out.

Chapter
Six

By the end of the week, Miss Lewis hadn't worn a trail between The Hatbox and the schoolhouse. As a matter of fact, since the first day, Lee had only caught glimpses of her bowed head in the window of the millinery as he sat beneath the shade of the tree and ate his lunch. Sometimes, he wondered where she ate her lunch, but most of the time, he was too busy trying to keep up with his students.

On more than one occasion, he actually found himself enjoying the little rascals. His greatest feeling of accomplishment had unexpectedly come when he strayed from his lesson plan to explain how numbers worked and why they were important.

"If hair ribbons cost two pennies each, and Jimmy Stellar has three girlfriends and wants to buy them each two ribbons, he's got to be able to figure out that he needs to take ten pennies to the mercantile," he said.

"He's gonna lose one of his girlfriends," Allie called out, smiling. "He's gonna need twelve pennies."

Furrowing his brow, Lee walked behind his desk and wrote the numbers on the blackboard, ciphering as he went. Red-faced, he turned to his class, dreading the snickers and laughter that would follow his announcement. "Allie's right."

A reverent silence filled the room. Shifting his stance, Lee wondered how to convince them he was still capable of teaching them even if he had fumbled the problem he was trying to explain.

Hal Anderson raised his hand. "Gosh, Mr. Daltry. We ain't never had a teacher admit to being wrong before—even when we could prove they were wrong. Sure makes me feel better knowing you're gonna listen to what we have to say." Then his face had split into a wide grin. "Reckon you might turn out to be the best schoolmarm we ever had!"

Lee certainly wanted to be the best teacher they'd ever had. It was the reason he was still in the classroom even though all his students, except one, had left for the day, heading home to chores and families.

The one student who remained was Jimmy Stellar.

Jimmy had visibly stiffened when Lee told him he wanted to speak with him privately after school. He hadn't even smiled when Lee tried to ease his discomfort by saying he wanted to talk with him "marm to man."

As Lee wrote the single sentence across the blackboard, he was acutely aware of Jimmy studying him. He felt like Minotaur, a monster intent on destruction. Only he hoped by destroying, he could build. "What did I write?"

Jimmy set his jaw stubbornly. "A bunch of words."

"What do the words say?"

"How come I had to stay after school?"

"Because you won't read to me."

"I don't got to prove I can read. I know I can. That's all that matters."

Slowly Lee shook his head. "You've got to show me

you can read. At first, I thought you were just hesitant to read before the class. I can understand that. I hated to read out loud when I was in school so I brought you up here while everyone else was busy and asked you to read to me quietly. You wouldn't do it.''

''I like to read the words to myself. Words lose their magic if you share them with everyone.''

Lee studied the boy, the way his hands were balled into fists until his knuckles were almost white; the way his brown eyes darted around the room whenever he spoke.

''But you know how to read?'' Lee asked quietly.

Jimmy gave a brusque nod and relaxed his hands a fraction.

''You know what the sentence I wrote on the board says?''

Jimmy glanced at the board, then met Lee's gaze squarely. His fists tightened. He nodded.

''And you don't want to read it out loud?''

Jimmy shook his head.

''You sure?''

Jimmy nodded, and Lee crossed his arms over his chest. ''I don't think you can read, Jimmy.''

Jimmy jumped to his feet and pounded his tightly balled fists on the desk. ''I can, I tell you! I can read! I know what that stupid sentence says!''

''What does it say?''

''It's a stupid sentence. Stupid just like you. Just like all your stupid teaching. I ain't gonna read out loud when I know how to read quiet! And you can't make me!''

''Do you want me to read the sentence to you?''

''Can if you want. Don't matter 'cuz I already read it to myself.''

''All right.'' Lee put his finger beneath the first word on the blackboard. ''Do you know what this word is?''

Jimmy lifted his chin defiantly. ''Don't you know?''

"I know, but do you?"

"Course, I do. It's 'if.' "

"And this word?"

"That's simple enough. It's my name."

Lee moved his finger so it was beneath the third word. "And this word?"

Jimmy crossed his arms. "You're trying to trick me again, and I ain't stupid."

"I don't think you're stupid, Jimmy. As a matter of fact, I think you're so smart that if you could read this sentence, you would, and you'd read it out loud. It says, 'If Jimmy reads this sentence out loud, I will pay him one hundred dollars.' "

"You're lying!"

"No, Jimmy, I'm not." Lee slowly, patiently placed the tip of his finger under each word and read it aloud again.

Jimmy jutted out his quivering lower lip. "I hate you!" he yelled just before he bolted from the room.

Lee tore out after him and caught Jimmy just before he passed the oak tree. He wrapped a strong hand around Jimmy's skinny arm and pulled him against his chest. Jimmy bucked like a wild horse feeling the weight of a saddle upon its back for the first time. The heel of his bare foot landed squarely on Lee's shin. Lee grunted, but didn't release his hold.

"Stop fighting me, Jimmy."

"I know what the sentence said," Jimmy wailed. "I just didn't want your blasted money!"

Lee held him close. "Ah, Jimmy, it's more than the reading I'm worried about. I never see you playing with anyone or talking with the other boys. If you can't read, you don't have to feel ashamed. I can help you, but you've got to want me to."

The boy went limp, but Lee had too many brothers to lower his defenses. He slumped against the tree, his arms still holding Jimmy as though he were a calf to be branded. "Can you read, Jimmy?" he asked in a low voice that blended in with the rustling of the leaves in the trees.

Jimmy tried to push away, but found himself held more firmly. "Some," he admitted reluctantly.

"Have you told your pa you're having trouble reading?" Jimmy shook his head.

"Would you like me to talk with your pa, see if he can help you?"

Jimmy pressed his face against Lee's chest, carefully avoiding Lee's gaze. "My pa . . . my pa's too busy. He's got real important things he has to do."

Lee didn't know why, but he knew if he couldn't reach this boy, if he let this boy walk away, he'd be a failure as a schoolteacher. It didn't matter if he taught something to every other child in that classroom, if he ignored the needs of this one, he may as well have never accepted the challenge of his grandmother's labor. But he also knew he couldn't do it alone, not when the boy's problem involved reading. Lee could only take him so far, and he had a feeling Jimmy was smart enough to want to go farther.

It seemed of late everywhere he turned, he was unwittingly hurting people and then finding himself unable to help them. Jimmy felt betrayed by Lee's trick to uncover the truth just as Meredith Lewis had felt betrayed when she was replaced as schoolteacher.

Lee still felt a pang of guilt whenever he thought of her working in the millinery when she really wanted to be teaching school. He'd wanted to find a way to make it up to her. An idea took hold in his mind, a small idea that grew as he continued to think about it. "Jimmy, what if I could get Miss Lewis to tutor you?"

It was only when Jimmy sniffed that Lee realized the child had been quietly crying. Lee slid to the ground, bringing the boy with him. He let one arm come away from the boy, but he had enough strength and agility from years of working a ranch to halt the boy if he tried to bolt again. He put a hand beneath Jimmy's chin and tilted his face. "You shouldn't feel ashamed because you can't read, but now you have the opportunity to learn. If you don't take advantage of that, then you should feel ashamed. Miss Lewis has a teaching certificate and could teach you to read."

Jimmy ran a finger repeatedly beneath his nose. "I can read."

"But you could read better," Lee said kindly. "With Miss Lewis's help you could learn to read every word that I wrote on that board."

Jimmy braved a half grin. "Think you might write that sentence on the board again someday?"

Lee smiled. "I might if I thought you could read it."

"You really reckon Miss Lewis could teach me how to read it?"

"I'm certain she can teach you. You're a smart boy."

Jimmy's dark eyes brightened up. "And you'll write that sentence on the board again?"

"Maybe."

Jimmy worked his way free of Lee's hold. "I gotta get home. Thanks, Mr. Daltry." He darted across the field.

Leaning against the tree, Lee hoped it would be easier to get Miss Lewis to agree to help Jimmy than it had been to get Jimmy to admit he couldn't read. He rubbed his shin. It wasn't nearly as sore as his thigh had been when Miss Lewis's book had struck it. Although her anger seemed to have diminished, he decided not to take any chances. He wanted to approach her when she didn't have a book in sight.

Early the next morning, he stopped by the boardinghouse on his way to school, but Miss Lewis had already left for the millinery. He walked to The Hatbox and gazed in the window. Meredith Lewis was holding a large hat pin in one hand. Backing away, he stumbled off the boardwalk.

Talking to her at the millinery wasn't going to work. No telling where the woman might stick that lethal-looking pin, or what she might do to him with scissors in her hand. Lee shuddered as he walked to the schoolhouse. He needed to arrange a meeting where they would be on neutral ground.

Throughout the day as he listened to recitations, watched the careful drawing of letters, and extended the lesson beyond books, he thought about Miss Lewis. Somewhere he'd heard that back East when a fellow took an interest in a lady, he wrote a poem to invite her on an outing, and a friend delivered it to her. She would then pen her own poem, accepting his invitation, and send it back to him. Since Miss Lewis came from Boston, Lee was certain she'd received her fair share of poems delivered by friends of young men who'd sought her company. He didn't want her to think he was some uncultured cowboy who didn't know the fine art of courting.

As the children left for the day, Lee pulled a blank sheet of paper from his desk, dipped the tip of the pen into the inkwell, and wrote:

> *Roses are red.*
> *Violets are blue.*
> *I sure would like*
> *to have dinner with you.*

He signed the note, careful to show his talent at handwriting to impress Miss Lewis. He folded the note in thirds and wrote her name on the outside. Glancing up, he wasn't surprised to see Danny Guslock sitting at his desk working. The child loved to be on Lee's good side and was forever offering to help with the erasers.

"Danny?"

Danny's head popped up.

"I was wondering if you could run this note over to Miss Lewis at the millinery."

The boy's face lit up like fireworks at the Fourth of July. He scrambled out of his desk, rushed across the room, and took the note, holding it in worshipful hands.

"Tell Miss Lewis that you'll wait for her to give you an answer."

Danny's face grew serious as he realized the importance of his errand. He gave a brusque nod before running from the building.

With his fingers intertwined behind his head, Lee leaned back in his chair and waited.

It wasn't long before Danny returned with his note. In small, delicate script, she'd written "No, thank you" across the bottom of the note. Lee stared at her reply as though he were Jimmy Stellar and didn't know how letters formed words and words formed sentences.

When the rejection finally took root in his mind, he pulled out another sheet of paper and wrote:

> *Red is the rose.*
> *Brown is the deer.*
> *We could eat*
> *at the Buccaneer.*

He signed his name just in case she had admirers in town who might be sending her poems at the same time, folded the note, scribbled her name across it, and handed it to Danny with the same instructions.

Lee shoved himself out of his chair and walked through the classroom, putting books into desks and picking up a crumpled paper that had probably been used to pass a thought across the classroom while he'd been teaching.

Breathless, Danny rushed in and handed the note to Lee.

Opening it, Lee was dumbfounded by the "Not interested" that she'd scribbled in the corner. "Wait here."

He walked outside and picked a handful of daisies from the field that ran along the edge of town. Returning to the schoolhouse, he sat behind his desk and took pen in hand. Obviously, the woman had been courted by the best and received some very convincing poetry. He rubbed his chin, then set pen to paper.

The truth is, Miss Lewis, I have a problum, and I need your help. Will swap a meal at the Buc for your time.

He handed the note and daisies to Danny, who'd been waiting expectantly for the next mission. As soon as the boy was out the door, Lee stood. He wasn't exactly nervous, but he'd never before had a woman rebuke his attentions, and it seemed Miss Lewis was intent on continually rebuking him. He'd rather have her throwing books.

He began wiping his words off the blackboard. He didn't like the fact that he was listening for the sound of Danny's feet running back from the millinery. He forced his attention away from Miss Lewis and thought about the frog that had escaped from someone's pocket that morning.

It had created havoc with the children alternately screaming and laughing. When they finally caught the creature, Lee placed it in a box on his desk. Then he held a frog-naming contest. For the remainder of the day, Homer had croaked. Chuckling, he wondered how Miss Lewis would react to a frog named Homer in her classroom.

"Mr. Daltry?"

Spinning around, Lee wished he had been listening for the sound of footsteps. He certainly hadn't expected Miss Lewis to walk into his classroom, holding his note in one hand, clutching his daisies in the other. Quickly he glanced around to make sure no books were in sight. Breathing a sigh of relief, he walked around his desk. "Miss Lewis, I'm so glad you came."

She arched a brow. "You left me little choice. I felt compelled to come and tell you that you had misspelled 'problem.' It's P-R-O-B-L-E-M not P-R-O-B-L-U-M."

He bestowed upon her the most charming smile he possessed. "Yes, ma'am, I know. I figured if the flowers didn't work to get you over here, misspelling a word would."

Meredith fought hard to hold back her laughter. Hercules Daltry looked like a recalcitrant schoolboy who'd just pulled the wool over the teacher's eyes. "You said you were having a problem?"

Lee looked at Danny who had returned to his desk and was busily working. He knew he could simply ask the boy to take the erasers outside and clean them so he could talk privately with Miss Lewis, but he'd just been struck with the realization that he actually did want to have dinner with her.

His smile grew, and he stepped closer. "Yes, and it involves a student. I'd rather discuss it over dinner at the Buc." He tilted his head slightly toward Danny. "Where little ears can't hear."

It was so obvious the man thought he would wile her with his charms, but Meredith wasn't a flighty female. She'd told herself repeatedly on the way to the schoolhouse that she had not been charmed by his poetry or his flowers. It was only genuine concern that the problem might involve a student—and the misspelled word—that had brought her here. He could tell her his problem without dinner. "I'm not certain dinner would be appropriate."

"Please, Miss Lewis. It'll be business . . . pure and simple. Nothing more."

Lee could tell from the thoughtful expression on her face that she was giving it some serious consideration. "Pretty please. I'll even bring the books so you can throw them if you feel a need."

"Will I feel a need, Mr. Daltry?"

The change in his grin was subtle, and if Meredith hadn't been studying it so intently, she might not have noticed, but it seemed at that moment to become sincerely tender and more a reflection of the man.

"I certainly hope not, Miss Lewis. I promise to be on my best behavior."

"I'm not certain—"

"Please, Miss Lewis. Please with sugar and cream and cinnamon and butter."

"All this sweetness to discuss business?"

"It concerns one of my students."

She didn't want to admit to him that she was impressed he'd go to such lengths to help a student—to wear a stupid grin, send silly poetry, and practically beg her for dinner—but she did reluctantly acknowledge it to herself. "Very well. I'll have dinner with you this evening."

He bowed slightly. "I'll pick you up at the boarding-house at seven if that's agreeable."

"It is."

His grin remained, and Meredith allowed a small smile to ease upon her own face.

"Mr. Daltry, sir?"

Lee's gaze darted over to Danny. "Yes, Danny?"

"That problem you gave the bigger kids—how many animals are in the barn if there are five horses, twenty-one cows, and two pigs? Is the answer twenty-eight?"

"Yes, Danny, it is."

"Boy howdy! I knew I could figure it out!"

Lee puffed out his chest, certain Miss Lewis would be impressed with his teaching skills, belatedly noticing the smile was gone from her face.

"That's the way you're teaching them?" she asked, disbelief laced through her voice.

"Yep, I'm taking a practical approach, relating everything to things that they already know or things they'll need when they start working a range—''

"And if they never work a range?"

Lee was taken aback, surprised by the condemnation in her voice. "Most of these children come from ranching families—"

"But what of those who don't? What of those who move to the city? How will they be able to relate what you're teaching them with what they'll need? They need to know their mathematics tables, not how many animals are in a barn."

Lee had never considered that, and even now, he didn't understand why his method wouldn't work. "I'm teaching them what they need to know—"

"You're teaching them what *you* needed to know, Mr. Daltry. You can't have such a narrow outlook—"

"*I* have a narrow outlook? You won't even give my method of teaching a chance. You're condemning it before you've even seen if it'll work."

"Because I care about children—"

"So do I, Miss Lewis. I care about these children in particular so I'll pick you up at seven like we'd planned. Now if you'll excuse me, I've got erasers to clean."

He gathered up the erasers and stormed from the building. Danny jumped to his feet and raced after him.

Meredith stared at the empty desks, heard the silence roar through her ears, smelled the lingering scent of chalk dust, and felt the familiar ache of loneliness.

This classroom, these students, should have been hers.

Chapter
Seven

It was business, pure and simple.

So why had Meredith spent the early evening pressing the wrinkles out of the blue dress she reserved for church? Why had she brushed her hair to a sheen, then pulled it back and secured it in place with a new black ribbon she'd bought at the mercantile on her way home from the millinery?

The answer was pure and simple. Hercules Daltry had a reputation with the ladies, and she didn't want him to feel embarrassed when he walked beside her to the Buccaneer.

Pure and simple.

So why did she even care that he might be embarrassed to be seen with her?

Why did she keep thinking about the glimpse of tenderness she'd seen in his smile?

Why did her heart leap when she heard a horse whinny, and why did her stomach flutter when she heard a knock on the door that carried itself all the way up the stairs to her room?

It was business . . . pure and simple. She glanced at her reflection in the cheval mirror and saw the truth staring back at her with distorted eyes and orange hair. It *was* business—pure and simple.

She walked into the hallway just as Mrs. Bennett hurried down the corridor in a flurry, patting her chest. "My dear, you should have told me Lee Daltry was calling on you. We could have done something with your hair."

She forced a reassuring smile. "My hair is fine, and Mr. Daltry is not calling on me. We're going to discuss some concerns he has about one of his students."

A small moue of disappointment formed on Mrs. Bennett's lips.

Meredith suddenly wished she hadn't changed into her blue dress. He might think she was expecting more than a business meeting, might think she'd anticipated this evening. He would no doubt enjoy laughing over her discomfort, but at least he had arrived. She'd been concerned after his curt dismissal at the schoolhouse that he might have changed his mind and not come, which was why she hadn't said anything to Mrs. Bennett. Disappointments were best handled alone, when no one else knew of their existence.

She riveted her attention to her feet as she descended the stairs, only daring to lift her gaze when she entered the parlor. Relief coursed through her at the sight of Hercules Daltry standing in the parlor wearing a brown jacket, a starched white shirt, and a black string tie. A bouquet of flowers filled one hand while his battered hat filled the other.

Taking an awkward step toward her, he extended the flowers. Bringing them near her nose, she inhaled the sweet unfamiliar scent.

"My mother has a flower garden," he said by way of an explanation.

"Will she mind that you took these?"

He offered her a small smile. "Only if she finds out."

"I've never seen flowers such as these, never smelled anything quite so sweet, but not sweet if that makes sense."

"My mother enjoys growing new kinds of flowers. She thinks a lot of them up herself. She calls those Hercules because they'll weather any storm."

Blushing, Meredith tightened her fingers around the sturdy stems. The heart-shaped petals were a blue that matched his eyes. "I should put these in some water."

"I'll do that for you, dear," Mrs. Bennett said as she bustled into the room. "I do so love Jane's flowers. She's trying to create a vine now that will run in all directions, and she's going to name it after my grandson Simon." She took the flowers from Meredith. "Now, run along, you two, and enjoy yourselves."

Lee crossed the room and shoved open the door. Gathering her courage, Meredith swept past him, trying not to put any significance to the flowers. He undoubtedly always brought women flowers when he ate dinner with them. A man of his charms would do so without thinking. It was business tonight. Business. She ran the litany through her mind as they walked the short distance to the Buccaneer.

Lee liked the way the flame from the candle highlighted Meredith's hair. In the dim light, her freckles were barely visible, and he discovered he missed them. He also found that he was able to do little more than smile at her. He felt like he'd left his tongue at the ranch and all his charms along with it.

As they ate their meal in an awkward silence, he was acutely aware of their utensils clicking against the plates. Every time he smiled at her, she dropped her gaze to her plate and ate more vigorously. She was obviously still upset about this afternoon.

Anger wasn't an emotion he enjoyed hanging on to, and

he usually released it as soon as possible. It appeared Miss Lewis liked to gnaw on her anger the way a mongrel pup chewed on a bone. He needed to get her mind off their little spat this afternoon. The flowers hadn't worked as he'd hoped, and she wasn't charmed by his smiles. So that limited his options. He gathered his wits about him and leaned across the table. "Listen, Red."

She snapped her head back, her eyes darting around the eating establishment. Then her gaze met his. "To whom are you speaking?"

And he thought he was dense. He smiled. "You."

She blinked her eyes rapidly. "My name is not Red."

"But Miss Lewis takes so much time to say, and your first name's not much better. I figured if I gave you a shorter name, we could get more talking done in less time."

Leaning forward, she whispered harshly, "I don't want a shorter name, and I certainly don't want to be called Red. My hair—"

"I'm not calling you Red because of your hair. I'm referring to how red your cheeks got when you saw my bare feet that first day of school."

Her cheeks flared to a brilliant hue. She moved her hands to her lap. Although the table obstructed his view, he would have bet money she was strangling the napkin she'd carefully laid in her lap earlier. "I was understandably surprised. It's hardly appropriate attire for a teacher."

"Have you ever gone barefoot?"

"Certainly not."

"You don't know what you've missed. The clover is like velvet caressing the soles of your feet; the petals of flowers are like the lips of wood nymphs kissing your toes."

Meredith was lured by the deep timbre of his voice into the depths of his blue eyes. Had the gods created a male siren and neglected to warn the world? Her feet actually tingled and her toes curled. The image his words conjured left her with the unsettling desire to bare more than her feet. Mentally she shoved the daunting thoughts away. "Mr. Daltry, I thought we were here to discuss business."

"No harm in enjoying each other's company a little bit."

Meredith thought a great deal of harm could be done to her heart if she dared entertain the idea of enjoying his company. Lowering her gaze, she gingerly wiped the corners of her mouth with her napkin. "It would be entirely inappropriate under the circumstances to enjoy each other's company."

"When would it be appropriate, Miss Lewis?"

Her gaze shot up to his. Lee propped his elbow on the table, rested his chin in his palm, and thrummed his fingers against his cheek. "When would it be appropriate to enjoy your company?" Lord, he'd never seen her eyes blink so fast. It was amazing to watch. "Are you nervous, Miss Lewis?"

She folded her napkin into precise squares. "No."

"I am."

"Why in the world are you nervous?"

"I've never had dinner with a schoolmarm before."

As she shoved her spectacles up the bridge of her nose, her hand covered what he thought was a small smile. When she placed her hand in her lap, her lips showed the barest remnants of a grin, the tiniest tilting at the corners.

"I've never eaten dinner with a schoolmarm either," she admitted.

Smiling broadly, he dipped his head down, peering up at her. "Good Lord, Miss Lewis, I can almost see a smile. I'd swear you were teasing me."

The corners of her lips went up a shade higher. Making her smile was like pulling a calf toward a branding iron.

"It's all right to smile," he said.

Immediately the corners of her mouth dipped down. "Mr. Daltry, I was under the impression we were going to discuss a problem you were having with one of your students.''

Lee shoved his plate out of the way and planted both elbows on the table. So much for teasing and enjoyment. ''It's not so much that I'm having a problem with my student. It's that I've discovered one of my older students, Jimmy Stellar, can't read.''

Her interest piqued. ''How did you discover he couldn't read?''

Lee rolled his massive shoulders into a shrug. ''He kept finding excuses not to read out loud in class. He was forever losing his assignments, and he wasn't playing with the other children.''

Despite her reluctance to do so, Meredith was impressed with his perceptions. ''You noticed him not playing with the other children?''

''Sure. Every time we played leap frog or crack the whip, he was wandering toward the outhouse or staring at the horizon.''

Closing her eyes, she rubbed her fingertips into her brow. She'd forgotten about the times she'd glanced out the window of the millinery and seen Lee Daltry hunched over, holding his knees while the children leapt over his back.

''Good Lord, now you're gonna tell me I shouldn't play with the children.''

It was an effort, but she managed to keep the censure out of her voice. ''I'm just not certain it's wise. The children should look upon you as an authoritarian figure. That's a little difficult when they're scrambling over your back.''

''I don't see anything wrong with having a little fun.''

''It's counterproductive.''

''Playing makes it easier for them not to be afraid of me.''

''But discipline must be maintained.''

Lee plowed both hands through his hair and released a

frustrated sigh. "Miss Lewis, I'm not here to discuss whether or not I should play with the children. I'm here to discuss Jimmy's reading problem."

"Reading is simple enough to learn, Mr. Daltry. The school year has only just begun. If you were to put him with your first-year students—"

"He's twelve years old, Miss Lewis. He's skinny as a willow branch, but he's twice as tall as a six-year-old. Can you imagine how he'll feel sitting in a desk where his knees keep hitting the desktop?"

"I realize it's a challenge when all the children don't progress at the same rate, but perhaps if you were to give Jimmy some extra attention—"

"He's too proud. I had to wrestle him to the ground to get him to admit he couldn't read."

"You wrestled him to the ground?"

"He left me little choice."

She removed her spectacles and rubbed the bridge of her nose. She actually had very small eyes and finely arched eyebrows. "Do those spectacles weigh heavy on your nose?" Lee asked.

"I am accustomed to their weight. The alternative is to live in an unfocused world."

She slipped her spectacles on and her owllike gaze returned. He wished she didn't remind him of an owl. Owls were wise creatures. She was probably as wise if not more so, which made her too smart for him. He needed to get his thoughts off her and back onto Jimmy. "Anyway, if I start spending time with him in the classroom that I don't give the other students, they're gonna realize he has a problem, and they'll start teasing him about it."

"You could keep him after school—"

"They'd think I was punishing him for something."

"Talk with his parents—"

"Jimmy's mother died several years ago. I suppose with

the grief and learning to adjust to his mother being gone, he must have fallen behind in his learning. I can't remember the last time I saw his father in town, but as I recall whenever he did business with us, he signed his name with an X so I'm assuming he can't read or write either. When Jimmy fell behind, he had no one at home to help him.''

"And his teachers didn't notice."

"I guess not."

Against her will, Meredith was impressed that Lee Daltry had noticed and more impressed that he wanted to do something to help the boy. "I'm sorry, Mr. Daltry, but you seem to have already considered and discounted every suggestion I've proposed. I just don't think I can help you."

"Actually, I wasn't looking for suggestions. I was hoping I could convince you to tutor Jimmy."

"Tutor?"

"Yes, ma'am. I figured if you tutored him on the sly, away from school, Jimmy wouldn't feel so uncomfortable. I thought I'd talk to his pa and see if he'd be willing to pay you."

Meredith felt the excitement surge within her at the prospect of teaching again—even if it was only one student. "Do you think he would?"

Lee shrugged slightly. "I don't know. If he won't, I will, but I want to ask the boy's pa first. That is, if you're willing to tutor."

"Oh, yes, Mr. Daltry. I welcome the opportunity to teach again. As a matter of fact, I'd like very much to go with you when you talk with Jimmy's father."

He gave her the tender smile she'd seen that afternoon, and it was enough to make her wish this dinner wasn't business, pure and simple.

"I'd like for you to go with me. I think it would make for a better argument if Mr. Stellar could meet you."

"When should we go?"

"How about right after church on Sunday? Most people take a day of rest then. I imagine we'll be able to find Mr. Stellar at home."

Once they agreed to visit Mr. Stellar on Sunday, their conversation came to an abrupt halt. As Lee escorted Miss Lewis to the boardinghouse, he didn't feel uncomfortable as they walked along in silence. Actually, he enjoyed it. There was always so much laughing and talking at his own home that he often felt he couldn't think a clear thought without somebody else's thought intruding. He took a deep draft of air into his lungs and felt the dry air of West Texas filter down and fill his chest, and he smelled the barest hint of lavender.

Watching her, he wondered what her hair would look like if he untied the black ribbon and allowed the fiery tresses to flow around her shoulders. The sharp edges of her mouth might soften if something silky caressed her cheek.

She pushed the spectacles farther up the bridge of her nose and glanced at him. He flashed his most charming smile because at the moment he couldn't think of anything to say except to ask her if he could untie the ribbon holding her hair captive.

Surrounded by moon shadows, she walked as though she balanced an invisible book on her head. From time to time, he'd seen Venus walk with a book perched on her head, practicing to become a lady. Venus put great stock in appearances and said a woman needed to walk a certain way to attract a man, though truth be told, Lee had never taken a woman's walk into consideration when deciding whether or not he wanted to kiss her.

They arrived at the boardinghouse sooner than he would have liked, but he could think of no reason to prolong their walk. Sometimes, it was a curse to have thoughts that moved slower than a river that a beaver had dammed up.

He'd probably come up with a good reason when he was halfway home.

Stepping upon the porch, she faced him. He removed his hat. "I appreciate you putting our differences aside to help Jimmy."

"I can't allow pettiness to interfere with education, Mr. Daltry. I wouldn't be a worthy teacher if I did."

He put his foot on the porch, and she jumped back like a frightened doe. He gave her a smile of reassurance and laid his forearm across his thigh. "Miss Lewis, since we've agreed to help Jimmy, and we're gonna spend time together, do you think we might do away with the formality? My family and friends call me Lee. I'd like it if you would, too."

She pressed a hand to her chest, and he wondered if the beat of her heart was rapid or steady and slow.

"It wouldn't be proper, Mr. Daltry."

"What's not proper about it?"

"I hardly know you. Calling a man by his first name indicates a certain degree of intimacy. I wouldn't want people to get the wrong impression. Besides, this is still a business arrangement."

He was tempted to step on the porch, take her in his arms, and send the business arrangement to hell with a kiss. Only his concern for Jimmy and his fear she'd take back her offer stopped him. Straightening, he removed his foot from the porch, settled his hat on his head, and touched his finger to the brim. "Good night, Miss Lewis."

Meredith watched him walk away. He was out of sight before she finally whispered to the night, "Good night, Lee."

Chapter
Eight

The fact that Hercules Daltry was an exceedingly large man crystallized in Meredith's mind the instant he took his place in the buggy beside her, and his broad shoulders had no choice but to brush up against her narrow ones. He'd removed the jacket he'd worn to church, folded it neatly, and set it beneath the bench seat in the buggy, but that hardly made a difference in the space between them. It only gave Meredith the opportunity to watch the muscles on his arms flex and tighten as he'd rolled up his sleeves.

Determined to enjoy this little outing, she turned her attention to the green plains rolling gently before her. She had not ventured from Paradise Plains since her arrival. Although the town was more developed than many she'd passed on the way, it was a far cry from all the conveniences available in Boston.

"Do you miss your home, Miss Lewis?"

Jerking her head around, she was surprised to find him watching her instead of the dirt road they traveled. She wasn't surprised, however, to find him smiling. She was beginning to realize that he smiled as easily as the sun warmed the land. His eyes were silently laughing, and she wondered if he ever had a moment when he wasn't filled with gladness.

She smoothed a nonexistent wrinkle in her skirt. "No, Mr. Daltry, I do not."

"Guess you saw a great deal of the country when you were traveling here."

"Yes, I did. I documented everything I witnessed. I'd planned—" She stopped, unwilling to continue with a conversation that would only serve to remind her of all she'd hoped for, all she'd lost.

"You'd planned?" he prodded.

She averted her eyes. "I'd planned to share the experiences with my students."

Lee felt the sharp stab of guilt, then chided himself for feeling guilty about something that wasn't directly his fault. He wasn't the one who'd decided on this labor. If he had his druthers, he'd be breeding a three-horned calf by now. "I'm sure those notes'll keep."

"Yes, Mr. Daltry, I'm certain they will, and now I can include the return trip."

Lee heard the curt dismissal in her voice. Damn, but she was all prim and proper this afternoon, acting like a schoolmarm and making him feel like he was sitting in a classroom. He hated sitting in a classroom, and he wasn't a boy. The urge was strong to take her in his arms and give her a lesson that would teach her he was a man.

That irrational thought caused Lee to direct his attention back to the road and concentrate on the purpose for this trek. He certainly didn't need to become entangled with a schoolmarm, especially one whose life he'd upset. He guided the horse off the road and onto a worn trail. At the end of the trail, he pulled the buggy to a halt and studied the dilapidated wooden structure. A frayed and dirty curtain had worked its way through the broken glass of a window, or someone had stuffed it through the hole so the wind wouldn't blow into the house.

Meredith surveyed the debris-filled yard, not even venturing to guess what some of the rust-coated objects and rotting wood had been at one time. "Why did we stop here?" she asked.

"Because this is where Jimmy lives."

"Their house is little more than a shack," she whispered, horrified that anyone would live in a building that looked as though it might topple over if someone released a deep sigh anywhere in its vicinity.

"Yep, it needs some repairs, that's for sure."

"What does Mr. Stellar do for a living?" she asked.

"Odd jobs mostly. A couple of times he's worked for us during roundup or sorting time."

The buggy rocked as he climbed out. She thought she heard an expletive or two before he came around to her side.

"There's animal droppings everywhere and no telling what else. Do you want me to carry you?"

An image of Hercules Daltry cradling her within his massive arms caused an unsettling warmth to suffuse her body. "No, thank you, Mr. Daltry. I'm perfectly capable of skirting manure."

"Well then, Miss Lewis, you'd best start skirting on your way down to the ground."

He held out his hand, and Meredith knew she'd be a fool not to accept his assistance. She placed her hand in his and leapt as gracefully as she could over the disgusting slop that coated the ground. As soon as she made contact with the ground, she released his hand and lifted her skirt so it rose above her ankles. Cautiously she walked through the yard as Lee followed. When she reached the door, she knocked timidly.

No one answered.

She knocked louder, but still no response came. "Mr. Stellar! Jimmy!"

Silence answered.

She lifted her gaze to Lee. "Did you see Jimmy in church this morning?"

"They never come to church, not since Jimmy's ma died anyway. You wait here, and I'll have a look around."

"Be careful."

He gave her a lopsided grin. "Thank you for caring, Miss Lewis."

He hopped off the porch and disappeared behind a shed. Meredith watched large brown bees crawl in and out of what appeared to be mud plastered to the eaves of the porch. Spiderwebs decorated the railing so it appeared someone had tatted lace along the rotting wood. When a large black multilegged bug skittered by her shoe, she decided she'd rather be inside than out.

She tested the latch on the door. With the gentlest of pressures, it gave way to her touch. She peered through the tiny opening into the gloom beyond. "Jimmy!" she called out softly.

She eased the door open farther. "Mr. Stellar?"

Slipping into the dwelling, she was assaulted by the smell of rancid meat and rotting fruit. She heard the flies buzzing around the dirty dishes scattered haphazardly over the table. Her stomach lurched as she clamped a hand over her mouth, her fingers covering her nose as she staggered back and hit the wall.

If she could locate some water, she'd wash the dishes in order to eliminate the odor surrounding her, but the only water available had a murky layer skimming along the top.

Unable to stifle her curiosity, she searched the kitchen

area for some sign of recent habitation. She found none. The cupboards were bare, not a staple in sight—no flour, no sugar, no coffee. She wondered if Lee had made a mistake, if perhaps the Stellars had moved to another house. This shack contained little save the table and a sofa resting before a barren hearth, a hearth as barren as the cupboards.

She crossed the single room and knelt beside the sofa, lightly touching the soiled pillow. Lovingly, she picked up a much worn blanket and spread it over her lap. Someone, Jimmy's mother she suspected, had embroidered the faded and frayed horses that must at one time have been as vibrant and alive as the woman herself. She imagined a small child, clutching the small blanket for comfort, tiny fingers plucking at the threads because it was all he had of the woman who had once loved him.

She was startled by a sound at the door and glanced over her shoulder. "Any luck?" she asked as Lee walked toward her.

Somberly he shook his head, hunkered beside her, and rested his elbows on his spread thighs. "Maybe they've moved on."

She touched the threadbare remnants of Jimmy's baby blanket. "No, they're still here—or at least Jimmy is."

"We can wait a while if you want, but I'd rather do the waiting outside. My stomach's about to heave up Persy's blueberry flapjacks."

"It's those dishes. If you could locate some fresh water, I could at least wash them, get rid of some of the filth and stench."

He grimaced. "Wouldn't it be better just to burn them?"

"Probably, but they aren't mine to burn. Besides, that would leave them with nothing to eat on."

Reluctantly he unfolded his body. "I saw a well out back. If I can find a bucket, I'll get you some water."

"Thank you."

"I have a feeling you'd appreciate it more if I couldn't find any water."

She watched him trudge out the door, then carefully folded the small blanket before laying it on the pillow. Standing, she unbuttoned her cuffs and rolled up her sleeves, inventorying the room, trying to decide how much she could do before Mr. Stellar returned, how much she could do without offending him.

Lee walked in, pushing the door wide open before setting the bucket down on the table with a thump. "Let's leave the door open so we can at least get some air in here."

"There's no reason for you to stay while I clean up."

His gaze slowly circled the room, and she could see the uncertainty written across his face. He didn't want to stay, but he felt an obligation not to abandon her.

"Honestly, you don't have to stay." She began placing the soiled dishes in the bucket. She had both hands in the bucket when he walked up behind her. She thought if she took a deep breath, her back would lie up against his chest. She resisted the urge to fill her lungs, her senses, with his masculine bay rum scent even though it would be much more pleasant than what lay before her on the table.

She saw a flash of red just before her nose and mouth were covered. Her hands flew out of the water, sending droplets over the table and her bodice. She touched the soft cloth. "What's this?"

"A bandanna. It'll stop some of the smell from getting to your nose."

"Where did it come from?"

"My pocket. A good cowboy never goes anywhere without one. Never know when the wind will pick up and bring a dust storm your way, or you'll get caught on the tail end of a herd."

Dipping her hands into the bucket, she worked to clean a plate. "I feel like an outlaw."

"Believe me, Red, you don't look anything like an out-law."

She glanced over her shoulder. His eyes and lips were smiling. "I thought we had agreed to keep the relationship businesslike."

"No, you agreed. I just went along until the time was right."

"Then you've made a grave error in judgment. This is hardly the time to be informal."

"Yeah, well, I don't see any books around so I figure I'm safe."

Against her will, she smiled, grateful the bandanna prevented him from seeing it. She watched his large hands rub his thick thighs.

"I'll see if I can find something I can use to fix that window," he said.

His retreating steps echoed around her, then settled into silence. She stilled her hands as an unfamiliar emotion swept over her. She was alone in this shack, and yet she felt no loneliness. He'd return soon to fix the window while she washed the dishes. They'd be working together to accomplish a goal the way she'd often imagined people in a family worked together.

Through her mouth, she blew a quick burst of air that made the bandanna billow briefly. The soft cloth had touched her heart more than the daisies, more than dinner at the Buccaneer, more than her introduction to Pegasus. It was a simple enough gesture to tie the cloth over her face, but the thoughtfulness behind it—to spare her some of the unsavory stench wafting through this room—touched her deeply. She had always longed for grandiose displays of affection—bear hugs, kisses, and enthusiastic greetings. Now, she just longed to have Hercules Daltry return to the room.

He walked into the room carrying an odd assortment of

boards in his arms and a hammer in one fist. Nails protruded from his mouth.

"I like that smile," she said.

He set everything on the floor by the broken window and looked at her, the smile of nails gone, replaced by a smile that showed his white teeth. "If I didn't know better, I'd think you were teasing me."

"Then it's a good thing you know better." She scrubbed the dishes, a smile easing onto her face.

Hearing his harsh curse, she glanced at him. He cradled his right hand against his chest while the other searched a pocket. His white shirt slowly turned crimson.

"Oh, my God!" She rushed over, untying the bandanna from around her face. "What happened?"

"Some glass in the curtain. Should have been paying more attention."

Gently taking his hand, she pressed the bandanna over the gash across his palm to stanch the flow of blood. "We should get you back to town, to a doctor."

"No doctor in Paradise Plains. Besides, the cut's not that bad."

"How can you say it's not bad?"

"I've broken bones, been gored by a bull, and tossed from here to Hades by an angry bronc. Just wrap the bandanna around it and tie it off. I'll be fine."

"I can certainly understand why you decided to give up ranching to become a schoolteacher. It's a much safer occupation."

"Teaching has its hazards," he said quietly.

She lifted her owllike gaze to his, and Lee wished he could confide in her, could tell her all the things about teaching that scared the hell out of him. As a teacher, she'd understand more than anyone his fear of making a mistake, doing something so the students would learn he wasn't as smart as they were. Then everything he taught them would mean nothing.

The very fact she was a teacher kept him silent, knowing a greater fear would be realized with his admissions. She'd see him as the dumb cowboy he was.

"What sort of hazards?" she asked.

"Sneezing fits when I clean the erasers."

"You should turn your head away so you don't inhale the chalk dust."

"Bellyache from eating a green apple."

"Why would you eat a green apple?"

"The little girl that gave it to me wanted me to eat it with my lunch."

"You should have explained it wasn't ripe."

"But she had big brown eyes. I have a hard time resisting big brown eyes."

Meredith blinked, suddenly unable to remember the color of her eyes. She thought they were brown, but with Lee watching her so intently, they could have been purple, and she wouldn't have cared. "I'd hardly call those incidents hazardous."

"You ever had a bellyache from eating green apples?"

"No."

"Believe me. It's hazardous."

She bit back her smile as she peered beneath the bandanna, grateful to see the bleeding had stopped. She secured the bandanna around his hand. "Are you certain you'll be all right?"

He flexed his fingers. "I'll be fine."

She wasn't convinced, but she returned to the bucket of water, putting the last of the dishes from the table into the bucket to soak. She feared standing close to Hercules Daltry for too long might prove hazardous to her heart.

"I did it on purpose, you know," he said.

"What?"

"Cut myself. It was the only way I could think of to get the bandanna off your face so I could see one of your smiles."

A look of horror crossed her face. "Are you insane?"

Shaking his head, he smiled. "I'm teasing you, Red. I didn't cut myself on purpose."

"Well, it wasn't funny to suggest that you had." She started scrubbing vigorously.

"Don't suppose you'd smile just for the heck of it?"

"Whatever makes you think I was smiling while I was wearing the bandanna?"

He didn't answer, but Meredith heard the pounding of a nail into a board as he returned to his task of covering the broken window. She'd scrubbed the table and stacked the clean dishes by the time he finished. With the hammer in his bandaged hand, he carried the bucket of water outside with his good hand.

Wrapping her fingers around the back of the wobbly, rough-hewn chair, she considered what else she could do to make this shack more closely resemble a home. She stiffened when Lee came to stand behind her, placed his arms around her, and rested his hands beside hers on the back of the chair.

"You guard your smiles the way Cerberus guarded the portals of death," he said in a low voice beside her ear. "Why is that?"

His breath was warm against her neck, a whisper across her flesh.

"I think I should sweep this floor."

A loud thump caused them to spin around.

Eyes wide, Jimmy stood beneath the threshold, firewood scattered at his feet. "What are you doing here?" he asked, his suspicious gaze darting around the room.

Reassuringly Lee smiled at the boy. "Remember when we talked about your reading problem?"

Jimmy gave a hesitant nod.

"That's why we're here. This is Miss Lewis. We wanted to talk to your pa about letting her tutor you. Is he here?"

Jimmy ran a grimy finger beneath his nose. "He's out courting some widow woman. He wants me to have a new ma. He says a new ma can help me with my reading, so we don't need your help 'cuz . . . 'cuz my pa's gonna take care of it."

The child was as unkempt as the house, his blond hair in need of a thorough washing and trimming, his face smudged with sweat and dirt, his clothes as tattered as his blanket. Meredith stepped forward, her hand extended. "Jimmy—"

"I told you we don't need you!" He darted out the door.

Burying the disappointment alongside the one Minerva Daltry had given her, she turned bewildered eyes toward Lee. "Do you believe him?"

"Nope."

"Do you think you should go after him?"

"Nope." He slipped his hand beneath her elbow. "Come on. We've done all the good we can do today."

She allowed him to escort her outside and help her into the buggy because she was too confused to do anything else. She'd seen the suspicious bulges in Jimmy's shirt and a carrot peeking out between the buttons.

Lee climbed into the buggy and set the horses into motion.

"Did you notice a vegetable garden when you were scouting around?" she asked.

"Nope. Didn't see anything in his shirt either if you're planning on that being your next question."

"What are you going to do?"

He heaved a frustrated sigh. "Take you back to Paradise Plains, then go to my thinking place."

"Your thinking place?"

"Yeah, it's a place I go to when I need to think things through."

Tipping his hat back off his brow, he studied the way the sunlight played with her hair. No one knew the location of his thinking place. He'd never shared it with anyone. It was one of the things he'd promised himself when he'd discovered the place. Come hell or high water, the place would remain his and his alone. So he was surprised when he heard himself ask, "Would you like to come with me?"

Chapter Nine

It was disgraceful. Scandalous. Heavenly.

The cool rushing waters tickled Meredith's toes and caressed her ankles. Every now and then, the strong waters nudged Lee's bare foot against hers, and she'd feel the warmth from his flesh run up her calf, jump over her knee, and race up her thigh, coming to settle somewhere in her nether regions.

She'd never in her life done anything so improper, never would have thought a grown man's thinking place would be a low tree branch stretching out across a river.

When they arrived, they strolled beneath the shade of towering trees until they neared the riverbank. Then he dropped to the ground, removed his boots and socks, and rolled up his trousers until his calves were exposed. The afternoon sun filtering through the abundant leaves suddenly grew warmer as she noticed the dark hair covering his calves and her gaze was inexplicably drawn to his feet.

Tilting his head, closing an eye against the sun's brilliance, he peered at her, his smile that of a naughty boy teasing an unwanted nanny. "My thinking place is sitting on the end of that branch, dangling my feet in the water. Are you gonna come with me?"

She glanced at the thick branch, then quickly down at his bared flesh before meeting his mischievous gaze. "It's highly improper."

He continued to grin, his smile transforming into that of a knowing man. He casually draped his arm over a raised knee. "Miss Lewis, I have three sisters. I've seen female toes before." He wiggled his own toes, his smile broadening. "They're not that much different. Maybe skinnier, a shade prettier."

Prettier? His toes looked as though they'd been tromped on and squished. She shifted her gaze, watching the waters catch the sunlight and carry it downstream. She had a feeling that even without sisters, he would have seen female toes before now. His name was whispered on the wind like a benediction around Paradise Plains. She'd known who he was long before she knew how he would impact her life.

"Who's gonna know, Red? I'm not one to kiss and tell."

She jerked her gaze back to his. His voice promised one thing while his eyes and smile promised something else entirely. It was the promise in his eyes that drew her, that forced her to accept the silent challenge.

"I assure you, Mr. Daltry, there will be nothing to tell." She flopped onto the ground, turned her back to him, and worked her shoes off. Discreetly she rolled her stockings down and stuffed them into her shoes.

"Definitely prettier."

She snapped her head back to find him standing behind her, his attention focused on her toes. She yanked her skirt over her bare feet. He chuckled, a warm, soothing sound that clearly stated her actions came too late—he'd seen what he wanted to see. He leaned down, his hand swallowing hers as he pulled her to her feet.

The grass was as thick as velvet beneath her soles as she followed him toward the riverbank. The wildflowers kissed her instep and toes, just as he'd promised.

He released her hand, gathered rocks, and stuffed them into his pocket before he climbed onto the thick gnarled branch. He hauled her up, holding her hand as he guided her toward the leafy end of the branch. He helped her sit on the bough before nimbly dropping into place.

In her lap, she now cradled the hand he'd held. She searched the recesses of her mind for one moment when someone had held her hand—not taken it and pulled her into a room—but held it as though it was something to be cherished. Her mind held no such memories—until now. She was amazed she could still feel where his rough palm had pressed against her hand even though his hand was now dangling limply across his knee.

She thought he came here to think because it was quiet, but the longer she sat, the more she realized it wasn't quiet at all. She listened to leaves dancing with the wind, water lapping against the shore, birds twittering in the branches overhead. Occasionally, she heard a fish splash in the river. She closed her eyes. A thousand different sounds mingled together to create tranquillity.

Opening her eyes, she watched the dappled sunlight play over Lee's features. His brow was furrowed, his deep blue gaze reflecting the waters. Leaning forward, he'd planted his elbows on his thick thighs. She wondered why he didn't topple over into the water. Perhaps because he was as much a part of Nature as she was a part of her books. When troubled, she buried herself in words; he buried himself in the sturdy oak. His thighs, his entire body, reminded her of the tree that housed his thinking place.

"Do you think Jimmy was telling the truth—that his father was off courting?" she asked quietly.

He gave her a sidelong glance. "Do you?"

Slowly she shook her head. "I think maybe Jimmy's being seriously neglected. The condition of that house—" She shuddered with the thought of the filth manifesting itself.

"It definitely needs a woman's touch, but I can't imagine any woman wanting to settle in there." In spite of the bandanna still wrapped around his hand, he reached into his pocket, withdrew a pebble, brought his arm back, and hurled the stone. It skidded across the top of the water, bouncing three times, before going under. "I can't remember the last time I saw Mr. Stellar in town."

"Jimmy's so thin. A boy his age, growing into manhood, shouldn't be scrounging for food."

Lee skipped another rock across water. "His pa's definitely not doing right by him."

"Are we going to do right by him?"

Resting his forearm on his thigh, he laced his fingers through hers. She lowered her gaze, studying the way his arm twined around hers in the same manner that the vines twined around the tree branches above. Her arm should have felt exceedingly uncomfortable twisted around his as it was, but instead it felt treasured. He squeezed her hand, and she lifted her gaze to his.

"I'll track Mr. Stellar down this week, have a talk with him. I'm sure there's something we can do to help Jimmy."

Her heart tripped over itself at the way he'd said we. It almost made her feel as though she belonged. He turned his attention back to the water, but his fingers remained threaded through hers. He had a strong hand, a strong arm. She was tempted to place her other hand over his arm just to see if he was as firmly built as he looked.

The waters pushed his foot alongside hers. He didn't move his foot away as he had previously, but allowed it to brush up against hers. Then he slipped his foot beneath hers, the top of his foot rubbing up against the ball of her foot. Her toes curled.

"When I was younger . . . it bothered me," he said quietly, staring at the water.

She felt her heart lurch, knew he was answering the question she'd asked the night before school started. She wished the question hadn't preyed on his mind, wished she'd never had the audacity to ask. She watched his Adam's apple slide up and down before he turned his head and his blue gaze captured hers.

"I always wanted my name to be Jack."

If he hadn't been holding her hand captive, she would have slid off the tree branch and let the water carry her away into oblivion. She felt the heat suffuse her face as she stammered, "I'm so sorry."

"It's not your fault. You didn't give me my name."

She shook her head. "No, I'm sorry I asked that question the other night. I was rude, cruel, callous—"

"It was rude of me to pretend I thought you were referring to my mother's name."

"No, no. Truly, I was the one that was rude—"

"Meredith."

It was the first time she heard her name rumble from his lips, and she was surprised to discover how lovely he made the syllables sound. His fingers flexed and tightened around her hand.

"Why don't we just admit we were both equally rude?" he asked.

She nodded in acquiescence, then asked softly, "Why Jack?"

He rolled his shoulders into a careless shrug. "It seemed plain, common."

"Did children tease you?"

He grinned, and his bandaged hand floated through the air from his head toward his feet. "This body didn't come about overnight. I was always bigger, always stronger than anyone surrounding me, except for my pa. Not a soul in this area would tease me without asking permission first.''

''You were a bully?'' she asked, disbelief resounding throughout her voice.

''Nope, but most people figured if they hit me, I'd hit back, and being as big as I am, my punch would hurt worse than theirs.'' His hand tightened around hers. ''You were the exception.''

In humiliation, Meredith closed her eyes. ''That's why you looked so shocked when I threw the books.''

He ran his thumb along her jaw, turning her face. Opening her eyes, she wondered if she hadn't fallen into the blue depths of the river.

''That and I honest to God didn't know I'd taken your teaching position. I'd been working the range all summer, and I hadn't had much time to pay attention to the goings-on in town.''

''But once you knew, why didn't you step aside? Why did you still feel a need to play schoolmarm?''

''I'm not playing, Meredith. Teaching school is not a game to me. I know you don't approve of my methods, but I am serious about teaching those children.''

She didn't want to ruin the moment by discussing school or his teaching methods. ''When did your name stop bothering you?''

''When I realized it could have been worse.''

''How could it have been worse?'' She slapped her hand over her mouth, her eyes growing rounder. ''I didn't mean that the way it sounded!''

Laughter rumbled from deep within his chest, then his twinkling eyes came to rest on her. ''It would have been worse if I'd been the second son C.J.''

''What's wrong with C.J.?''

"Nothing's wrong with C.J. It's just that I can't see people calling me Cupid."

"Cupid?" An image of a bare-bottomed cherub floating through the air skipped across her mind. "No, I can't see anyone calling you Cupid." She slipped her spectacles back into place. "So, there's Persephone and Cupid. Who else?"

"Venus. She's the prettiest thing this side of the Rio Grande. I reckon we spoil her, but it's hard not to. My other sister is Atalanta, but she likes to be called Allie. Then there's Atlas. He's the baby in the family. Most of the time we call him Bub."

"Such a large family. I'll confess, Mr. Daltry—"

"Did you know that it's an unwritten law that if you've seen a man's toes you can't call him mister anymore?"

She felt a sweltering heat consume her body.

"If you won't call me Lee, I might have to tell Mrs. Bennett about your pretty toes."

Her eyes widened in horror, her lips moving, her voice locked into silence. When her words finally escaped past her knotted throat, she sounded like a babbling brook. "But you said you never kiss and tell!"

He bestowed upon her a devilish grin that caused her heart to flutter.

"Ah, but, Meredith, we haven't kissed. When we do, I promise I won't tell, and if you'll call me Lee, I won't tell anyone about your toes either. No one in Paradise Plains will ever learn how cute they are, how perfect, how tiny—"

"You're despicable!"

"No, just desperate to get past this formality. I've never brought anyone to my thinking place before, and it doesn't feel right that you keep calling me Mr. Daltry. If you won't use Lee, then don't use anything."

"I've never addressed a man by his given name."

"Boston must be a heck of a formal place. No wonder you left."

"I left because I wanted to bring some semblance of culture to the children here." She swallowed, feeling a need to exchange a confession for the one he'd willingly provided, but hers seemed more painful, didn't want to move from the far corner of her heart into this lovely place. Gently clearing her throat, she studied his hand. "And there was nothing—no one—holding me there." She brushed her knuckles beneath her spectacles, moving them back into place. "You see, part of the reason I threw the books at you was because you had someone in your life who obviously loves you very much."

"What about your family?"

This part was the hardest. She'd listened attentively to the explanations and pretended they didn't hurt when they cut into her heart. "One night, someone, my mother I suppose, left me on the orphanage doorsteps wrapped in a blanket with no note, no explanation."

"No one ever adopted you?"

"No."

"I imagine that must have hurt," he said with understanding woven through his deep voice.

"At first. When I was younger, I would dream that a family adopted me, a family that had a mother and a father and maybe a sister or brother. But over time, the dream began to fade and reality took root."

Working her hand free of his, she reached back and tightened the ribbon holding her hair.

"Why do you do that?"

"Do what?"

"Always wear your hair pulled back."

"It's less obvious that way."

"What's less obvious?"

"The color. It's so hideous."

"Why would you think that?"

"I happen to own a mirror, although there are times I wish I didn't."

He dug into his pocket, then skipped a rock across the water. Five skips, an accomplishment that normally brought a smile to his face. He scowled. "Why wouldn't you want to have a mirror?"

"Because it reminds me of the truth."

"Which is?"

"That I'm so plain no one would ever want me."

"That's not true!" he protested.

"Mr. Daltry—"

"Lee."

Shaking her head, she pursed her lips.

"Call me Lee or I'll tell Mrs. Bennett how cute your toes are."

Meredith couldn't hold back her smile this time. "You're impossible."

"Because I'd like to hear you say my name?"

He bestowed upon her the most sincere smile she'd ever seen, and it broke her resolve to keep up the formal pretense. She was beginning to feel anything but formal with this man. She wondered what he'd say if she told him she thought he had ugly toes, and it was that unattractive appearance that made them adorable.

"All right, Lee." She forced an irritation into her voice that she didn't feel.

"Thank you," he said tenderly. "Now, tell me where you got this crazy notion that you're plain as a rock."

She heaved a sigh. "Not a rock. A duck, and it's a long story."

"I like stories."

"You'll continue to pester me, won't you?"

"Yep. I've got five brothers and sisters. Pestering comes easy to me."

His smile was infectious, and she couldn't help but smile at his persistence. As she began the story, however, the smile slowly faded from her face. "When I was five, a man and woman came to the orphanage. It was an exciting morning. They were wealthy. She was beautiful, he was handsome. They smiled and spoke a few words to me. Then they walked out holding the hands of a little girl with curling blond hair.

"I was heartbroken. I went outside, sat beneath a tree, and cried. One of the matrons found me. She told me the tale of an ugly duckling that grew into a beautiful swan. She meant to be kind, I knew that in my heart, but I also knew that in her tale, I was the ugly duckling. I knew in real life, ugly ducklings did not grow into beautiful swans. Life became easier after that for I no longer had the hope of being adopted. I suppose one of the things that made me angry at you was that I resented the fact you had a family. It must be wonderful to have so many brothers and sisters, to be surrounded by so much love."

Lee rubbed the side of his nose. "I suppose, but sometimes there's so much noise, so much going on, that I feel like I'm gonna go crazy. That's when I come here. I love my family. I truly do. I can't imagine not having them around, but sometimes, it's nice to be by myself."

"I think if I had a family, I'd never want to be by myself."

Lee took a rock from his pocket and skipped it across the water. "I guess people are always wishing for things they don't have."

"Why would they wish for things they did have?" Meredith asked.

"I mean people are never happy with what they have. I'm surrounded by family, and I wish for solitude. You're surrounded by solitude and wishing for family."

"This place seems like a nice compromise," she said.

''You have your family, and you can come here when you need solitude.''

He gave her a big smile. ''You like this place?''

She bestowed upon him a full smile that spread from one cheek to the other. ''I like it very much.''

His knuckles grazed her cheek. ''Did you smile at that man and woman who were looking to adopt a child?''

''Of course I did.''

''Was your hair pulled back?''

She frowned. ''No. No, I think I was wearing it down that day.''

He reached behind her, and she felt the tug on her ribbon. Her hand flew back, covering his large hand, stopping his actions. ''What are you doing?'' she asked.

''I want to see what your hair looks like when it's loose.''

''Please, don't.''

''Why?''

''Just don't. I'm not one of the ladies of Paradise Plains that you can charm into doing anything. I like wearing my hair back.'' She slapped his hand away. ''And if you don't mind, I prefer to keep it bound.''

''Ah . . . but I do mind.''

Before she could react to the slight tug, he was grinning broadly and dangling her ribbon in front of her face. Reaching behind her, she felt her unbound hair spreading across her back.

If she weren't on a tree branch, she would have lunged for the black silk. ''Please return my ribbon.''

He stuffed it into his pocket.

''Mr. Daltry—''

''Lee,'' he reminded her.

''Do you enjoy making me angry?''

He gave her a devilish smile. ''You're not angry. Shake your head and let the wind play with your hair.''

She sat as stiff as a poker. "It'll get all tangled."

"I'll brush out the tangles."

Meredith couldn't help herself. She laughed, a small laugh that waltzed with the leaves surrounding them.

"You have a nice laugh," he said as he draped her hair over her shoulder.

"I don't use it very much," she said quietly, suddenly embarrassed that she had laughed over something so inconsequential.

"I know, and I'm sorry."

A distant rumbling sounded. Meredith's eyes widened. "What was that?"

Lee glanced over his shoulder. "Storm moving in."

She looked behind her at the blackened sky. Lightning zigzagged down to earth. "But the sky is blue before us."

"I've been in the middle of a herd when it only rained on the cattle to the right of me. You never can tell with Texas storms when they're gonna move in and how far they're gonna travel, but I do know we need to move out. Otherwise, the buggy will get stuck in the mud, and we'll have a heck of a time getting back to the road."

Chapter
Ten

As the buggy slowly traversed the muddy road, Lee lifted his arm and draped it around Meredith's shoulders, drawing her near, shielding her as much as possible from the slashing rain.

Despite the dampness of his shirt, with her cheek pressed into the crook of his shoulder, Meredith was acutely aware of the warmth of his flesh, the taut muscles that lay just beneath the cloth. In spite of the steady harsh staccato beat sounding above her head, the whipping winds that accompanied the rains, the resounding thunder, and the occasional lightning, she felt safe.

The storm ushered in the night as they rode toward Paradise Plains. Dark clouds hovered before the moon so its light was but a pale reflection on the barren land. When lightning filled the heavens and whispered across Lee's chiseled profile, she realized he was not lured into the storm's trance as she was.

While one hand pressed her tenderly against his side, the

other clenched the slippery reins, telegraphing to the skittish mare with an occasional tug on the leather that he, and not the storm, was master.

"Damn," he muttered when a gale of wind buffeted the buggy. "Maybe we should have stayed by the river. I don't like being out in the open like this."

She thought if she spoke the wind would carry her words away, so she remained silent. Without taking his eyes from the horse or the road, he lowered his face until she could feel the warmth of his breath fan her cool cheek.

"It won't be much longer. I can see the buildings of town in the distance when the lightning flashes."

She squinted, but the raindrops glistening on her spectacles deterred her vision more than normal. Closing her eyes, she trusted Lee to get her back to the boardinghouse safely.

"Meredith?"

The thunder rumbled her name, deeply, tenderly near her ear. She smiled softly as warm breezes blew along her ear.

"Red?"

The breezes were so tiny she didn't think they could have traveled far. Jerking awake, she realized the buggy was no longer in motion, and the warm balmy breeze she'd felt had traveled no farther than Lee's mouth. The storm still surrounded her as did his arm, but the branches from the willow tree near the boardinghouse provided some respite from the rain. She lifted her gaze.

"I thought you were playing possum at first," he said, his smile broad.

"Have we been here long?"

His smile softened. "Awhile. I kept thinking the storm would let up some, but it doesn't appear it will."

She shivered as he withdrew the warmth of his arm, his chest. The buggy rocked as he climbed out. As he walked around, she edged toward the side, preparing to step down.

He came into view. As she was about to duck from beneath the covering of the buggy, he lifted her into his arms.

"What are you doing?" she cried, throwing her arms around his neck, pressing her face against his chest, allowing the wide brim of his hat to shield her from the rain.

"The mud will ruin your shoes," he said as he carried her to the porch and set her beneath the eaves.

She stepped back so the rain no longer touched her. A lamp burning brightly in the front window cast a faint glow over his features. Smiling broadly, he joined her on the porch and removed his hat.

"Sorry about the rain and getting you back so late."

She combed her fingers through her wet hair. "It was an adventure."

His smile grew, and she realized he owned a cadre of smiles, each one genuine, each one conveying something different.

"You slept through most of it." The smile eased off his face. "Meredith, I was wondering . . . since you've never had a family, and I have such a large one—" He looked at the thunderous skies before returning his gaze to hers. "I was wondering if you'd like to share my family?"

She was speechless. No one had ever offered to share something so wonderful with her.

"Course you might not want to make that kind of a decision without getting to know them better. Would you like to come to the house for supper next Sunday?"

She nodded slightly, then smiled brightly. "I'd like that."

"Good. I'll pick you up Sunday evening."

He dropped his hat on his head and jaunted toward the buggy. Halfway there, he skidded a crazy dance, one leg sliding out, the other unable to catch up. He landed on his backside. Meredith screeched and rushed off the porch, hitting the same slippery patch of earth, sliding and landing beside him.

She covered her mouth, but the laughter tumbled out anyway. "Are you hurt?" she asked.

He scowled. "You're laughing."

She laid her hand on his arm, laughing until she felt tears mingle with the rain streaming down her face. "You looked so funny. You were so graceful walking across the tree limb this afternoon, and now you couldn't even walk across the yard. Did you hurt yourself?"

The rivulets ran down his face as his smile once more took shape. "Only my pride, and after all the trouble I went to carrying you, you've ruined your shoes anyway."

"And my dress."

Struggling to stand, he wrapped his hand around hers and brought her to her feet. Then he lifted her into his arms.

Giddy with the sensation of the rain pelting them, she laughed. "My shoes and dress are muddy. You don't have to carry me."

"I know."

Something deep within his voice, something she didn't recognize, caused her laughter to subside. He stepped onto the porch and set her in the shadows. Although she now stood, his arms hadn't come away from her. One arm shifted, and he laid his hand tenderly against her throat, his thumb pressing gently against her pulse.

"She was wrong, you know," he said in a low voice.

"Who?"

"The lady who compared you to an ugly duckling," he murmured just before his lips touched hers.

His mouth was warm, his supple lips moving over hers in ways she'd never imagined a man would move his mouth. She felt the tip of his tongue brush over her lower lip. Gasping, she drew back, covering her trembling lips with her shaking fingers, grateful the shadows kept his expression and hers a secret. He moved his thumb slowly beneath her chin.

"Dear Lord, Meredith, don't tell me no man has ever kissed you."

She ducked her head, but with the gentlest of pressures from his fingers, he tilted her face upward. In spite of the shadows, she could see a smile gracing his face, not mockingly, but tenderly, as though he'd just discovered a wonderful, hidden truth.

Fleetingly his lips touched hers. "Do you want to be kissed?"

"I don't know. I've never had anyone hold my hand as you did this afternoon, or shelter me from the storm. They're things I've dreamed of, Lee, and I'm afraid it'll hurt."

"Kissing doesn't hurt, Meredith."

"But if you've never had something, you can't miss it. I just think it might be better not to know what I've missed, what I'll never have."

"If you'd never eaten blackberries, and I brought you a bowl filled with them and said you could only eat one—wouldn't you eat that one just for the simple pleasure of knowing what it tasted like?"

She couldn't contain her smile. "Are you saying kisses are like blackberries?"

"Better," he promised in a husky voice just before his mouth claimed hers in a series of small, tender kisses, each lingering longer than the one that had come before.

Then his lips settled over hers as though they were planning on taking up residence. His large hands cupped her face, and his rough thumbs slowly circled her cheeks. This time when his tongue tasted her trembling lower lip, she couldn't have pulled back if she'd wanted to.

He teased the corners of her mouth, his tongue swirling across her lips in figure eights as she'd once seen a cowboy twirl a lasso. Slowly he moved his hands around to her back, wrapped his arms around her, and drew her closer until her breasts were pressed against the wide expanse of his chest. She felt soft and delicate against his hard muscles.

She wanted to taste his lips as he was tasting hers, crazily wondering if he tasted like blackberries. She didn't know how she'd slip her tongue past his, but she thought if she darted quickly . . .

She parted her lips. Warmth and a deeper kiss rushed in. She gasped in surprise, then sighed as a myriad of sensations rushed over her. She felt his kiss as though it had touched her entire body. His tongue took its sweet time exploring all the different facets of her mouth. She felt as though she was again sitting on the tree branch, experiencing something scandalous and heavenly at the same time.

The door to the boardinghouse opened and light spilled onto the porch, chasing away the shadows. Meredith jerked her head back, but Lee continued to hold her. Her breathing came in great gasps that sounded harsher than the thunder. His breathing was deep, his smile tender as he glanced toward the door. Slowly Meredith turned her eyes toward the light.

Mrs. Bennett stood in the doorway, a lamp in one hand, the other hand patting her chest. "Oh, my! Oh, my!"

Lee's smile broadened. "Evening, Mrs. Bennett. How's Simon?"

"You children shouldn't be out in the storm. Please, come inside before you catch your death."

He moved his hand to the small of Meredith's back and prodded her toward the open door. She stopped at the threshold and studied her muddy shoes. "I'll need to take off my shoes first."

"Nonsense, dear. Get inside. We can wash the mud off the floor later."

Meredith lifted her eyes to Lee. His tender gaze was

focused on her. "I can't stay, Mrs. Bennett. I need to get the buggy back to the livery and pick up Pegasus. My family will worry if I tarry much longer."

"I don't think they'd want you out in this downpour, dear."

"I'll be fine." He touched Meredith's cheek. "I'll see you next Sunday."

It was all she could do to nod her head.

"Take care of her for me, Mrs. Bennett," he said before he flashed her a wide smile and jumped off the porch.

"Be careful!" Meredith called out after him.

"Thank you for caring, Miss Lewis!" came out of the darkness, followed by his laughter.

The lightning flashed, and she watched him climb into the buggy. She heard the horse slosh through the mud, heard the wheels turn slowly, taking him away. She touched her lips at the sudden realization that she'd never tasted blackberries.

Lying in bed, Lee listened to the rain pattering against his window. The storm had lessened, but it wasn't the rain or distant rumble of thunder that kept him awake. It was thoughts of Meredith crowding into his bed that had him tossing and turning.

Cradling her in his arms during the storm made him want to cradle her in his bed. Just lay his body next to hers and feel her warmth and her innocence.

He'd kissed a fair amount of girls in his life, usually just for the fun of it. He'd never been serious about anyone or in love. Yet he couldn't remember anyone's lips feeling as soft as Meredith's had.

He threw the covers back and dropped his heavy feet on the floor. Her feet were so tiny next to his, and she did have the cutest toes he'd ever seen.

Reaching across the bed, he grabbed his pants and

stuffed his legs into them, then reached for a shirt and shrugged into it, not bothering to button it. He didn't imagine anyone was awake at this hour, but he didn't want to be caught parading around in the altogether if someone was wandering the halls.

He eased up the flame in the lamp beside his bed and carried the lamp into the hallway. A peaceful quiet emanated through the house as he crept down the stairs and walked to the library at the far end of the house.

Shelves lined the walls, books lined the shelves. He ambled to the shelves, placed his finger on the spine of a book, and read its title in order to get his bearings. Sometimes, Atlas arranged the books in order according to their authors. It appeared he had recently arranged them according to their titles for which Lee was grateful because he didn't know who had written the book he was looking for. He only knew that Meredith had been reading it at breakfast that first morning when he'd approached her, and it had been the first book to come sailing toward him. When he'd picked it up from the floor, the sight of its worn corners and title had been emblazoned in his mind.

He pulled *Great Expectations* off the shelf and carried it to the family room. He set the lamp on a small table and drew the curtains back from the windows. Sitting on the window seat, he leaned his back against the wall and gazed at the black abyss stretching before him.

The rain had stopped. Surrounded by distant stars, a sliver of the moon hung in the velvety blackness. He wondered if Meredith had ever wished on a star.

It seemed odd to miss someone after he'd spent most of the day and part of the evening with her.

He set the book in his lap and turned back the cover, thumbing through the pages until he came to the beginning of the story. He wondered how far along she'd gotten, if she knew how it ended. It would take him a month to read a book with this many pages, but for now, if he couldn't curl up with Meredith, he'd be content to read something she was reading.

He pulled her ribbon out of his pocket where he'd stuffed it after he'd taken a bath and put on clean clothes. He laid the ribbon over his raised knee and caressed it with his thumb as he settled in for a long night of reading.

"Good morning, Sunshine."

Meredith snapped her head up and gazed out the window into Lee's smiling face. The hat she'd been sewing rolled off her lap and tumbled across the floor. "So, you made it home all right," she said, grimacing at the inane comment.

"Were you worried?"

"No, not really." She shifted her spectacles. "Well, a little."

His smile broadened, and he leaned in the open window of the millinery. "Was it better than blackberries?"

Meredith felt the pulsating heat racing the length of her body. She studied her hands, trying to appear unaffected. "I really wouldn't know. I've never eaten blackberries."

"That occurred to me on my way home last night." He extended his hand over her lap, a small dark blue fruit nestled within his palm, just above the bandage covering his wound.

"Where did you get a blackberry this time of year?" she asked.

"From one of Persy's jars. Her kitchen knows no season. You can find anything you want anytime of the year you want it."

Before she could take it, he snatched his hand back. "Open your mouth." He held the perfectly shaped blackberry between his thumb and forefinger.

She did as he bid, her breath stopping as the succulent fruit touched her tongue and his fingers touched her lips.

She closed her mouth, and he withdrew his fingers. She felt the juice squirt into her mouth from a hundred different directions.

"Well?" he asked.

She licked her lips. "Shouldn't you be ringing your school bell?"

"Aren't you gonna answer my question?"

Blushing, she shook her head.

"Then I'll ask another one. Were you reading *Great Expectations* because my name was in it?"

Startled, she couldn't hide the surprise from her face. "What?"

"Pip said Joe was as strong as Hercules."

"Oh, I'd forgotten about that." She gave him a rueful smile. "I haven't read the entire book in ages."

His face fell, the smile disappearing. "But you were reading it the morning I saw you at the Buc."

"Only my favorite passages. Are you reading it?"

He glanced toward the schoolhouse. "Yeah, I started reading it last night." He yawned. "Couldn't sleep." He unfurled his body. "Guess I'd better get those rascals into their seats. Don't forget about Sunday."

"I won't," she assured him.

She watched him saunter toward the school. She licked her lips, again tasting the blackberry. She smiled. It paled in comparison to the kiss Hercules Daltry had given her.

Chapter
Eleven

Lee's deep laughter rumbled through the open window of The Hatbox. Meredith glanced at her watch. Ten minutes before eleven.

Two days had passed since the storm, but already the land had absorbed the water, and the puddles of mud had turned back into dust. She should have known he'd have the children out of the classroom and playing in the sunshine as soon as it was possible.

Moving away from the counter, she peered through the window. Lee carried a large wicker basket and set it beside the wide trunk of the tree. Older boys struggled to carry other large baskets to the tree while the girls spread quilts beneath the shade.

"What are you looking at?" Miss Lavender asked.

At the unexpected question, Meredith jerked up and banged her head on the open window. Gingerly rubbing the small knot that was forming on the back of her head, she glanced over her shoulder at the proprietor of The Hatbox.

Miss Lavender was busily tying one of the many bows that adorned the dress covering her sparse frame. The woman was a walking advertisement for her shop.

"I could hear the children and was curious as to what they were doing."

Her tiny feet clicking a rapid tattoo, Miss Lavender crossed the room, bent her graying head, and stared out the window. "Appears they're having a picnic."

"They should be studying."

"But they need to eat."

"The midday meal should be at noon."

"I'm certain Lee knows what he's doing."

Meredith spun away from the window. "But he has no experience teaching. Listen to that laughter. He's not taking it seriously."

Miss Lavender's frown caused her wrinkles to shift over her face. "Perhaps you should speak with him on the matter."

"Would you mind if I did it right now? I fear he'll allow the children to play all day if nothing is said."

"Certainly, you should do what you feel is best."

Meredith strolled as calmly as she could from the millinery. She rounded the corner and saw Lee sitting beneath the tree, a wide grin spreading across his face. She felt her heart flutter and took a deep breath to calm it. This was business, pure and simple.

As she approached, he stood. "Meredith, what a pleasant surprise."

"I need to speak with you, Mr. Daltry."

His smile rapidly vanished. "Mr. Daltry? I thought we'd agreed to do away with the formality."

"This is business."

"Business? Can't it wait until after our picnic?"

"I think not."

"But we're in the middle of a lesson."

Her eyes widened in disbelief, and she waved her hand in a semicircle. "A lesson? You call this a lesson?"

"Certainly, Miss Lewis. That's what teachers do. Give lessons."

"I am fully aware of what *teachers* do, Mr. Daltry. I have yet to determine what it is *you* do."

"Then why don't you join us? Maybe you'll learn a thing or two."

"I assure you, Mr. Daltry, I don't need any lessons on teaching."

"Who said anything about teaching, Meredith?"

His blue eyes darkened, challenging her, igniting her curiosity. She thrust her chin upward. He tilted his head toward the quilts. "Please join us." When she hesitated, he looked to the children for support. "How many of you want Miss Lewis to join us?"

Hands shot up, fingers waving. Several of the smaller children held up two hands, but it wasn't the hands that convinced Meredith to stay. It was the smiles.

"This is highly improper."

"Ah, Meredith, when are you gonna learn that highly improper is usually a lot of fun." He took her elbow and supported her as she knelt on the ground.

"Where did all this food come from?" she asked.

Lee sat beside her, his knee brushing up against hers. "Persy made it. She loves to cook."

"What's the occasion?"

"It's Alpha's birthday," Danny Guslock said.

Meredith raised a brow. "Alpha?"

"Yeah, the boy king who made up the alphabet."

She nailed Lee with a look of complete disapproval, a look she would have given an unruly boy to still his naughtiness. "The boy king who made up the alphabet?"

Lee's face turned as red as the apples resting in a basket beside him. He shrugged. "This is just a picnic in honor of the alphabet. We have most of the letters here. What food begins with the letter 'A'?"

A chorus of "Apples!" resounded around them, and Lee tossed the apples toward the smaller children.

"And what about 'B'?"

"Biscuits!"

"Let's find them and get to eating."

The children scrambled over the quilts, searching out the food, calling out the letters as they loaded their plates.

Meredith spotted Jimmy on the outskirts, tentatively watching, chewing on his bottom lip. Parted unevenly down the middle, his dark blond hair was plastered to his head as though he wanted desperately to look as though someone cared for him. She felt an ache in her chest watching his thin face as he studied all the activity around him. His skinny wrists dangled over his knees as he sat Indian style.

"Jimmy!" Lee called out, catching the boy's attention. "Everyone! This is a celebration. See how many different foods you can eat. Start with the apple." He tossed a large red apple into Jimmy's waiting hands. "Or start with something else and take the apple home, but we've got to eat it all, otherwise, we'll hurt Persy's feelings. She went to a heap of trouble to cook all this food. The least we can do is eat it for her."

"Gosh, Mr. Daltry, I ain't never seen so much food," Danny said around the chicken in his mouth, his cheeks resembling a chipmunk's.

Lee leaned against the tree. "Then everybody should go home with a full belly today. Fill up your plate, Meredith." Smiling, he took a big bite out of an apple.

Meredith slid her gaze toward Jimmy. He stuffed cheese into his mouth while heaping sliced beef and chicken onto his plate, and she realized this picnic had nothing to do with boy kings or the letters of the alphabet.

*   *   *

In the late evening Meredith stood unobtrusively in the dark corner of the classroom. A solitary lamp on the edge of the desk chased the shadows from Lee's face. Hunched over a book, he was obviously preparing the next day's lessons. She knew how time consuming that task could be. He had nineteen children in his classroom. Since it was the standard to teach children according to their ability and not age, a teacher often had to devise as many as forty different lesson plans for a group of students this size.

She'd been staring out her back bedroom window when she noticed the pale yellow glow spill from the schoolhouse into the night. She walked to the building and slipped inside without his noticing her. Now, watching him in silence, she had a strong urge to thank him. She had learned something at the picnic that afternoon.

Once she settled in to enjoy the celebration, she noticed the children had their slates by their sides. Lee told her they were keeping a tally of the foods they ate that began with different letters.

Every now and then, he called out a letter. Children jumped to their feet holding something that began with that letter. For "B," they held biscuits, bread, and beef. When Lee called for "K," a small girl held a piece of cake.

On the verge of explaining it was a common mistake for children to believe cake began with "K," Meredith felt Lee gently squeeze her hand, and she quickly shut her open mouth.

He drew the tiny child onto his lap and created an elaborate, fanciful tale explaining why cake wanted to sound like it began with "K," but wanted to be spelled with "C."

His methods were outlandish, but while he spoke not one child chewed, not one child uttered a word, and Meredith was left with the distinct impression that once he finished the tale, every child would remember that cake began with "C."

The picnic lasted most of the afternoon. Sometimes, he called on the older children to spell a food; sometimes, he asked a younger child how many biscuits were left.

"If we started with forty biscuits and only eight are left, how many did we eat?" he then asked the children and hands were frantically waved for his attention.

He never called on a child who didn't want to answer; he gently corrected a child who gave a wrong answer.

She was brought from her reverie as he scraped the chair across the floor, stood, and began to write on the blackboard. The word half formed, he turned his attention back to the book.

"Burning the midnight oil?" she asked quietly.

He jerked his head up, alarm clearly registered on his face. "What are you doing here?"

Smiling, she walked farther into the room. "I didn't mean to startle you. I was gazing out my window and saw your light."

Lee combed his fingers through his hair. The last thing he wanted was Meredith in his classroom right now. He always came late at night to do his writing on the blackboard. Once his students arrived, he didn't write anything on the board unless he was absolutely sure of what he was writing. He closed the book on his desk. "Well, I'm all done now."

"It looks like you've only just begun."

He glanced over his shoulder at the word he'd started writing on the board. Quickly he picked up an eraser and wiped the letters away. "I was just breaking in a new piece of chalk."

"Breaking in a new piece of chalk?"

"Yeah, haven't you ever noticed how much they squeak when they're new?" He shuddered. "Hate that squeaking sound."

She ran her finger along the edge of his desk. "I came

over here because I wanted you to know I figured it out.''

Lee slammed his eyes shut. He didn't know why he thought she wouldn't be able to see through him to the truth—after all, she was a teacher.

''You were trying to make certain Jimmy had something to eat.''

His eyes flew open, and he studied her expression. It contained no censure, no disgust. As a matter of fact, a wealth of tenderness filled those big brown eyes. ''Jimmy?''

''Yes, the picnic this afternoon. Its purpose was to feed Jimmy.''

Releasing a sigh of relief, he smiled. ''Yeah, the boy's got a lot of pride. Tried to share my lunch with him yesterday, and he'd have nothing to do with it.''

''Have you had an opportunity to talk with his father?''

He moved around until he was standing in front of his desk and leaned back. ''No, but I made some inquiries around town. Seems no one's seen him in a good while. Jimmy said he's working on a ranch, but he couldn't remember the name. A few ranches are scattered a distance away. He might be working on one of those. I've got C.J. asking around when he's out riding the range.''

''You don't think he leaves Jimmy alone all the time, do you?''

''No, I reckon he must get home late in the evening; probably heads back out once he sends Jimmy off to school. If he wasn't around, Jimmy wouldn't be coming to school. He'd be off fishing like a normal boy.''

She intertwined her fingers. ''I'm just not certain he should be left alone at all.''

''This isn't Boston, Meredith. Out here, boys grow up fast. Went on my first cattle drive when I was ten.''

''But you didn't go alone.''

"No, but I learned responsibility, and I learned how to take care of myself."

"Still, it seems a lot to expect of a child. Will you let me know if you discover anything about his father?"

"Sure will." He shoved himself away from the desk. "I'll walk you back to the boardinghouse."

"It's not really necessary."

He wrapped his hand around hers and began walking through the building. "But Pegasus would be disappointed if I denied him the pleasure of escorting you home."

Once outside, he locked the door and whistled. The horse appeared, and Lee lifted Meredith onto the saddle. Without warning, he pulled himself onto the back of the stallion.

"This is highly improper," Meredith said, acutely aware of his chest pressed against her shoulder. She stiffened as his arm came around her, and he tugged on the reins. He guided the horse along the back of town avoiding the main street and occasional glow of a lamplight.

"Relax, Red. There's not even a moon tonight so no one will see us."

"I envy you," she said quietly, keeping her back straight as though someone had rammed a rod down its center.

"Because I'm teaching?"

She folded her hands in her lap. "No, because you're so comfortable with touching. You must have grown up with a lot of touching in your family."

"I reckon there wasn't much touching at the orphanage."

She glanced down at her hands. "Very little."

He trailed a callused finger along her throat. "You know I spend a lot of time thinking about touching you."

If she were standing, she thought her knees would have gone weak. "You shouldn't speak of such things."

"Why?"

"Because it's highly improper."

"Not as improper as my thoughts."

She twisted her head around, lifting her gaze to his, unwittingly giving him easier access to her throat. He wrapped his large hand around her neck and rubbed his thumb beneath her chin. She could smell chalk dust mingled with the scent of man.

He was a silhouette against the night, and she could well imagine how the gods on Mount Olympus had persuaded mortal women to lie with them, without shame, without marriage. Pegasus stopped walking, but Meredith kept her gaze focused on Lee's face, not wanting to discover that they'd arrived at the boardinghouse.

"I can't recall ever spending as much time thinking about a woman as I spend thinking about you, Red."

"It's because we both want to help Jimmy—"

"My thinking has more to do with your toes than Jimmy." He brushed his lips along her temple. "I think about kissing your toes. I think about kissing your lips. I think about kissing every hill and valley in between."

He kissed behind her ear, and Meredith felt as though she'd suddenly turned into molten lava. She wondered why she didn't just flow off the horse's back. Perhaps because Lee had one arm holding her firmly in place.

"You ever think about me?" he asked, his breath fanning her neck.

"Never," she said, embarrassed that her breathing sounded as though she'd just run from the schoolhouse.

He trailed his warm lips along her throat. "Never?"

"It would be improper."

He chuckled low in his throat, and she had a strong urge to press her fingers against his neck and feel the vibrations.

"You ever dream about me?" he asked.

"No," she squeaked, hating her voice for its betrayal.

"I dream about you every night. I want to be in your dreams, Meredith."

His hold on her tightened, and he lowered his mouth to hers. Meredith thought she'd just fallen into a dream. He bestowed upon her a lazy trance-inducing kiss, the kind she imagined a man might give a woman upon first awakening in the morning after a night of sleeping in each other's arms. Only she thought she'd never want to wake up.

His mouth left hers, and she lifted her heavy eyelids to gaze upon him. She could see his tender smile in the shadows. He wrapped his arm around her and lowered her to the ground.

"Sweet dreams, Red."

She watched him gallop into the night before she walked into the boardinghouse. Did he think a kiss could influence her dreams?

She prepared herself for bed and snuggled beneath the covers. Sleep claimed her with a gentleness reminiscent of Lee's kisses.

While the sun lifted itself over the horizon, Lee straddled the pointed roof of the schoolhouse and watched his father mark off his points of reference. "Should I use that old cowbell this morning?" he asked.

"Nope, I should be able to get the framework erected and the bell hung right quick. I'll close in the tower this evening. Wouldn't want my pounding all day to distract your students."

"Thanks, Pa. I appreciate you taking the time to build the bell tower."

His father slowly shook his head. "Don't know why no one ever noticed the school needed a dang bell."

Lee removed his hat and wiped his brow. He was ready for the autumn winds to arrive and blow away the sultry mornings. "Pa, when you were working on your labor, did you ever feel like maybe you wouldn't succeed?"

"Sure. That's the whole point of the damn thing—to put

you through hell so you can reach heaven.''

In all the years Lee had heard his father talk about his labor, he'd never heard him speak of it negatively. ''I thought you figured it was a grand idea that Grandma gave you a labor.''

''Hell, no. When she assigned the first one to my oldest brother, I asked to be put up for adoption.''

Lee tried to peer around his father's broad back so he could see his face. The man had to be joshing with him. ''But she wouldn't hear of it, huh?''

Odie hammered a nail into a small board, securing it to the roof. ''She said it was fine with her, but when I turned twenty, she'd track me down and give me a labor to perform anyway.'' He shrugged his massive shoulders. ''So I figured I might as well stay. Didn't sleep for a week before my twentieth birthday.''

''You never let on that you felt that way about your labor.''

Guiltily his father peered over his shoulder. ''Didn't want you worrying about something you had no control over.''

Lee scooted closer to his father and glanced around the area as though to make certain the gods of Mount Olympus weren't eavesdropping. ''Did you ever feel like it was going too easy?''

''Yep.'' Releasing a melancholy sigh, his father reached back and patted Lee's knee. ''It's not the labor, son. The labor's easy. It's when the reason behind the labor rears its ugly head that you've gotta watch out. Sometimes, the labor is connected to the reason, sometimes it's not. The only thing you can be sure of is that before the year is out, the labor will draw the reason to the surface. And when it does—'' He patted Lee's thigh, pursed his lips, and nodded sagely. ''You'll do just fine. Now, don't worry about it, and let me get this bell tower put up.''

As his father began his steady, rhythmic pounding, Lee climbed down the ladder and walked to the schoolhouse door. That conversation hadn't ended the way he'd hoped. He thought he'd met the test and was easily on his way to passing it. He didn't like hearing he had yet another test awaiting him.

Slipping the key into the lock of the schoolhouse door, he heard a harsh, desperate whisper.

"Mr. Daltry, sir."

Over his shoulder, he could barely see Jimmy Stellar's brown eyes peering around the corner of the schoolhouse. He smiled. "Morning, Jimmy."

Jimmy eased a crooked finger around the edge of the building and motioned him forward. Lee glanced around, wondering if Jimmy had gotten himself into some kind of trouble. In long strides he walked around to the side of the schoolhouse and froze, his eyes widening in disbelief.

Jimmy was in trouble all right. A heap of trouble.

"Gawd Almighty, Mr. Daltry, help me! It was Miss Lewis's doing! She bushwhacked me!"

Lee pretended to rub his jaw in thought when he was actually trying to hide his enormous grin. Jimmy clutched a straw hat with ribbons wrapped around the brim and dangling over the edge. His black trousers came just below his knees to reveal red stockings and lace-up shoes. A black velvet coat with fancy edging around the collar and sleeves partially covered a ruffled shirt.

"How'd she manage to . . . uh?" He cleared his throat.

"She's a sly one, Mr. Daltry. Yesterday afternoon, she told me if I was to come into town a little earlier this morning and sweep Miz Bennett's porch, she'd feed me some of Miz Bennett's biscuits with gravy. You'd have to be downright loco to pass up a offer like that so I come in. When I was done sweepin', she had this tub of hot water waitin' on me. Said I had to bathe before I could come to

Miz Bennett's table. Figured them biscuits was worth a bath, but while I was bathing she tossed out my clothes and brung me these to wear. Didn't see no choice but to put 'em on.''

"Where is she?" Lee asked.

Jimmy swallowed. "Working at The Hatbox already."

"She meant well, Jimmy."

"I know." He looked down at his clothes, then his worried eyes shot back up to Lee. "But you'll help me, won't you? I can't go to school lookin' like this!"

"Yeah, I'll help you, but we don't want to hurt Miss Lewis's feelings. Hightail it around to the back of schoolhouse. You can use my pa's horse, and we'll ride to my house, see if we can find you something decent to wear."

Jimmy tore off like his tail was on fire. Lee looked toward The Hatbox. Whatever had the woman been thinking to dress the boy like that?

"Morning, Red."

Meredith nearly jumped out of her skin. She pressed her hand to her chest and tried to calm her breathing before she glanced toward the window. The hat in her lap took on a distorted shape as the fingers of her other hand closed unmercifully around it. "Morning."

"How'd you sleep?"

"Really, Mr. Daltry, my sleeping habits are none of your concern. Besides, shouldn't you be ringing the school bell?"

"I was gonna wait until my pa finished putting it up."

"What?"

Crooking a finger, he encouraged her to lean out the window and glance toward the school. She saw a man sitting on top of the school building. She'd heard the sound of a hammer echoing across the land, but she'd paid little attention to it. Her mind had been occupied with memories of the dreams she'd had last night.

"What is he doing?" she asked.

"Building a bell tower. I didn't like that little bell I was using so I ordered a proper one for the school. It came in yesterday. Soon as Pa's done putting it up, I'll ring it."

"It'll make the children tardy if you wait."

"A little maybe, but Pa's pretty experienced at building things. Shouldn't take him much longer."

Reaching through the window, he laid a brown parcel on her lap.

Meredith shifted her spectacles before tugging on the string and moving the paper aside. Her heart sank to the pit of her stomach. "These are the clothes I bought Jimmy." Hurt and confusion mirrored in her eyes, she looked at Lee. "Why isn't he wearing these?"

"Those are city clothes. A boy can't wear those out here."

"The mercantile only got them in this week. They're the best money can buy."

"I know, but sometimes the best money can buy isn't always the best thing to get the job done."

"Is he running around with his backside bared?"

He smiled. "No, ma'am. I took him home, and we found him some of C.J.'s old clothes to wear."

She slumped her shoulders. "But I wanted to do something for him."

"I know you did." He trailed his finger along her chin. "Meredith, I think what you did for Jimmy this morning was the kindest thing I've ever seen."

"It was no different from the picnic you held so he wouldn't spend the day hungry."

"It was a lot different. I could build the boy a new house, and it wouldn't empty my pockets. It's easy to give when you'll always have something left for yourself. I have a feeling you didn't leave anything for yourself when you bought Jimmy's clothes.''

"I didn't mind. I wanted to buy Jimmy those clothes. At the orphanage, we wore uniforms. When I saw these in the mercantile, I was reminded of how much I wanted fancy clothes when I was a child. I guess I transferred those feelings to Jimmy.''

"You can take those back to the mercantile, and Hank'll return your money.'' He tugged on the ribbon holding her hair in place. "Maybe you could buy yourself a new hair ribbon for Sunday. You are still planning on coming with me, aren't you?''

She gave him a small nod.

"Great. I gotta meet with some of my friends at the Buc that afternoon. Soon as I'm done with them, I'll come by and pick you up. Will that suit you?''

"That'll suit me perfectly.''

A bell tolled in the distance, and he smiled. "Told you it wouldn't take Pa long to build that tower. Reckon I'd best get to school.'' He touched the tip of her nose. "See you Sunday.''

Chapter
Twelve

"I'll confess, I'm anticipating this visit. I've heard so much about Mount Olympus," Meredith said, glancing at Lee as the buggy traversed the dirt road.

Only one side of his mouth tipped up. "Oh, you have?"

"Everyone in town talks about it."

"They do?"

"They all say your ranch is very grand." She gave him a sidelong glance. "Some people even laugh when they talk about Mount Olympus, but I think they're just envious."

"Could be."

She flicked an imaginary piece of dirt off her skirt. "I'll also confess that I'm a bit nervous about meeting your family."

"No reason to be. My family's very friendly."

"I suppose everyone will be there?"

Furrowing his brow, he glanced at her. "C.J. probably won't be there; he likes to spend his Sunday afternoons courting." He covered her hands with one of his own. "Relax, Meredith. You'll do just fine.''

They rode along in companionable silence for long moments before he pointed forward, drawing the buggy to a halt. ''There's our ranch.''

Meredith gazed at the arched beam through which they would pass. At its zenith, a ''D'' sat in the middle of a circle. Weathered, wooden fencing stretched out on either side of the gateway.

''Does the fence go all the way around your land?'' she asked.

''No, we've got too much land to fence it in with wood. Pa just built this so we'd have an entrance. The Circle D is our brand. It's what we put on our cattle to mark them as ours.''

''I would have thought you would have used something that symbolized the name of your ranch.''

''We did.''

She twisted her head around, her brow furrowed. ''What did you use?''

''The Circle D.''

She shook her head. ''I don't understand. If your ranch is called Mount Olympus—''

''But it's not.''

Meredith touched her cheeks, wondering if she'd suddenly developed a fever. ''Your ranch isn't called Mount Olympus?'' she squeaked.

Struggling to hold back his smile, he shook his head.

''What is the name of your ranch?''

''The Daltry Ranch.''

''Not Mount Olympus?''

''Nope.''

''But in town, everyone . . . oh, my.'' She released a small sigh. ''With your family's history of names, when people referred to your ranch as Mount Olympus, I just assumed . . . I didn't know . . . I mean, I thought.'' She buried her face in her hands, shaking her head. "Please, tell me you knew they called your ranch Mount Olympus."

Silence surrounded her, suffocating her. Through splayed fingers, she peered at him. He was wearing a lopsided grin. "Tell me you knew."

"I suspected, but no one ever dared call it Mount Olympus to my face." His grin righted itself. "Except for you, of course."

"Is there a hole near here that I can just drop into?"

Lee tilted his head back and laughed. She'd turned the shade of red that made her freckles disappear.

"It's really not funny," she said as she pushed her spectacles back up the bridge of her nose.

"Yes, it is."

"No, it's not. I thought they were serious. Why didn't you tell me?"

"I thought you were being Miss High and Mighty calling it Mount Olympus. I didn't know that's what you honestly thought it was called."

"Miss High and Mighty? If you thought that, why did you approach me about tutoring Jimmy?"

"Because I like the color of your hair, the freckles on your face, and the shape of your toes."

"You didn't know what my toes looked like."

"But I do now."

"I never should have gone with you to your thinking place."

He brought her hand to his lips. "But I'm glad you did, and whether this place is the Daltry Ranch or Mount Olympus doesn't really matter. You're here now."

Meredith fell in love . . . with Lee's home.

Everything spoke of joy and happiness. Everything was well maintained—from the stables to the tiniest chick. She held the little ball of fur in her hand, listened to its cheep-

ing, and every motherly instinct she'd buried long ago burst
to the surface.

By the time they walked the dirt path to the house, Meredith had a clearer understanding of all that was lacking in
her own life. It was an understanding she would have preferred not to possess.

Smiling, Lee shoved open the door, and Meredith preceded him inside. The aroma of nutmeg and ginger greeted
her. "Something smells good."

"Glad to hear it. That means Persy's cooking. Come on,
and I'll introduce you."

He wrapped his hand around hers, and they walked to
the end of the hallway. Meredith's courage faltered as she
heard a myriad of voices and jubilant laughter. Lee
squeezed her hand, and she looked into his smiling face.
She returned his smile just before they walked into the
kitchen.

Four females of various ages circled a large table, but
only one woman seemed to be working. Efficiently she
chopped onions and carrots, a soft smile on her face, while
those around her talked. Wiping a tear from the corner of
her eye with the back of her hand, she looked up. Her
mouth fell open.

One by one, the others glanced toward the door, their
voices falling into silence.

"Why's everybody staring?" Lee asked.

His mother moved away from the table. "No reason. We
just forgot you were bringing company for dinner."

"We didn't forget," Venus said. "He didn't tell us."

Persy lightly punched Venus's shoulder and gave her a
pointed look. "He did tell us."

"He did not."

"Venus, don't you need to brush your hair?" Lee asked,
realizing he had forgotten to tell them.

Her hands flew to her blond curls. "Has a strand fallen out of place?"

"It looks pretty messed up from where I'm standing," he assured her.

Venus popped off the tall chair. "This is embarrassin'. I do wish you'd told us to expect company. You'll just have to introduce me later when I look presentable." Gracefully she glided from the kitchen.

"Well," Jane said. "Now that we've all remembered you were coming for dinner, I'm Lee's mother. We're glad to have you here."

"I'm happy to be here," Meredith said, finding comfort in the woman's kind blue eyes.

Jane took her arm. "Lee, why don't you make sure everyone else remembered we were having company for dinner, and I'll introduce her to your grandmother and Persy."

As Lee walked out, Meredith followed his mother to the table. When he had invited her to dinner, she hadn't realized she'd see his grandmother again, would again face the woman who had destroyed her dreams.

"I've had the pleasure of meeting Miss Lewis before," Minerva said, laughter shading the soft gray of her eyes.

"Oh, I hadn't realized," Jane said. "Persy, have you met Miss Lewis?"

"No." She lifted her flour-coated hand. "I'm Lee's oldest sister."

"And the only one among us who has any talent for cooking," Jane added.

Persy gathered up the chopped vegetables and dropped them into a pot. "Miss Lewis, would you like to help me with the dumplings?"

Meredith smiled. "I'd like that, but please call me Meredith."

A door slammed, and boots thumped down the hall just

before Allie skidded into the kitchen. "Lee sent Hal home."

"That's because we're having company for dinner," Jane said.

Allie scrunched her face, stomped across the room, planted her elbow on the table, and laid her chin in her palm. "He coulda waited. We still got a couple more hours of daylight."

"I'm sure Lee was doing what he thought was best," Persy assured her.

Allie snorted. "Yeah, he thought I needed some time to get ready for dinner since Miss Lewis is here. Said I needed to put on a dress." She shuddered.

During the next half hour as Meredith made awkward attempts to help Persy, she discovered this family showed their affection for one another with gentle teasing. For the first time in her life, she witnessed the easy camaraderie between mother and daughters, observed the gentle smiles shared, and listened to conversation steeped in years of memories.

Leaning against the table, Minerva stood. "Miss Lewis, would you walk with me to the gazebo? My legs have grown too old to carry me that far without assistance, and I'm too proud to use a cane."

Meredith studied the older woman's challenging gaze. The woman looked as fit as a fiddle. No doubt she just enjoyed using people. If Meredith weren't a guest here, she would have told the woman to lean on someone else. Instead, she walked away from the table and forced a smile she didn't feel. "I'd be happy to."

Minerva slipped her arm through Meredith's. They walked painstakingly slowly through the house and out to the gazebo. Minerva eased onto a bench. Meredith gazed past her to where Lee leaned against the corral, talking to the man she'd seen on the roof of the schoolhouse.

"My son, Odysseus," Minerva said. "Lee very much resembles his father, don't you think?"

"Yes, it seems he does," Meredith said as she turned to go back to the house.

"I don't tolerate rudeness well," Minerva said.

Meredith spun around. "I don't mean to be rude, but you did after all steal my dream."

"Is your dream so small then that one person has the power to take it away?"

"I don't see that you have the right to judge the size of my dream, and I intend to reclaim it. I'm earning the money now to achieve it."

"But if you hadn't been rude and stormed from the sheriff's office, you would have already had your dream."

Meredith blinked her eyes. "What?"

"Did you honestly think I would take one opportunity away from you without offering another in its place? It was important that Hercules teach the children of Paradise Plains. It was unfortunate I didn't realize it in time to stop your journey, but I had compiled a list of schools in Texas that needed a teacher. Had you heard me out, you could have had your choice of positions, and I would have gladly paid your travel expenses."

Meredith sank onto the bench. "Why didn't you tell me that before now?"

Minerva tilted her head slightly. "As I said, I don't tolerate rudeness well. When you rushed out of the sheriff's office, you took your opportunities with you."

Meredith angled her chin defiantly. "I can make my own opportunities."

"Or you may have back those you left with me in the sheriff's office. You need only ask."

"And if I ask?"

"You may teach elsewhere, and I'll provide the means to get you there."

"And I'll leave Paradise Plains," Meredith whispered more to herself than to the woman sitting beside her. She saw Lee walking toward the gazebo, a smile spread across his face.

She tried to convince herself it was only a smile, and he smiled at everyone. As he neared, however, she couldn't help but feel the smile he gave her was more personal, was more of a caress than a greeting. She stood as he stepped into the gazebo. He slipped his arm around her waist.

"Grandma, do you mind if I borrow Meredith for a while? I want to show her something in the barn."

Minerva smiled, more at Meredith than Lee. "No, I don't mind. Remember, Miss Lewis, you have but to ask."

"Thank you, Mrs. Daltry, but I won't be asking."

As they walked away from the gazebo, Meredith glanced over her shoulder in time to see Minerva walk briskly back to the house.

"She walked by herself."

Lee looked back. "Grandma? Why wouldn't she?"

"She said she needed help."

Her gave her an apologetic smile. "She does that from time to time. She told me once that she can tell a lot about people when she walks beside them."

"What do you think she learned about me?"

"That you're special." He wrapped his arm around her. "Now, come on. I want to introduce you to a friend."

"There he is," Lee said quietly.

Meredith followed the direction of his finger and saw a small owl nestled within the rafters. "Is he asleep?" she whispered.

"Yep. He comes awake at night. I found him when he was a baby. He had a broken wing. After I tended him, he just stayed around here."

Sitting in the hayloft, surrounded by the scent of hay with

dust motes dancing in the sunlight, Meredith shifted so the straw wasn't sticking into her backside.

He draped his arm over his drawn-up knee and trailed his finger along her cheek. "Did you dream about me?"

His blue, beckoning gaze burned into her. She looked at her hands. "Yes," she whispered as though the admission caused her pain.

"Want to tell me about your dream?"

Meredith almost scoffed. Dream? She'd had more than one. She'd had hordes of dreams, but she wasn't about to tell him about any of them. "It was highly improper."

"Those are the best kind."

She peered at him. "You don't understand. I've never even contemplated having dreams like these. Proper ladies don't entertain these sorts of thoughts."

He bestowed upon her a tender smile and grazed her cheek with his knuckles. "But it was just a dream. Nothing improper is gonna pass between us unless it's what you want."

"I just wish you hadn't put these ideas in my head."

"Was I kissing you in the dream?" he asked.

She sighed. "Sort of."

He touched her lips with his thumb. "Must not have been kissing your lips. Was I kissing your toes?"

She squirmed. "I don't wish to discuss what you were kissing."

Wearing a lazy smile, he stretched out, bracing himself up on an elbow. "I'll bet you've never rolled in the hay, have you?"

"Certainly not."

"No hay in Boston?"

"Whether or not there is hay is beside the point. Why would a person want to roll in it?"

"Because it's fun."

She pursed her lips. "For children maybe—"

"For adults, too."

She glanced around the loft. Hay was in abundance, but she couldn't imagine lolling around in it would be much fun.

"Why don't you give it a try? A person shouldn't live their whole life without rolling in the hay at least once."

She arched an eyebrow. "I suppose it's better than blackberries?"

He sat up, his eyes silently issuing a challenge. "It can be."

"Oh, all right." Feeling like a fool, Meredith lay on the straw and rolled from her stomach to her back, the straw prickling her skin. She gazed at the rafters and heaved a sigh. "Yes, you're right. It was quite refreshing."

"But you did it wrong."

She dropped her gaze from the rafters and stared at Lee's serious face. "How could I have done it wrong?"

Before she could move, he lay with half his body covering hers. "You did it alone."

Working his arms between her back and the straw, he rolled her across the loft, stopping her shriek by covering her mouth with his own. The kiss felt like a smile, bright and shining, and filled with joy, edging toward laughter.

When they stopped, she was on her back with his body pressed against hers and his mouth bringing her dreams to life. He trailed his mouth beneath her chin and along her throat.

"In your dream, did I kiss you here?" he asked as he dipped his tongue into the hollow at the base of her throat.

"Yes," she said in something that resembled a moan.

"Did I kiss you anywhere else?"

The kisses he pressed to her throat seemed to paralyze her voice, and she could do little more than nod.

"Where?"

She shook her head. "This is improper. Your family will be looking for us."

He lifted his face and gazed down on her. "Did you touch me?"

She wet her lips. They suddenly felt as parched as a desert, and she had a strong urge to drink from his mouth to quench her thirst. Her cheeks burned with the thought.

"Did you touch me in your dream?"

"I don't want to discuss my dream."

"You never touch me, Meredith."

She became acutely aware of her arms lying like dead weights at her sides while his arms were wrapped firmly around her.

"You don't stop me from kissing you or taking your hand, but I'm wondering now if it's just that you're too kind to say you don't want me to touch you. Maybe there's something about me you don't like."

The genuine concern and doubt swimming within the blue pools surprised Meredith. He always seemed so confident, so sure of himself. She found it disconcerting to realize she gave him such insecurities. "I like you, Lee, it's just that I grew up in a world where people didn't touch each other. I'm just not accustomed to touching people."

"Then what did you do in your dream that makes your cheeks turn so red when you think about it?"

She slid her eyes closed and released a sigh. "I touched you."

"Where?"

She opened her eyes, surprised by the longing in his voice. She worked her hand up so she could wave it freely in the direction of his face. "On your face."

He shifted his body, moving one arm away from her so he could take her flailing hand. He pressed a kiss to her palm, then laid it against his jaw. "Here?"

She looked at her hand pressed against his strong jaw,

her fingers feathering up to touch his cheek. She nodded slightly and gently cleared her throat. "Only you were smiling, and I touched the dimple your smile creates."

His face transformed beneath her touch until her finger touched the small dimple nestled in the side of his cheek.

"Does it feel like what you were expecting?" he asked.

She met his warm gaze. "The dimple yes, but your jaw—" She stroked his jaw. "I expected it to feel coarser."

"It would have if I hadn't shaved real quick after I left you in the kitchen."

"Why did you shave after you left me in the kitchen?"

"Because I didn't want nearly a full day's growth of beard to cause you any discomfort when I did this."

He settled his mouth over hers, and she felt his kiss with her fingers as much as she did with her lips and tongue. She eased her other hand up, touching the other side of his face, feeling the movements of his jaw and cheeks as he mated his mouth with hers.

He lifted his mouth slightly. "Come to me, Meredith," he whispered hoarsely.

When he lowered his mouth, it was only his lips that touched her, leaving a void between them. From the first moment he'd kissed her, she'd wondered what the depths of his mouth felt like, but she hadn't dared explore the regions that beckoned to her now. Tentatively she slipped her tongue past his lips, his deep groan reminding her of thunder rolling over the plains. She relished the feel of his tongue welcoming hers, waltzing with hers, drawing her deeper into the kiss.

"Lee?" Atlas's voice echoed through the cavernous barn.

Lee's groan was nothing like the ones she'd elicited from him. He lifted his mouth from hers.

"What?" he called out.

"It's time to eat."

"We'll be down in a minute."

He gave her a wry smile. "Guess we'd better go eat."

Sitting beside Lee, Meredith wanted to smack the smile from his face when he reached behind her, plucked a stray piece of straw from her hair, and slipped it between his teeth while everyone else settled into their chairs.

As soon as Lee's father reached for the chicken, pandemonium broke loose as everyone started filling their plates and passing dishes across the table.

Lee leaned close, and Meredith felt his breath fan her neck. "You just have to grab something when it comes by, Red."

"Don't call me that," she whispered harshly.

"Why not?"

"Not here, Lee." She glanced over at him. "Please."

"It'll cost you."

She would have gotten angry if it weren't for the warmth filling his blue eyes. "What will it cost me?"

"A walk to the gazebo in the moonlight."

"Just a walk?"

The smile he bestowed upon her promised more than a walk, and she felt the heat warm her face.

"Lee, either put some potatoes on your plate or pass the bowl down here 'cuz me and Bub is getting tired of waiting on 'em," Allie said.

Meredith was afraid she was redder than the tomato stew Persy had made. Lee dropped a dollop of potatoes on her plate and his before passing the bowl on to his sister. As other dishes came by, Meredith took a sampling from each, trying to ignore the way Lee's thigh brushed up against hers every time he reached for a platter or bowl. She ate in silence, listening to the conversation surrounding her.

"So, Lee, have you adjusted to being the new school-teacher?" Minerva asked.

Lee glanced quickly at Meredith before meeting his grandmother's laughing gray eyes. "Yes, ma'am, I have."

"Persy told me you're using some new methods."

"Yes, ma'am, I'm taking a practical approach to teaching."

"Practical?" Meredith scoffed. "Your methods are hardly practical."

"My methods are real practical. Why just this week—"

"I know, you had them out roping cattle."

"You saw us, huh?"

Glancing over at him, Meredith could not believe the pride radiating from his face. "I couldn't miss the spectacle. I looked out the window of The Hatbox and saw a whole herd of wooden cattle dotting the landscape."

"Pa carved the cattle. I thought he did a good job. Didn't you think they looked close enough to the real thing?"

Meredith shifted her gaze to Lee's father. He wore the same satisfied expression on his face, his deep blue eyes radiating pride. She smiled weakly. "From what I could see, they very much resembled cows."

"C.J. branded them for us."

Shaking her head, she tapped her fingers on the table. "You don't understand. School is not the place to learn to be a cowboy. School is where a child should learn reading, writing, and ciphering. It should be a disciplined, structured environment where every child knows what is expected and can meet those expectations. If these children move to the city, they won't need to know how to rope cattle."

"The lesson had nothing to do with roping cattle."

"That's what they were doing."

"No, they weren't."

"Lee, I sat there and watched."

"You should have come over and watched."

"Being closer would not have changed what I saw."

"Could you see the brands?"

"No."

Lee slapped his hand down on the table. "Bub, why don't you tell Miss Lewis about the brands since you were the one to figure out which brands to use?"

"Oh, well, see Lee figured some letters aren't used very much so they're the hardest to learn. I went through my reader and tallied up how many times each letter was used. We took the letters that weren't used so much and branded them on the cattle. When Lee hollered out a letter, we ran through the herd and roped a cow with that letter branded on it."

"So, what do you think?" Lee asked. "Pretty smart way to do it, huh?"

"It was a game," Meredith said. "It didn't teach them anything."

The smile left his face. "Why? Because they weren't looking in a book? You think everything of value has to come out of a book?"

Meredith sighed in exasperation. "You have not been certified to teach. You couldn't possibly understand."

"You think I'm dumb?"

"I didn't say that."

"But it's what you're thinking. Every teacher I ever had thought I was dumb when I was just bored. My students don't have time to get bored, and they're learning, Miss Lewis. You might not be able to see it from your window at the millinery, but they're learning."

An awkward silence hovered around the table. Meredith clasped her hands in her lap, staring at the food that was becoming a blur on her plate, fighting back her tears, wondering how the evening had turned into a disaster so quickly. She jumped when Lee shoved his plate across the table.

"Who do you think is the smartest kid in school, Lee?" Allie asked.

"They're all smart," he said evenly.

"The strangest one is Jimmy Stellar," Atlas said.

"That's 'cuz he's an orphan," Allie said.

"He's not an orphan," Lee said. "His ma died, but he still has his pa so he's not an orphan. An orphan is someone who doesn't have a ma or a pa."

Allie shrugged. "But the girls at school say he doesn't have a ma or a pa. That's why he looks like nobody loves him—'cuz nobody does."

Lee and Meredith looked at each other, the truth becoming perfectly clear.

"We gotta go," Lee said as he shoved himself away from the table and pulled back Meredith's chair. "Thanks for the fine meal, Persy."

"Why didn't we figure it out?" Meredith asked as Lee placed his hand on the small of her back and escorted her from the room.

"Reckon we were just too busy trying to prove which of us was the better teacher."

Chapter
Thirteen

Lee halted the buggy before the Stellar house. All was dark except for a small glow slipping out between the boards Lee had nailed in place over the broken window.

"Watch where you step," Lee said as he helped Meredith clamber out of the buggy.

Keeping his hand wrapped around her arm, he led her through the darkness to the house. As they stepped on the porch, they heard the boards moan an ominous protest. Meredith knocked softly on the door. A muffled rustling sounded within the house, followed by the light patter of bare feet across a wooden floor.

The door squeaked open, and Jimmy peered out. Yawning, he rubbed his eyes and squinted into the night.

"Hello, Jimmy," Lee said.

"Hey, Mr. Daltry. My pa's still out courting that widow woman."

"We came to see you," Meredith said kindly.

"Oh." He glanced over his shoulder, and they could see

the battle raging across his young profile. Finally, with the look of a defeated warrior, he stepped away from the door. "I reckon you want to come in then."

Meredith and Lee slipped through the open door. A solitary lamp sitting on the table lit the room, its golden glow hovering over a Bible and a schoolbook.

Resting her hand on Jimmy's shoulder, Meredith felt his protruding bones through the worn nightshirt. She led him across the room to the couch and pulled him down beside her. Lee crouched before them, resting his forearm over his thigh.

Jimmy's hair stood up on one side, grooves marred his face as though he'd fallen asleep on an uneven surface.

"Were you reading, Jimmy?" Meredith asked.

He nodded and rubbed his finger beneath his nose. "Some. Reckon I fell asleep."

"What did you eat for supper?" she asked.

"Food."

"Are you hungry now?"

"Nope. Told ya I ate."

Lee put his hand on Jimmy's shoulder. "Jimmy, we heard a rumor tonight that you were living alone. Is that true?"

Jimmy's gaze dropped to the floor. He placed one bare foot on top of the other and clenched his hands in his lap.

"We want to help you," Lee said.

"I'm learning to read—"

"I'm not talking about reading. Where's your pa?"

"I told ya. He's out courting some widow woman."

"Which woman? What's her name?"

"How the heck should I know?"

"How long has he been courting her?"

He shrugged his narrow shoulders. "Awhile."

"When do you think he'll be back?"

Jimmy shrugged haplessly.

"Then I guess we'll wait."

Jimmy jerked his gaze up from the floor, his wide eyes searching Lee's face. "You're gonna wait?"

Lee nodded. Jimmy turned his gaze to Meredith. "Sometimes, he don't come back till it's late, really late. You don't got to wait for him."

Meredith lightly brushed the blond hair off his brow. "We want to wait for him. We want to make sure you're all right."

"But sometimes, he don't come back till mornin'. You can't wait here all night."

"We can wait here all week if we have to, Jimmy," Lee said.

Jimmy slumped against the couch, closing his eyes, lolling his head slowly from side to side in defeat. "He ain't coming back," he said in a hoarse whisper. "Not tonight, not ever."

"Did something happen to him?" Lee asked.

The boy squeezed his eyes, but the tears escaped, trailing down his cheek as he shook his head. "He just up and left 'bout a month or so ago. I wasn't good enough, I reckon, so he didn't take me with him."

Meredith understood completely the pain of rejection. She wrapped her arms around Jimmy, pulling him against her breast, comforting him as she'd never been comforted. "No, Jimmy, his leaving had nothing to do with you."

"Why'd he leave then? Why didn't he take me with him?" He sobbed, his thin body wracked with grief long held at bay.

"I don't know," she whispered, brushing her fingers through his hair, rocking him until his sobbing subsided. She looked at Lee. "What are we going to do?"

Lee forced his gaze away from Meredith's face, bathed in concern and compassion. He didn't think he'd ever seen anything as beautiful in his life. He studied Jimmy, peering at him with half his face buried against Meredith's shoulder. "Jimmy, get dressed." He glanced at the sparse furnishings. "Gather up whatever is important to you. We'll go into town, talk to the sheriff, see what he has to say." Unfolding his body, he took Meredith's arm. "We'll be waiting outside. You just come on out when you're ready."

As soon as he had Meredith outside and closed the door, Lee wrapped his arms around her. She pressed her face to his chest, and he felt her shoulders quaking as she grieved.

"Oh, Lee, how could his father have left him?"

He pulled her tighter into his embrace. "I don't know, Red." He laid his cheek against the top of her head. He'd seen the look of worthlessness in Jimmy's eyes. At Jimmy's age, he'd seen that same expression reflected in his own mirror when his guard was down. It was easy to cover, but the feeling never truly went away. Some days, it still snapped at his heels with a vengeance.

"What are we going to do?" she asked.

"We'll have to see what Sheriff Sampson says."

"Did you see the books on the table?"

"Yep."

"I think Jimmy was trying to teach himself to read."

"Yeah." Lee figured Jimmy was trying to give himself some self-worth. He wondered if the boy thought his reading problem was the reason his father had left. If Jimmy's father ever showed his face in Paradise Plains, he was going to feel the full wrath of Mount Olympus bearing down on him. Lee'd see to it. He rubbed his hands up and down Meredith's slender back. "It's gonna be all right, Red."

Sniffing, she pulled away from him. "It's just that I know what it feels like to be unwanted."

And Lee knew what it was to feel like a failure. Reaching into his pocket, he pulled out his bandanna and handed it to her. She blew her nose and wiped her tears.

He glanced around, his senses suddenly alert.

"What is it?" she whispered.

"It's taking Jimmy too long to get ready." He pounded his fist on the door. "Jimmy?"

Silence came from within.

He shoved the door open. A lonely room greeted him.

"Damn!" Stepping off the porch, he saw a shadow streak toward the barn. He ran after it, his long strides eating up the distance. He wrapped his arm around the shadow before it disappeared into the grove of trees.

"I ain't going!" Jimmy yelled as he flung his bag over his shoulder.

Lee felt the blow to his head and closed his eyes against the blinding light as he staggered back, refusing to release his hold on Jimmy. Jimmy flailed his arms and legs. Lee grunted against the succession of sharp pains randomly slicing through his body. "Damn it, Jimmy! Be still."

"Let me go! I ain't gonna go to jail just 'cuz I ain't got a pa!"

"No one's taking you to jail!"

"But you said—"

"I said we were gonna talk to the sheriff. We need to find out who's gonna take care of you."

Jimmy went limp, his feet dangling above the ground. "I ain't goin' to jail?"

"No. If I let you go, do you promise not to run?"

Jimmy nodded, and Lee released him. "Come on, let's go."

They walked to the buggy where Meredith was waiting, hands clasped before her. "Oh, my God, you're bleeding!" she exclaimed as they neared.

Lee touched the sticky wetness above his eye. "What the hell did you have in your bag?"

"My books," Jimmy said.

Lee released a rueful laugh. "You and Miss Lewis ought

to get along just fine, then, since she likes to throw books at me, too.''

She drew up indignantly as she pressed his bandanna to the gash. ''Maybe you should stop giving me your bandanna. It seems I always have to give it back. Are you going to be all right?''

''Yep, but I'll confess I'm starting to develop a real dislike for books.''

While Lee went to fetch the sheriff, Meredith took Jimmy into the boardinghouse. As they sat on the sofa in the parlor, she took Jimmy's hand. ''Everything's going to be all right.'' She issued a silent prayer that she was telling the truth.

It seemed an eternity passed before Lee walked through the door, Sheriff Tommy Sampson in tow. The sheriff removed his hat.

''Evening, Miss Lewis, Jimmy,'' he said in his slow drawl.

Jimmy tried not to feel nervous as the man scraped a chair across the floor and deposited it before him. Miss Lewis squeezed his hand, and he gave her a quivering smile. He sure as heck didn't want to be arrested for being without a pa.

Sheriff Sampson planted his elbows on his thighs and turned his hat in his hands. ''Now then, boy, Lee here tells me your pa ain't about. That true?''

Jimmy nodded.

''You know where he'd be?''

Jimmy shook his head.

''He didn't say where he was going?''

Jimmy shook his head.

''Or how long he'd be gone?''

He shook his head.

Sheriff Sampson's tongue slid out of his mouth, caught

the corner of his mustache, and brought it between his lips where he gnawed on it absently. He glanced up at Lee. "You say his pa's been gone for a month?"

"That's about what he figures."

"Then I'd say we've got us a case of abandonment."

Lee looked at Sheriff Sampson as though the man had lost his mind. "That's what I told you when I knocked on your door."

He blew the end of his mustache out of his mouth. "Don't go getting smart with me. I gotta sift through the evidence, can't be taking people's versions of what happened. I've done my sifting and came to the same conclusion you did."

"So what are you gonna do about it?"

Jimmy stiffened, waiting for the handcuffs to be put on his skinny wrists and to hear the jail door slam in his face.

"Only thing I can do. Send him to an orphanage. Nearest one I know about is in Fort Worth."

"An orphanage?" Meredith glanced at Lee, then back at the sheriff. "I've lived in an orphanage. You can't expect him to be happy there."

"Got no choice, little lady, unless I can find someone in town to adopt him."

"I'll adopt him!" two voices sounded at once. Meredith looked at Lee. He was looking at her. He gave her a sad smile.

"Meredith, Jimmy would be better off with me."

Her mouth dropped open. "I beg your pardon. What do you know about raising a child?"

"More than you."

"I think not. You believe children should be tossed out windows!"

"Not children. Just Si—" He stopped and looked over his shoulder, grateful they hadn't disturbed Mrs. Bennett. "Just Simon," he finished in a whisper.

"Now, just a minute you two. This is my decision, not yours," Sheriff Sampson said.

Lee braced his legs apart into a stance he used when he was about to toss a steer down to the ground for branding. "And what's your decision?"

Sheriff Sampson scratched the bare spot on top of his head. "Gotta hear the evidence before I make a decision as to who should adopt the boy."

Lee took a step forward, towering over the man. "I'd make the better parent. I've got a big, loving family, which is what Jimmy needs right now. Stability. We're not going anywhere. Miss Lewis is planning on going back to Boston."

Meredith jumped to her feet. "I wouldn't go to Boston and abandon Jimmy in the process. He needs a mother and attention. I've been around your family. Jimmy would get lost, would have to vie for attention. With me, he'd have the full, undivided attention he deserves."

"I have a home he can live in."

"There's an empty room next to mine upstairs."

"He can share a room with Atlas and C.J."

"He can have his own room. Besides, I know what it feels like to be abandoned. I can help him deal with those feelings."

"And I know—" Lee stopped himself from admitting the truth. "I know what it feels like to be raised in a loving family. I can share that with Jimmy."

Sheriff Sampson chewed on his mustache again. "You've both got good arguments so I tell you what I'm gonna do. I can't figure out with your words which of you would make the better parent, so I'll have to judge you on your actions. Until I make a decision, you'll both be responsible for the boy. He can spend the days during the week with Miss Lewis, Saturday and Sunday with Lee. With Lee being the new schoolmarm, he don't need to be worrying about the boy during the week. He can just go back and forth till I figure out what's best.''

"That's hardly a stable environment," Meredith said in protest.

Sheriff Sampson shrugged. "It's either that or the orphanage 'cuz I'm too dang tired to sit here any longer and listen to you two bicker about it." He pulled himself out of his chair and pointed his finger at her. "You get the boy first." He dropped his hat on his head. "And remember— I'll be watching."

He trudged out of the front door.

Although they'd forgotten about Jimmy during all the arguing, he was wearing a big grin.

"Why are you smiling?" Lee asked.

"Never had nobody fighting to keep me before."

Jimmy snuggled beneath the blankets. The clean sheets felt strange next to his clean skin. He'd begrudgingly taken another bath because Mr. Daltry had told him it would make Miss Lewis smile, but two baths in one week could give a boy nightmares. He surely hoped Miss Lewis wasn't planning on making him scrub his body down every night.

He didn't think he'd be any better off with Mr. Daltry, though. The man had gone back to the Daltry Ranch and located some clean clothes so Jimmy wouldn't have to put his dirty clothes back on after his bath.

He supposed there were worse things in life than two people wanting him who thought being clean was important. No one at all could want him.

He'd sure been surprised when Mr. Daltry and Miss Lewis had been arguing over him. He'd thought they liked each other—a lot. He'd peered through the crack in the door before making his escape and seen Mr. Daltry holding Miss Lewis close—real close. He figured they'd forgotten all about him, holding each other as they were. He'd been wrong.

Miss Lewis drew the covers up to his chin. She'd washed and trimmed his hair. He knew he wasn't, but he felt nearly bald. He couldn't remember the last time his hair was this short.

"Good night, Jimmy. Sleep well," she said, a soft smile on her face.

"Miss Lewis?"

"Yes, Jimmy."

He balled his hands around the covers. "I was wondering if you might talk to me a minute till I get used to being here."

"Certainly." She sat in a chair beside the bed. "What would you like to discuss?"

"Uh, what's it like being in an orphanage?"

Reassuringly she placed her hand over his where it gripped the covers. "You don't have to worry about that. We won't let you go to an orphanage."

"Was it so gawd-awful?"

"It seemed so at the time, although in retrospect, I realize it was only my own dreams that made me discontent. No one abused me. I was never hungry. I had clothes to wear. I was warm in winter."

"But no one loved you?"

A sadness swept over her face. "No, no one loved me."

"My ma loved me. Thought my pa did, too."

"I'm sure he did."

"Why'd he leave then?"

"I don't know, Jimmy, but if he hadn't left, I still wouldn't have anyone to love."

His eyes widened. "You love me?"

"I care about you very much. I have since the first time I saw you with the carrot sticking out of your shirt. I don't think it'll take much for me to come to love you."

"I'm awful sorry I didn't keep those clothes you give me."

"That's quite all right. They really weren't the proper clothes for a growing boy to wear. I saw them at the mercantile and was reminded of children I'd seen in Boston. I'm not even sure why they were stocked at the mercantile. They're hardly suitable for this part of the country."

Jimmy yawned. "If you adopt me, will my last name change?"

"Only if you want it to."

He rolled over. "Sure smells nice in here. Like flowers."

She patted his back. "Why don't you try and go to sleep now?"

For long moments, Meredith sat and watched him sleep. She'd never hoped to have a son. The responsibility weighed heavily on her shoulders, lightly on her heart. She knew love was taking root, knew she wouldn't let any member of the Daltry family yank another dream away from her.

Chapter Fourteen

"Hurry up, Miss Lewis!"

"Now, Jimmy Stellar, you just calm down," Meredith said with an even tone in her voice although her heart was skipping wildly within her breast.

"But I see 'em! They're almost here."

He stuck his head out the window, and Meredith reeled him back in, "You're not going until you look proper."

"What's to look proper? We're gonna see a circus! I ain't never been to no circus."

"Don't say 'ain't.' " Running the comb through his hair, she realized her gesture at making him look cared for was futile. She wished she'd spent the time making herself more presentable. She hadn't seen Lee except at a carefully guarded distance all week. She heard his deep voice as he brought the horses to a halt. It took every ounce of willpower she possessed not to peek out the window to catch a glimpse of him.

Jimmy possessed no such willpower. Eagerly he stuck

his head out the window, yelled he was on his way down, and then proceeded to carry out his promise. Meredith rushed after him. "Jimmy, you're going to wake everyone." But he was down the stairs and out the door before she could catch him.

At the bottom of the stairs, she drew a cleansing breath, wiped her sweaty palms on her black skirt, and walked sedately into the parlor and out the front door.

Lee's laughter reached her as he helped the overly excited Jimmy clamber into the back of the wagon with the other children.

"Enjoy yourself, Jimmy," Meredith called out.

Lee spun around, and the smile eased off his face. Removing his hat, he walked toward her.

He halted just shy of the porch. Meredith didn't remember his eyes being so blue and wondered if it was a reflection of the deep blue sky as dawn eased over the horizon. She also didn't realize how much she'd come to enjoy his smiles and wished she wasn't the one responsible for making them go away, but she refused to give Jimmy up for a smile.

"I'll have him back tomorrow evening before sunset," Lee said.

"That'll be fine."

He squared his jaw, gave a brusque nod, turned on his heel, and walked back toward the wagon. Meredith forced a smile and waved at the laughing children.

Lee concentrated his efforts on getting to the wagon without looking back. Being a mother agreed with Meredith. Strands of her hair had escaped her ribbon and formed a feathery frame around her face, and she was too concerned over Jimmy to notice. He gazed into the back of the wagon. "Everybody ready?"

A chorus of enthusiasm rose up around him. "You be sure you keep your butts on the floorboards. Use the blankets if you want to take a nap before we get there.''

"When will we get there?" Atlas asked.

"Around noon."

"Then what?" Allie asked.

Lee looked at the two huge baskets in the back of the wagon. "We'll probably eat the food Persy cooked for us."

"When will we see the circus?" Hal asked.

"After we eat," Lee assured him. "Now, let's go." Plopping his hat on his head, he peered at Meredith standing alone on the porch, her arms wrapped around the beam. Jerking his hat off, he stalked to the porch.

"Is something wrong?" Meredith asked, releasing her hold on the beam.

Lee cleared his throat. "Do you want to come with us?"

"I beg your pardon?"

Heaving a sigh, Lee planted a foot on the porch and braced his elbow on his thigh. "Look, Meredith, I don't see why we can't share some of our time with Jimmy."

"But the sheriff said—"

"The sheriff was just doing his job because you were being so stubborn."

Meredith drew herself up, balling her fists.

"Want me to fetch you some books to throw at me?" Lee asked.

"I want you to admit we were both stubborn."

Lee's mouth curled up into a half smile. "All right, Red. We were both stubborn." His smile warmed. "I was just thinking about the first time I saw a circus. Jimmy can tell you about everything he sees, but it's better if you see him seeing it." He furrowed his brow. "I just mean I wouldn't like it much if you were the one taking him to the circus, and I was the one watching him go. So do you want to go with us?"

She looked at the wagon filled with four laughing children, then to the man who would no doubt see to it that the entire day was filled with laughter. A day filled with laughter. In her entire life, she'd never had one. "I'd like very much to go with you."

"Then go gather up what you need."

"What do I need?"

Slowly he shook his head, his grin broadening. "Good Lord, Red, don't tell me you've never been to a circus."

"I've never been to a circus."

The warmth of his laughter spread through her heart and soul to the tips of her toes.

"Shoes that don't hurt your toes, a bonnet, and a shawl. It'll be evening before we head back, and it'll be cooling down."

"Should I bring some money?"

"I'll take care of the money part. Just hurry up."

Moments later she returned carrying her reticule and a shawl. He was still standing by the porch, waiting.

"I don't have a bonnet," she said. "As bright as the sun is here in Texas, I know I need one, but after sewing hats all week, I can't bring myself to buy one."

"We'll figure something out." He held out his hand. She stared at the broad palm, the long fingers.

"Today's not business, Red," he said in a low voice.

"Do you know what it is?"

"Nope, I just know what it's not, and what I think I'd like it to be."

"And what's that?"

"A day we'll always remember."

Somehow, she thought she'd always remember every moment she'd ever spent with Hercules Daltry, every silly grin, every tender smile that crossed his handsome face. She slipped her hand into his and felt his strong fingers wrap around hers.

"Bub, I need your hat," he said as they approached the wagon.

"How come?"

"Because my head is too big, and Miss Lewis doesn't have a bonnet."

"So you're gonna let her wear my hat?"

"Yep, or we can wait until the mercantile opens—"

The hat sailed through the air. Lee dropped it on Meredith's head.

"I feel like a cowboy," she said, touching the brim.

"Believe me, Red, you don't look anything like a cowboy," he said as he lifted her onto the bench seat of the wagon. Then he climbed up to join her. "Ready?" he asked.

Peering past the broad brim of the hat, she nodded.

"Ready back there?"

"We been ready!" Allie yelled. "We coulda walked there by now."

Lee clicked his teeth and flicked his wrist, setting the team of horses into motion.

"Persy didn't want to come?" Meredith asked.

"Nah, she's a homebody, and Venus wouldn't be caught dead outdoors."

"I guess C.J. is out courting."

Lee smiled victoriously. "Nope. Today he's working the range. When you give the men the day off, somebody's gotta fill in behind them. He wanted the responsibility of managing the ranch, and now he's got it. While he's working, I'm gonna enjoy the circus."

"Lee, do you know what all we're gonna see there?" Atlas asked.

"All sorts of things. Why?"

" 'Cuz I'm making a list of all the things we're gonna see."

Glancing over his shoulder, Lee leaned back far enough to see the paper and pencil clutched in Atlas's hand. "Why don't you wait, and after we've been to the circus, you can make a list of everything we saw?''

Atlas smiled. "I didn't even think about that! I'll make a list of what we think we'll see. Then I'll make a list of what we saw. Then I'll make a list of the things we thought we were gonna see, but we didn't see and one of the things we saw that we didn't know we were gonna see! Thanks, Lee.'' He pressed the paper against his thigh and scribbled.

Lee rolled his eyes heavenward. Meredith rested her hand on his arm. "It's an excellent exercise. We should probably have all the children make a list."

"Nope. Today's got nothing to do with reading, writing, or ciphering. Today is just to enjoy."

"Done!"

"Me, too!"

Looking at the full plates sitting on the quilt, then at his brother and sister, Lee shook his head. "One bite's not enough."

Allie shoved a biscuit into her mouth. Atlas shoved his plate away. "I want to save room for the popped corn. You promised we could have some. I don't know why Persy made all this food when there's so much here to eat."

Hal and Jimmy stared at Lee. Neither one had taken a bite since Allie and Atlas had declared they were finished.

Lee waved his hand through the air. "Go on. Get out of here."

"Jimmy!" Meredith called as the four children began to run off.

All the children stopped. Meredith looked at Lee. "Shouldn't he stay with us?"

"Nah, let him run around with the others. He's gonna want to look at things you won't be interested in."

"Like what?" she asked as all sorts of horrors raced through her mind.

"Dog-faced women and contortionists."

"What if something happens?"

"They'll be able to find us easy enough." He turned his attention to the waiting children. "Catch up with us in front of the big tent just before the show starts—and stay together. No straying off to find your own adventures."

"Yes, sir!" they hollered in unison before they ran off.

Lee loaded everything back into the wagon. Then he wrapped his hand around Meredith's. "Want to see if we can fill up the day?"

"I don't think that'll be a problem. How do you know where to start?"

"We'll just walk around. Whenever you see something you want to look at, just let me know and we'll stop."

Meredith had never in her life seen such sights. She'd read about circuses and seen sketches of men balancing on a wire strung high in the air, but what lay before her made everything else pale in comparison.

She touched her first elephant and watched a snake charmer handle an assortment of snakes. After going into a small tent and staring at Siamese brothers, she was grateful Lee didn't suggest they visit any other exhibits boldly proclaiming freaks of nature. She had a feeling he'd felt as uncomfortable as she had looking at people who couldn't help the way they were.

He bought her taffy and lemonade, and they watched a man eat fire. They passed a colorful tent. The sign announced that Madame Futura was reading palms and predicting the future.

"Want to know your future?" Lee asked, just before he popped another piece of taffy into her mouth.

"No." She chewed the sweet confection. "No one can tell the future."

"I know that, Red. It's just for fun. Just to see what she'll say. Come on, let's do it." He tugged on her hand.

"Are you going to let her read your palm?"

"Might. Depends on what she says about yours."

They stepped inside the shadow-filled tent. A bent and aged woman sat at a round table where a solitary candle lit the darkness. A smoky scent filled the air. A blue and red scarf surrounded her head, hiding the color of her hair. Her black eyes glowed as she extended gnarled hands toward them.

"Come, let me reveal your future."

Meredith took a step back. "Maybe another time."

"It'll be years before another circus passes this way," Lee said as he nudged her forward. Reluctantly Meredith sat beside the woman. Lee took a seat beside her and set a coin on the table.

Madame Futura slid the coin off the table into her lap. Then she smiled at Meredith and held out her hand. "Give me the hand closest to your heart, my child."

Meredith placed her balled fist on the table. Madame took it and gently stroked her gnarled fingers over Meredith's hand until her muscles relaxed and her hand unfurled. Madame moved her hand closer to the candle.

"Now, then, let us see what we can see." She trailed her finger over Meredith's palm. "I see a long life filled with children."

Meredith glanced at Lee. He was engrossed in the spectacle. A long life was an easy enough statement to make. Who could ask for their money back if they didn't have a long life? And a life filled with children . . . she was a schoolteacher. Of course, she'd have a life filled with children, but then she realized Madame didn't know that.

"The children will have many labors."

The table shook when Lee dropped his elbows down and leaned forward. "Labors?"

Meredith was surprised by his reaction. "Lee, what person doesn't go through life with labors?"

He gave a brusque nod. "Oh, yeah. Right. What else do you see?"

"A river," the old woman rasped. "A moon. A swan. That is all." She folded Meredith's fingers over her palm.

Meredith moved her hands to her lap and eyed Lee speculatively. "Now, it's your turn."

"Oh, sure." He laid another coin on the table and extended his right hand.

Madame took the coin. "I need the hand closest to your heart."

"I want you to read this hand," Lee said.

"Come on, Lee," Meredith urged. "You wanted me to play along, now you have to play. Besides, that's the hand you cut at Jimmy's house and scars might interfere with her ability to see the future."

Lee scooted the chair back. "You're right, Red. It's just a game. Let's look at the rest of the exhibits."

"No, sir." Grabbing his wrist, she pulled his hand across the table. "Let's hear your future." She nodded toward the wizened woman. "Go ahead." Then she smiled at Lee.

Holding her gaze, Lee smiled and unfurled his fingers, hoping his future could be told quickly. He felt the warmth from the flame of the candle touch his palm.

"You have unusual lines, carved deeply, lines the scars cannot hide."

Meredith averted her gaze from his and leaned with interest over the table. It was the last thing he wanted. Lightly she touched his palm, trailing her fingers over ancient wounds, and he felt as though she'd laid the flame of the candle against his flesh. Furrowing her brow, she looked at him. The questions were in her eyes, the knowledge within her reach. His mouth went dry, and his palms began to sweat.

"Forget the scars. What do the lines say?" he rasped.

"A long life."

"Wonderful," he said impatiently. "And many children, and they'll have labors. I'm much obliged." He pulled his hand, but the old woman's grasp remained steadfast.

"I see a choice; a truth that must be faced." She released his hand.

"We appreciate your thoughts." He stood and helped Meredith to her feet. Taking her elbow, he escorted her from the tent.

They both squinted against the bright sunlight. Playfully he tipped her hat down to shade her eyes.

"Well, that was fun," he said as he glanced around. "So what do you want to see now? There's supposed to be a pony around here with a twelve-foot tail. Want to see that?"

Meredith slipped her hand into his. "How did you get the scars on your palm?"

"Hell, I don't remember. Cowboys get all kinds of scars."

"But these are from burns, and you don't have them on your right hand."

He heaved a sigh, his eyes studying far horizons. "Probably got 'em when I was first learning how to brand. Was careless, I reckon." He shifted his gaze to hers and smiled. "Now, what do you want to see?"

Shaking her head, she released a skeptical laugh. "I don't believe you. When we were at your thinking place, I told you all about me—some things were painful to share—yet I shared them, but now you don't trust me enough to tell me how you got the scars on your palm."

"I told you."

"No, you didn't, and do you know how I know you didn't? Because of your smile. I have finally figured out that's the smile you use whenever you want to distract me from something. It's a beautiful smile, and I imagine most of the ladies in Paradise Plains swoon every time you show it, and if I wasn't beginning to know you as well as I do, I'd probably swoon as well.''

He furrowed his brow. ''What do you mean, 'if you weren't beginning to know me so well'?''

Reaching up, she touched the corner of his mouth. ''You have a host of smiles. Some like the one you just gave me are designed to cover something up. Then you have a smile you use when you're teasing. And then there's my favorite smile.''

''The one with the nails,'' he said as he gave her a teasing grin.

Smiling, she shook her head. ''No, this one's different. Usually one of your other smiles slips into it unexpectedly. It's very tender, very caring. I'm not even certain you're aware it exists, but whenever you use it, it makes me want to know everything there is to know about you. Please, tell me about your hand.''

''You're gonna keep pestering me about this, aren't you?''

She folded her arms beneath her breasts and tilted up her nose. ''Yes, Mr. Daltry, I am.''

''Oh, hell, then let's find some shade to sit under.''

He grabbed her hand, and they walked past the hustle and bustle of the circus activity. Meredith fought to hold back her laughter as he found something wrong with every tree they passed. It wasn't tall enough, the shade didn't cover a wide enough area, too many birds twittering. He had an excuse for every tree until Meredith finally stopped walking and pointed to a tree.

''That one.''

''Shade's on the wrong side.''

''Hercules Daltry, you're just putting off the inevitable.''

He lumbered to the tree, dropped beneath the shade, and glared at her like a petulant child. She walked over and knelt beside him, taking his hand and lightly trailing her fingers over the faint scars. "Just start talking whenever you're ready."

Lee watched the way her fingers moved over his palm. He'd never be ready. He cleared his throat, but it didn't make the words come out any easier.

"I had a teacher when I first started school. She was real strict and boring as hell. I spent a lot of time gazing out the window, dreaming about different things. So I wasn't always prepared with the answer when she called on me, and when I wasn't—" He cleared his throat. "She had a magnifying glass, and she'd make me stand by the window where the sun was coming in. She'd hold my hand and let the sun burn through the magnifying glass onto my palm."

Horror swept across Meredith's face. "I've heard of teachers using that method of punishment, but I didn't believe it. Didn't you tell your parents?"

He shook his head. "I didn't want them to know I'd gotten into trouble. The only one who knows is Persy, and that's because the teacher was still there when she started school."

"Persy saw her burn your hand?"

Nodding, he swallowed, trying to dislodge the lump in his throat that always surfaced when he thought of Persy's gentle tears. "She cried. Lord, how she cried because the teacher was hurting me. I told her it really didn't hurt. I just hollered so the teacher would stop."

"But it did hurt."

"Yeah, it hurt, but the burns didn't hurt as much as watching Persy cry. I hated that teacher for making Persy cry. She left at the end of the year, but the damage was done."

"I just don't see what she hoped to accomplish by hurting you."

"Guess she figured I'd start paying attention."

"Did you?"

"Not much. Like I said, she was boring."

"Is that why you take the children outside so much?"

"Yep."

She brought his hand up to her lips and pressed a kiss to the center of his palm. He watched a tear trail slowly down her sun-kissed cheek. "Ah, Red, don't cry."

"She had no right to hurt you, Lee."

He cupped her cheek. "Being gored by a bull hurt a lot worse, and you didn't cry when I told you about that."

"I didn't care about you then."

Tenderly he wiped the tear from her cheek with his thumb. "And you care now?"

Slowly she nodded her head.

"Will you take off your spectacles so your tears don't look so big?"

"Oh, my, I even got the lenses wet." She removed her spectacles and began to clean the lenses with her skirt. "Really, I seldom cry. Tears never accomplish anything."

"Oh, you'd be surprised what tears can do, Red," Lee said as he cupped her face in his large hands and lowered his mouth to hers.

The kiss was infinitely tender, remarkably sweet as though she were delicate spun glass to be cherished. She released her hold on her spectacles and moved her hands so her palms pressed against his chest. She felt the steady rhythm of his heart, heard the pounding echoing within her ears.

The ground began to vibrate, and she realized the pounding she heard was that of children's feet.

"What in the heck are you doin' all the way out here?" Allie cried. "We been lookin' all over for you!"

Meredith pulled back and began to search within the folds of her skirt for her spectacles. She felt the heat rushing to her cheeks as the children's feet stopped hitting the earth. She could feel them standing behind her, and she prayed they hadn't seen what was going on beneath the shade of this tree. She felt Lee's hand graze by hers just before he placed her spectacles back on the bridge of her nose and brought the wire into place behind her ears. She blinked, her world coming back into focus to reveal his special smile. "That's the one," she said quietly. "The smile I like best."

He ran his thumb over her lips, still tingling from his kiss. "I think you're the only one who's ever seen it."

"We're gonna miss the show!" Allie cried.

"No, we won't," Lee assured her as he unfolded his body and reached down to bring Meredith to her feet.

"We gotta hurry," Allie said.

"All right, then, let's go," Lee said as he grabbed Meredith's hand, and they ran toward the big top.

As the wagon rolled along in the moonlight, Meredith drew her shawl more tightly around her.

"Cold?" Lee asked in a hushed voice.

Smiling softly, she glanced at him. "A little."

"Reckon I can try and wrestle a blanket away from one of the young'uns . . . or you could snuggle up against me."

Meredith looked over her shoulder at the children sprawled over and beneath the blankets. Their gentle snores escaped into the night. They'd been so vibrant after watching the circus performers, their excited voices recanting each feat of wonder they'd witnessed: the high-wire artist, the clowns, the bareback riders, the wild animal tamer. Then one by one, their voices had drifted into silence. "I hate to disturb them. They look so peaceful."

"Yep, and they're finally quiet. It'd be like opening up Pandora's box if I woke them." He lifted his arm. "Come here, Red."

She scooted across the wooden bench seat. He wrapped his arm around her, drawing her against his side. She nestled her face into the crook of his shoulder.

"Better?" he asked.

"Much."

She looked at the stark, dark landscape that melted into the black heavens above. A partial moon graced the sky, but darkness was the predominant force tonight.

"Are you certain we shouldn't have waited until the morning to travel back to Paradise Plains?"

"Why would we wait?"

"What if we get lost?"

"We won't." He pointed one of his fingers holding the reins. "There's the North Star."

"Where?"

He raised his finger so she could follow its path to the heavens.

She sighed. "I can't see it. I guess you know all the constellations?"

"Know the ones I need so we don't get lost when we're driving the cattle north, or when we're coming home after a trip to the circus."

"I never can see the constellations. People point them out to me, but all I see are a thousand little bits of light."

"I see the Big Dipper. Want me to point it out to you?"

"No, I'd just get frustrated. I'll just enjoy all the stars and not try to figure out their patterns."

"Are you enjoying the stars, Meredith?"

"Yes."

He closed his arm more securely around her. "Just the stars?"

"No."

She felt him lay his cheek against the top of her head.

"What was your favorite part of the day?" he asked.

"Sitting beneath the tree after we saw the fortune-teller. Thank you for trusting me."

Lee felt a twinge of guilt because he hadn't trusted her

completely. No, it wasn't that he hadn't trusted her, it was just that he knew how she'd feel about the truth. With her teaching certificate and belief in teaching by the book, she'd never accept him as he was, but he'd become skilled at hiding the truth. For the moment he was grateful he had. He pressed his lips to the top of her head, the hat she'd worn all day tossed into the back earlier. "It was my favorite part, too."

The wagon rolled through the arched entrance to the Daltry Ranch. They rode the remainder of the way in silence, Meredith relishing the feel of Lee's closeness, wondering at his ability to stay warm when she felt chilled.

He pulled the wagon to a halt before the house. He vaulted off the wagon, then helped her down. Reluctantly the children woke up and shuffled into the house, Lee and Meredith following.

Jane and Odie Daltry greeted them at the door. "We'll put them to bed if you need to get Miss Lewis home," Jane said as she prodded the children up the stairs.

"Good night, Jimmy," Meredith said softly.

He stopped, one foot on the step. Then he turned around and hugged her. "Night, Miss Lewis."

"Enjoy yourself tomorrow."

"Yes, ma'am. I will."

He peered at Lee through sleep-filled eyes. "Thanks, Mr. Daltry. This was the best day I ever had."

Lee ruffled his hair. "I'm glad, Jimmy. Now, get on to bed."

"Yes, sir." He tromped up the steps.

Persy stepped out of the family room. "I guess they'll tell us all about it tomorrow."

Lee sighed deeply. "They'll probably be talking about it for a week."

"Would you like me to make you something to eat?"

"Appreciate the offer, Persy, but I need to get Miss

Lewis back to the boardinghouse. It's been a long day for her, too.''

He opened the front door. They stepped outside and walked along in the moonlight. Unexpectedly he took her hand and pulled her into the gazebo.

''I thought you were taking me back to the boarding-house.''

''I lied.''

He sat at an angle in the corner of the gazebo, putting one foot on the bench. He pulled her down so she was sitting between his thighs, her back pressed against his chest. It seemed an exceedingly intimate position in which he'd placed her.

''Relax, Red,'' he whispered near her ear, and she felt the chills travel along her spine.

''This is exceedingly—''

''I know. Improper.'' He trailed his finger along the nape of her neck. ''Look at the sky, all the stars. Isn't it beautiful?''

''Yes,'' she admitted in a voice that didn't sound at all like hers. ''I think if we sat side by side—''

''We'd get a crick in our necks looking over our shoulder, and we wouldn't enjoy it near as much. Just take a deep breath and settle in against me.''

''Lee—''

''If you didn't want to be here, Meredith, you would have already gotten up. I don't know why you won't admit you want to be here as much as I want you to be here. It's just like tasting blackberries.''

Sighing, she nestled the back of her head within the crook of his shoulder. ''It's nothing like tasting black-berries.''

He slipped his arm beneath her knees and brought her legs up to the bench, then brought his other foot up so she was nestled firmly between his thighs. He wrapped his arms around her. "My father knew what he was doing when he made the benches extra wide."

"What if someone sees us?"

"What if they do? What are we doing that's so gawd-awful wrong? I'm holding you, and we're looking at the stars; no harm in that."

"It's beautiful out here," she said, placing her hands over his, rubbing her thumbs over the hair covering his wrists.

"Think you'll remember today?" he asked quietly.

"Always."

"I want you to remember tonight, too."

He placed his hands on her shoulders, turning her ever so slightly so she was looking up into his face. Then he removed her spectacles and set them aside.

"I can't see without my spectacles. You're just a blur."

"You don't need to see me. Besides, you're fixin' to close your eyes."

"I am?"

"Mmm-huh."

One arm went around her, supporting her. One hand cupped her cheek, tilting her face. His lips touched hers, and she did close her eyes.

His mouth moved slowly, provocatively over hers, teasing and tempting her to respond. She shifted her body so she could put one arm around his back, the other up over his shoulder. Her fingers toyed with the curls along the nape of his neck. Groaning, he deepened the kiss, and somewhere Meredith thought she heard a cat purr.

He moved his hand to her rib cage, and through her bodice, she felt his thumb stroke the underside of her breast. Then he moved his hand until her breast rested in his palm and his thumb began a lazy exploration around her tautened nipple. She wanted to melt into him, to touch him in ways that he touched her, but she dared not.

His mouth left hers, trailing kisses along her throat.

"Lee?"

"I know. It's highly improper." He nibbled at her ear, and she shuddered. "But you have to admit, it's better than blackberries," he whispered just before he returned his mouth to hers.

With an abandon she never would have expected of herself, she welcomed his kiss, raking her fingers through his hair. The night felt incredibly hot and sultry, and she wondered why he'd thought she'd need a shawl to keep warm.

Abruptly he slid down, and she found herself pinned along the length of his body. His finger replaced his lips on her mouth.

"Somebody's coming," he whispered.

"I didn't think we were doing anything wrong."

"It doesn't always matter to this person. Just lay still. We're in the shadows, and he won't see us. If we're quiet, he'll just walk on by."

He shoved her spectacles into her hand, and she worked them into place, moving as little as possible. In the distance she could hear the jangling of spurs. They neared, then fell into silence as a silken voice caressed the night. "So, brother, how was the circus?"

With her hand pressed to Lee's chest, she felt more than heard his groan.

"It was fine."

"See anything interesting?"

"Saw a lot. I'm sure Atlas will read off his list in the morning. Don't you have anything better to do than lean against the gazebo?"

She heard a clink as though someone was placing one spurred boot over the other.

"Not really."

She could feel Lee's frustration through the tenseness in his body.

"Hey, you know anything about a red-haired lady working at the millinery?" the voice asked.

She felt Lee's body tense further.

"Yeah, why?"

"Clay Masterson at the newspaper office was thinking of calling on her. What's her name? Mary or Merlin?"

"Meredith."

"That's it. Any idea if she's nice?"

"Yeah, she's nice."

"Pretty?"

Meredith pressed her face against Lee's chest, wishing she could cover her ears. She didn't want to hear the truth pass through lips that had been kissing her just moments before. Silence eased in around her, embarrassment rolled out before her. Lee's warm palm cradled her cheek and tilted her face away from his chest. He brushed the pad of his thumb over her lips as his tender gaze held hers.

"I think she's pretty."

Boots and spurs echoed across the gazebo, then silence again filled the air.

"I don't think I've had the pleasure," a mirth-filled voice said.

Meredith looked at the hand that had suddenly appeared before her face. Lifting her gaze, she stared into the smiling face of a blond Adonis. She wondered why Lee had neglected to mention this strikingly handsome brother.

"I'm C.J."

"You're Cupid?" she asked.

"So, you've heard of me, have you?"

Meredith could do little more than nod and slip her hand into his. She thought the intensity of his gaze, even when ensconced in shadows, could serve him as effectively as Cupid's arrow.

"And you are?" he asked.

"Meredith," Lee barked.

C.J.'s smile increased just before he placed a kiss on the back of her hand.

"She's too old for you," Lee growled.

C.J. laughed heartily. "Miss Lavender is the only woman too old for me. How old are you, Meredith?"

"Nineteen."

"See there, brother. She's not too old. What are you doing out here anyway?"

"We were trying to watch the stars—in private," Lee said.

"You can see the stars from down there?" C.J. hunkered beside them and peered up. "So you can. I never realized that before. Think I'll just lie over here—"

"Not if you want to live to see tomorrow," Lee said in a voice ominously low.

"But it's such a clear night."

"And if you don't head out, you're gonna be squinting at it through two black eyes."

"Lee, you don't mean that?" Meredith asked, unable to believe he'd talk so harshly to his brother.

Her concern only seemed to increase C.J.'s smile. "Oh, he means it all right. The stories I could tell—"

"C.J.!"

Meredith had a feeling if Lee could have extricated himself from the compromising position they were in without falling off the bench first, C.J. would already have those black eyes. C.J., however, just grinned more broadly and winked at her.

"I'll tell them to you another time. Meanwhile, enjoy the stars." His laughter followed him out of the gazebo.

"See why I have my thinking place?" Lee asked. "There's no privacy around here. Atlas bothers us in the hayloft; C.J. bothers us out here."

He grazed his knuckles along her cheek. "I'm sorry about that. You know though, for all the teasing he did, he won't tell anyone he saw us.''

"Would you have really given him a black eye?''

"Mmm-huh,'' he murmured just before closing the gap between their mouths.

It was a careful mating of the tongues, a giving and a taking. Then he lifted his mouth from hers and pressed her cheek against his chest. "Will you remember tonight?'' he asked in a low voice.

"Always.''

For long moments he simply held her, and she listened to the hard, steady pounding of his heart.

Chapter Fifteen

As the church bell summoned the parishioners, Meredith pulled her hair back and tied the black ribbon in place.

Although she'd only taken care of Jimmy for a short time, she felt a strong maternal attachment for him. She was proud of his small accomplishments when they worked together to improve his reading skills. She enjoyed sitting with him at the table for the evening meal as he recounted his day, listening intently for any mention of Lee.

Slowly Jimmy was making friends. From her window at the millinery, she often saw him play crack the whip with the other children or share Lee's lunch beneath the shade of the oak tree. It was obvious Jimmy worshiped the man. Yesterday at the circus had proven to her that Lee was good with children.

He allowed them the freedom to run when Meredith would have tethered them. Perhaps children needed a mother and a father to balance out parental involvement.

She picked her reticule off the bed and left her room.

She would miss the feeling of family that she'd experienced yesterday with Lee at her side and Jimmy talking excitedly about all that he'd seen. She'd miss having Jimmy sit with her in church as he'd sat beside her inside the circus tent. She'd miss having Lee so close throughout the day that she could smell his bay rum mixed with the now familiar scent of horses.

She'd almost decided not to attend church this morning. It would hurt watching Jimmy sit with the Daltry family at the front of the church while she sat at the back alone. However, until the sheriff made his decision, she would no doubt experience many moments like this—when Jimmy belonged and she didn't. She couldn't let those moments dominate her life. She stepped into the morning.

"Miss Lewis!"

Her heart soared at the sound of Jimmy's voice. Standing beneath the willow tree, he wore brown pants with a matching brown jacket. A black string tie circled his throat beneath the collar of his white shirt.

Wearing almost identical clothes, Lee stood beside him. While Jimmy wore the exuberant smile of youth, Lee wore a much warmer smile, a smile that made her blush with the memory of their time in the gazebo.

Jimmy rushed forward and took her hand. "Mr. Daltry thought we should go to church together."

She met and held Lee's blue gaze. "Oh, he did?" she asked softly, surprised she had any voice at all.

"Yes, ma'am, and after church we're gonna go on a picnic. We was hoping you'd go with us."

"Were you?" she asked softly, her gaze remaining on Lee.

"Yes, ma'am," Jimmy assured her.

"I don't want to impose on all your time with Jimmy," she said.

"I get to spend time with Jimmy during the week at

school. We talked it over and agreed we'd like you to spend the day with us—if it's what you want.''

''I'd like that as long as you're sure—''

''We're sure,'' Lee said as he extended his arm toward her.

Jimmy waited. Lee waited. Meredith felt as though she'd stood at the precipice of belonging for most of her life with no one ever inviting her into the welcoming abyss. She braved a step forward and slipped her arm through Lee's. Cradling her cheek, he tilted her face toward his. ''Morning, Red,'' he whispered just before he lightly brushed his lips over hers.

She felt as though he'd just applied a red-hot brand to her heart.

After church, Meredith stared at the three horses that had been waiting patiently behind the boardinghouse.

''Why can't we use a buggy?'' she asked.

''Because we want to go someplace that a buggy can't get to,'' Lee explained for the third time.

Jimmy fought so hard to hold his smile back that his eyes almost bulged from his head. Pursing her lips, Meredith planted her hands on her hips in a practiced gesture she would have used in a classroom. ''Do you know where we're going, Jimmy?''

''Yes, ma'am.'' He almost choked on his words as his smile broke free and raced across his face.

''Would you like to share that information with me?''

He shook his head vigorously, then turned his back on her, his shoulders shaking with the force of his suppressed laughter.

''Why don't I feel as though I can trust you two?''

''Ah, Meredith, you're hurting our feelings,'' Lee said, but his eyes were filled with so much laughter she could almost hear the chuckles. He patted the horse's flank.

"Now, come on and hike up your skirts so we can get going."

"You don't honestly expect me to sit astride that beast, do you?"

"You've ridden before, Meredith. This is no different."

"Riding your horse from the schoolhouse to the boarding-house two times"—she waved two fingers in front of his face—"hardly makes me an experienced equestrian. Besides, he was following you the first time, and you were guiding him the second. I did little more than hang on for dear life."

"Were you afraid?" Lee asked, furrowing his brow.

"I was apprehensive."

"Mr. Daltry, do you understand half the words Miss Lewis says?" Jimmy asked.

Lee rubbed the back of his neck, a grin forming. "I think she's afraid to ride Hades."

Her eyes widened. "You were going to put me on a horse named Hades?"

Lee's deep laughter rumbled out to overshadow Jimmy's guffaw. "We call him Hades because he's pitch-black. Besides, he's nearly twenty years old. He was the first horse any of us rode, and he won't do anything you don't want him to do."

"Unlike his master," she said, giving him a pointed look.

Bending over, he cupped his hands. "Come on, Red. Jimmy's been looking forward to this all morning. It was the only reason he sat still during church."

She placed her foot on his palms. "This is highly improper."

He boosted her onto the saddle, then wrapped his hand around her exposed calf. She tried to slap his hand away and nearly fell from her perch. Laughing, he tugged her skirt down before whispering, "Your calves are prettier than your toes."

"They are certainly prettier than yours."

"And all this time, I thought you hadn't noticed."

His laughter echoed around her, and she wished she'd kept her mouth shut. With a wide grin, he pulled himself onto Pegasus and leaned across, placing his hand over hers. "Relax your fingers, let the reins hang down and give the horse his lead. Just pull back firmly if you need him to stop."

"How do I make him go?" she asked.

"I'll do that for you. Once we get going, he'll just follow along beside Pegasus."

"Is Jimmy's horse safe?"

Jimmy maneuvered his horse around them, pride clearly reflected in his face.

"All the horses are safe," Lee assured her. "Now, let's go have a picnic."

It was unlike any picnic with which she was familiar.

Meredith stared at the slimy-looking creatures crawling over the bottom of the bucket and over each other. Then she glared at Jimmy and Lee. "Surely, you jest."

Lee had obviously given Jimmy smiling lessons because the boy's face nearly split in two from the force of his grin. "No, ma'am. We ain't funning."

"I thought you said we were going on a picnic."

"Yes, ma'am, but you gotta catch your own food!"

She gazed into the galvanized pail. The bucket, along with fishing poles, had been waiting beneath an oak tree for them when they arrived. She thought Lee had planned to take them to his thinking place, but this area was more rugged, the vegetation wild and ungiving. She had a feeling when he referred to it as his fishing spot that he had told as many people about it as he had told about his thinking place. She wondered if there was any part of the land with which this man was not intimate, and she had a feeling the fish here wouldn't dare not take his bait.

The brown, white, and gray creatures slithered within their prison. She couldn't tell the back end from the front end, and she wasn't about to risk touching the back end of anything. It would be a cold day somewhere before her flesh touched theirs. Straightening her back, she eased her spectacles back into place. "Then I suppose I shall go hungry."

"Ah, come on, Meredith. It's not so bad," Lee assured her as he reached into the bucket and plucked out one of the worms.

She shuddered and had a strong urge to wash her own hands.

"You just take this little fella and work him onto the hook."

He threaded the hook through the wriggling worm as though he were sewing a piece of cloth. Meredith was grateful they hadn't eaten yet. She thought she would have brought up any food resting in her stomach. "Doesn't that kill him?" she asked.

"Nah, Miss Lewis, that's why worms make such good bait. They just keep wiggling around on that hook, drawing the fish to them."

"So you put them on the hook and toss them into the river to drown?" She shook her head vigorously. "No, I just don't think I could send a creature, even one as ugly as that, to such a cruel death."

"They don't drown, Meredith," Lee said.

"They don't?"

He smiled. "Heck no. They get eaten before they drown."

She shrieked and hit his arm as Jimmy fell to the ground laughing. "That's horrible! You two are horrible!"

"Good Lord, Meredith, half the food you eat was alive at one time."

"Yes, but I didn't know them before they were killed."

Lee shrugged and held up the baited hook. "Homer here doesn't mind."

"Oh, my God, they have names?"

Jimmy's laughter increased to a high squeal and his face turned purple as he held his stomach.

"Are you about to be ill, Jimmy?" Meredith asked.

He shook his head vigorously, but it didn't ease her fears that the boy would expire out here in the middle of nowhere. She'd never seen anyone laugh so hard in her entire life.

"If I toss this out into the river, will you at least hold on to the pole?" Lee asked.

Jimmy's laughter came to an abrupt halt. He took a deep breath and sat up. "But, Mr. Daltry, you said everyone had to bait their own hook."

"I know, Jimmy, but Miss Lewis is city-bred and a mite dainty for these back woods. I'm thinking maybe we ought to show her some sympathy."

She tilted her nose on the verge of explaining she was in no need of sympathy when Lee swung the baited hook before her eyes. She cleared her throat. "I'll hold on to the pole."

"Good. You might want to take off your shoes. We'll be at the river's edge."

Meredith glanced at Jimmy who had already discarded one boot and was working on the other. "That would be highly improper in front of Jimmy."

"You're practically the boy's mother. Nothing improper about it at all."

Jimmy looked up at her with an exuberant smile she couldn't resist. She sat on the ground and took off her shoes and stockings.

"You were right, Mr. Daltry. She does have cute toes."

Sputtering, Meredith stared hard at Lee. He was partially bent over with laughter. She threw her shoe at him. He sidestepped, and it landed in the river. She scrambled to her feet and rushed to the water's edge. Her shoe bobbed once and, with a gurgle, sank beneath the murky brown depths.

Lee came up behind her, wrapped his arms around her, and drew her against his chest. She could feel his silent laughter as his chest quivered. "Will you please stop laughing?"

He touched his lips to the sensitive spot behind her ear. "I didn't tell Jimmy about your toes. I just told him to say those words if we managed to get you out of your shoes." He kissed the nape of her neck. "I'm sorry, but you're so much fun to rile, Red."

She would have crossed her arms beneath her breasts if his arms weren't already there. "I'm relieved to hear that I bring you so much pleasure."

"You bring me much more pleasure than you know."

His words, the subtle tightening of his arms around her, his lips grazing behind her ear caused her knees to grow weak. If he weren't holding her, she would have slid along the muddy bank into the water and joined her shoe. At least the water would be cool. Right now, she felt as hot as a furnace. Placing her hands over his, feeling the coarse hair covering his wrists, she leaned into him.

"Mr. Daltry, you want me to try and get Miss Lewis's shoe?"

Lee glanced down at the eager face. "Nah, we'll just buy her a new pair."

"Can we get to fishing then?"

"Yep, I reckon so."

Wading out until the water was lapping at his calves, Jimmy tossed his hook into the water. Lee released his hold on Meredith and retrieved the pole he'd already baited. He tossed the hook into the water, then extended the pole toward Meredith.

"What exactly do I do with the thing?" she asked.

"I'm so glad you asked," he said, grinning. "Take the pole."

She did as he bid. Standing behind her, he nestled up against her and placed his hands over hers on the pole. "You just hold it like this."

"You could have just told me."

"But showing you is so much more fun."

She laughed, and Jimmy glanced over his shoulder.

"You have to be quiet, Miss Lewis, or you'll scare the fish away."

"You weren't too concerned about scaring the fish away when you were laughing."

"That was different. We weren't fishing yet. Now, we gotta be serious."

He turned his attention back to the river.

"How will I know if I've caught a fish?" Meredith asked Lee.

"You'll feel a little tug like this," he said as he took the lobe of her ear between his lips and tugged.

Reflexively her shoulder came up as a shiver raced down her spine. "The fish is going to tug on my ear?"

"Nah, he'll tug on your line, but first he's gonna nibble on your bait like this." He nipped at the nape of her neck. Meredith moaned. "Shh, you don't want to scare the fish away," Lee reminded her. "Otherwise, you'll never feel that tug." He nibbled just below her ear, then tugged on her lobe again.

"I felt it!" she cried.

"I'd hope so," Lee said.

"No, not you! The tug on my line." She began hopping around like a bird after worm. "Something tugged on my line." The pole dipped down. "Oh, I've got something! What do I do? What do I do?"

"Hold on," Lee said. "Pull back on your pole slowly." He waded into the water and grabbed the line, pulling it out of the water. A fish broke through to the surface, thrashing in protest.

With a wide grin, Lee held her catch in the air and stalked over to her. She wore a smile brighter than any he'd ever seen on her face. "You caught the first fish, you get the prize."

Breathless from the excitement, she gazed up at him. "The prize?"

"Yep." He wrapped his free arm around her, drew her against him, and lowered his mouth to hers. He kissed her deeply, drinking of her excitement, feeling the rapid beat of her heart against his chest. The radiant look on her face had transformed her into a goddess. He planned to spend the entire day baiting hooks for her.

"I sure as heck am glad I didn't catch the first fish," Jimmy said.

Lee lifted his mouth from hers. "Yeah, me, too."

"Is there a prize for the person who catches the second fish?"

Laughing, Lee shook his head.

"Then I'm going back to fishing," Jimmy said before trudging toward the bucket to get a new worm. His had apparently drowned, but he wasn't about to tell that to Miss Lewis and spoil her excitement.

Lee worked the barb out of the fish's mouth, walked over to a flat rock, and laid the flapping fish down. He picked up a knife.

"You're not going to kill it, are you?" Meredith asked.

Lee's hand stilled, and he glanced up at her, wishing he hadn't. The excitement had dissipated and left dread in its place. "Unless you're wanting to eat it alive."

"I don't want to eat it at all."

He sighed and sat back on his haunches. "Meredith, the whole purpose of fishing is to catch something to eat. Why don't you just go watch the water while I do what needs to be done?"

She threaded her fingers before her, her knuckles turning white. He wished she hadn't done that. Her eyes began blinking rapidly, and before she spoke, he knew they weren't going to be eating the damn fish.

"Can't we just put him back in the river?" she asked quietly.

"Meredith—"

"Please. It was a joy to catch him, but I won't enjoy eating him."

Lee looked over at Jimmy who was wearing a look of complete disgust on his face, a worm dangling between his fingers.

"I knew we shouldn't have brought a girl fishing," Jimmy said.

"Ah, well," Lee said as he unfurled his body. "If Miss Lewis wants to go hungry, that's her choice." He carried the fish back to the river and set it free. He washed his hands in the rushing waters, then stood and faced her. He was damned glad he had given in to her wishes. Her eyes held a warm softness, and they weren't looking at the damn fish, they were looking at him.

She touched her fingers to his chest, and he could feel them shaking. "Thank you," she whispered. She rose onto the tips of her toes and pressed a quick kiss to the corner of his mouth. "Thank you."

He smiled broadly. "My pleasure."

"I know Jimmy's disappointed, but maybe we could find some berries or something to satisfy our stomachs until we get back to town."

"Maybe we can at that." He took her hand. "Jimmy,

we're gonna go see what we can rustle up to replace that fish. Call us if you catch something."

"We probably won't catch nothing else now that she let that fish go back into the water to tell his friends we're out here lookin' for 'em."

As they walked away from the riverbank, Meredith asked, "Do you know which berries are poisonous and which aren't?"

"Sure do."

He stopped walking, slipped his arm around her, and pointed toward a tree branch. "There's a squirrel. I've got my rifle if you've a hankering to eat some squirrel."

She shuddered. "That would be worse than killing the fish."

"I could search out some deer."

"I was thinking more along the lines of vegetation. Something that we don't have to kill to eat."

"In that case, this bush looks promising." He led her toward a thick-leafed bush.

"I don't see any berries on it."

"That's because this kind of bush only grows berries on one side."

"How strange."

"Yep." He walked around behind the bush. She could see his shoulders rolling with his movements. "Found some blackberry."

Meredith's eyes grew wide as he held up a triangular piece of pastry. She stormed around the bush and stared disbelieving at the picnic basket and quilts stacked beside it. "You brought food?"

"I wasn't planning on spending the whole day fishing. I wanted to do my own nibbling."

"Then why did you insist I go through the torture of fishing?"

"I didn't realize it was torture. Besides, I can't imagine

going through your whole life not knowing what it feels like to catch a fish. Even if you didn't want to eat it, that one moment of enjoyment couldn't have been torture.''

"No, it wasn't torture," she admitted.

"It was fun, wasn't it? Like rolling in the hay and kissing beneath the stars?''

"I have a feeling, Hercules Daltry, that not many people fish with a man's mouth pressed up against their neck.''

"I wanted it to be a time you'd never forget.'' The smile eased off his face. "When you go back to Boston, I want you to remember what it was like fishing out here.''

She knew she'd remember, but her memories wouldn't revolve around a fish or the tug on her line. They would revolve around Lee's gentle nibbles and his tugs on her heart.

"You did it wrong again, Red.''

Meredith glared at the man whose head was resting in her lap.

"Try again," he ordered. He opened his mouth. She plucked a blackberry from the bowl and dropped it into his mouth. "Wrong again.''

"I don't see any other way to do it.''

He heaved a frustrated sigh. "Take another one and give me your hand this time.''

Taking her wrist, he brought her fingers toward his mouth. "Now, don't let go of the blackberry until I tell you.''

He opened his mouth and closed his lips around her fingers. She felt his tongue lave her fingertips, circling the fruit.

"Now," he mumbled.

She released the blackberry. His hand prevented her from pulling her fingers free. She felt his mouth move over her fingers as he ate the blackberry. She closed her eyes, understanding at last why mortals fed the gods.

"Think you got it now?" he asked.

She opened her eyes and nodded. He raised up on an elbow and picked up a blackberry.

"Open your mouth."

She swallowed before parting her lips slightly. She closed her mouth around the fruit and his fingers.

"Lick my fingers, Red."

She did as he bid, tasting the salt of his flesh. Decadent. He tasted decadent. The blackberry rolled onto her tongue and the juices filled her mouth. Removing his fingers, he slipped them into his own mouth. "Good," he said.

Smiling, he lay back down, his head in her lap. "That's blackberries à la Hercules. Now, isn't that better than just plain old blackberries?"

Her laughter floated around them.

Jimmy walked over and dropped beside them.

"Fish stop biting?" Lee asked.

"Yep."

"Saw you with my pa this morning before we left for church."

"Yep. He was teaching me to whittle. Miss Lewis, you ought to see all the stuff Mr. Daltry's pa has made. They got beds stacked on top of each other and beds in the walls, and everything's got all this fancy carving on it."

Lee sat up. "Bring me my saddlebag."

Jimmy scampered off and came back carrying the leather bag. Lee folded the flap back and reached inside. He took out a leather case. Carefully he opened it and withdrew a knife. "My pa gave me this knife when I was twelve years old."

Jimmy's eyes widened as Lee turned the knife in his hand. The sun reflected off the steel blade. Within the ivory handle, inlaid bits of turquoise formed the letter D.

"You're only supposed to use it for whittling," Lee

explained as he slipped it back into its case. He extended it toward Jimmy. "It's yours."

Jimmy's mouth fell open in disbelief. He shook his head. "I can't take it."

"Why not?"

"Your pa gave it to you. My pa never gave me nothing like that. You ought to hang on to it so you can give it to your son."

"Right now, you're my son."

"But what if the sheriff decides different? What if he gives me to Miss Lewis?"

Lee took Jimmy's hand and wrapped his fingers around the leather. "Then you'll have something to remind you of the time when you were mine."

Meredith removed her spectacles and wiped the lenses with her skirt. They made her eyes look enormous, her tears even larger, and she didn't want either one of them to see her tears. Her resolve to keep Jimmy at all costs was slowly slipping away.

Chapter
Sixteen

Softly Lee tapped on the door Mrs. Bennett had told him led into Jimmy's room. That morning, Meredith had sent a note to let him know Jimmy wasn't feeling well and wouldn't be at school.

And she'd told him not to worry.

Seeing the anxiety etched so clearly in her face as she opened the door and peered into the hallway, he wished he'd ignored the last part of the note and come over right away like he'd wanted instead of waiting until school was over.

"How's Jimmy doing?" he asked, concern for her as well as for Jimmy woven through his voice as she ushered him into the room.

"He slept most of the day. I can't get his body to cool down. He says it hurts to swallow so he won't eat."

"When did all this start?"

"I'm not sure. He ate very little supper last night and went to bed immediately afterward. When I came to check on him later, he was feverish. He didn't tell me he was feeling badly because he didn't want to be any trouble. I spent most of the night sponging him down, but it doesn't seem to help.''

He cradled her cheek with his large palm. ''When did you last eat?''

She stared at him, her eyes blinking rapidly. He sighed deeply. ''Meredith, you've got to take care of yourself, too. You won't do Jimmy any good if you get sick.''

Her spectacles enlarged the tears welling in her eyes. He wrapped his arms around her and drew her against his chest. She released a pitiful little sob. ''I just don't want Jimmy to die.''

He pressed his lips to the top of her head. ''He's not gonna die.''

She sniffed. ''How do you know?''

''Because he's got you caring for him.''

She pounded her fist into his back. ''Oh, Lee, that's hardly a guarantee.''

With his thumbs stroking her cheeks, he tilted her head and gazed deeply into her eyes. ''You'd be surprised what love can do, Meredith, and now, you've got someone to help you take care of him as soon as I've taken care of you.''

Meredith knew the kiss was coming, and she was powerless to stop it or protest that it was completely inappropriate in a sick room. But when his mouth touched hers, it held no passion, only comfort. Instead of making her feel weak with desire, it renewed her strength and gave her the hope to carry on.

When he lifted his mouth from hers, she almost believed she saw love reflected in the depths of his blue eyes. She wished she hadn't drawn the curtains on the windows to shield Jimmy's fevered eyes from the harsh sunlight, wished more than a low flame in the solitary lamp on the bedside table illuminated the room.

"Now, then, I'll get Mrs. Bennett—"

"No, I don't want to impose on Mrs. Bennett. We're her boarders, not her family."

"All right, then I'll run to the Buc and get you something to eat and have them rustle up some broth for Jimmy. Whether he wants to eat or not, he needs to eat. Then we'll see about getting his fever down."

"Do you think we need to find a doctor?"

He gave her a reassuring smile. "There's a buggy doctor that covers this county. Finding him won't be easy, but I will if we decide Jimmy needs a doctor. Let's give him another day and see how he does. Atlas complained of his throat hurting and had a fever last spring. It only lasted a couple of days, then he was right as rain."

Meredith breathed a sigh of relief. "Oh, I hope that's all this is."

"I'm sure it is. Soon as I get you fed, I'll ride home and ask Ma what she used to ease his discomfort and bring his fever down."

Sometime later Meredith watched as Lee spooned a syrup-like concoction into Jimmy's mouth. Grimacing, Jimmy swallowed.

"Gawd, Mr. Daltry," he croaked, "now I know why your sister does all the cookin'."

"This isn't food, Jimmy. It's something to ease the ache in your throat so you can eat some of that broth I brought you earlier."

"What's in it?" Meredith asked.

"Honey and garlic," Lee said.

She stuck out her tongue and shuddered. "Sounds lovely. Remind me never to complain of my throat hurting."

"Is she joshing, Mr. Daltry?"

Lee smiled. "Yeah, Jimmy, I think she's finally getting a sense of humor."

"Least she's using little words. I can't hardly think with this pounding in my head."

"Let's get some broth into you, and I'll see about making something to help that headache and your fever."

"I'm really not hungry."

"Having a fever is like being in the desert. You go too long without putting something wet in your belly, and you'll dry up until you're nothin' but bones."

"You have the most interesting bedside manner," Meredith said.

Lee winked at her. "Yeah, but it works. Why don't you try spooning some of that broth into him? I'm gonna scrape some bark off that willow tree out there and make something to help with the fever."

As he left the room, Meredith sat on the bed, the bowl of broth in her lap. "Open your mouth," she urged as she held the spoon over the bowl.

Jimmy grimaced and shook his head. She tapped the spoon on the edge of the bowl. "Eat this or you'll turn into a desert."

He gave her a weak smile and opened his mouth. She brought the spoon to his lips, and he slurped the contents.

"Is Mr. Daltry gonna stay with us tonight?" he asked.

"I think so," she said as she spooned more broth into his mouth.

"I'm glad."

His eyes drifted closed. Meredith set the bowl aside and brought the covers up over his shoulders. She was glad, too.

Lee returned some time later and made Jimmy drink another concoction he'd brewed. As Jimmy fell asleep, Meredith took his limp hand and stroked the calluses on his palm. "Being a parent hurts sometimes, doesn't it?" she asked.

Sitting on the other side of the bed, Lee had begun to wipe a damp cloth across Jimmy's skinny chest. "Yeah, I reckon it does."

"I want to do what's best for him, but I don't want to hurt him doing it," she said.

"I don't think anyone wants to hurt their child, Meredith, and you've come to think of Jimmy as your son."

She scooted forward in the chair. "Actually, I was thinking of my mother."

"I didn't think you knew who she was."

"I don't, but all these years I thought she left me at the orphanage because she didn't want me. I looked at her abandonment through the eyes of a child and always imagined that she hated me. Since Jimmy's been in my life, I'm beginning to view things differently, through the eyes of a mother, and I'm wondering if maybe she did love me after all."

"Because she wanted to do what was best for you," Lee said, his voice low.

She nodded. "The night we discovered Jimmy had been abandoned, I wanted him because I understood what he was feeling, and I was being selfish. I saw him as someone who needed love, and I had love to give, but now that I've come to love him, if I truly thought someone else could take better care of Jimmy than I could, I wouldn't hesitate to let him go, even though it would nearly break my heart."

Lee dropped the cloth into the warm water. "Are you asking me to give up my claim to Jimmy?"

"No, I think you love him as much. I was just trying to explain that I think my mother loved me, and whatever her reason for leaving me, I understand now that it would have been hard for her to do." She lifted her spectacles and wiped her eyes. "She's not here so I can't tell her I understand." She sniffed. "So I wanted to tell you."

The bed squeaked as he stood and walked around to kneel before her. "I would imagine your mother loved you a great deal." Taking her hands, he rubbed his thumbs in circles over her knuckles. "With your orange hair and freckles, and your spectacles that make your eyes look so big and round."

She offered him a small, tremulous smile. "I wasn't born wearing spectacles, and I probably didn't have freckles."

He pressed his lips to her fingers. "But she would have loved you anyway. I don't see how any woman cannot love a child she carried around inside her. She would have felt the first time you moved, heard your first cry. Maybe she thought you'd cry less if you were pressed to someone else's bosom instead of hers."

"And she had no way of knowing no one would ever want me."

He wanted her, wanted her with a desperation that was frightening at times, but he didn't think she'd be content with him—not for the long haul. "I can't speak for all of Boston, Meredith, and I don't know why no one adopted you, but out here, I think a man can sense your worth."

"Mr. Daltry?"

He turned his attention to Jimmy. "What, son?"

"Would you read to me?"

He unfolded his body, his hands slowly sliding away from hers. "Why don't we let Miss Lewis read to you? She sponged you down last night. Tonight, it's my turn."

"Will you read to me, Miss Lewis?"

"Certainly." She pulled a book from the stack she'd brought in the night before to keep her company while she held vigil at Jimmy's side. She moved the lamp on the bedside table closer so its yellow glow illuminated the book.

Jimmy's eyes drifted closed, then sprang back open.

Affectionately Lee watched her as he gently wiped the wet cloth over Jimmy's narrow shoulders. She wondered why she'd ever thought it was enough to have books by her side while tending Jimmy. Soon, they'd make a decision about Jimmy's adoption, and all she'd have of Lee would be the memories of the time they'd shared. Tonight, she relished the comfort his presence provided.

She gave them both a small smile before turning her attention to the book. "I think you'll enjoy *Moby Dick*."

With reverence, Lee listened to the flawless flow of Meredith's soft voice as she read the words. She could probably write words as easily as she read them. She was a teacher. He wondered why she kept his company as often as she did.

After he rinsed the cloth, he wiped the beads of sweat from Jimmy's neck. The boy was the reason she went places with him. It was a good theory, but it didn't hold a lot of water because she'd gone places with him before they had Jimmy. She wanted a family.

He needed to hightail it to his thinking place and think these thoughts through, but he didn't know if the trip would do him any good. He'd gone earlier in the week, after their fishing trip, and all he'd been able to think about was Meredith's smiles and laughter. He hadn't been able to keep a serious thought in his head all evening.

It was long past midnight when he heard a slight pause in the reading and turned his attention to Meredith. She bobbed her head, blinked her eyes, and began reading again, her voice distant. Jimmy had fallen asleep. It was time Meredith did as well.

He dropped the cloth into the bowl, got up from the bed, and walked over to her. Gently he took the book from her hands.

With slumberous eyes, she looked at him. "But I haven't finished reading the story."

"You can finish reading it tomorrow."

"But Jimmy—"

"He's asleep now." Before she could protest further, he slipped one arm beneath her knees, the other behind her back and lifted her.

She wrapped her arms around his neck and lay her head against his shoulder. He could have sworn it was where she belonged, next to his heart. He carried her from the room and down the hall.

The door to her room stood ajar. Lee nudged it open with his foot and walked into the room, laying Meredith down on the bed. He walked to the dresser to retrieve a button hook. Two ribbons, folded neatly, decorated the dresser. He thought of all the colorful ribbons and delicate bottles of perfume on Venus's dresser, the flowers his mother arranged in the rooms of the house, the lace scarves his grandmother covered dressers and tables with, the little things that made a house a home. Meredith had none of that. This room had nothing in it to make a person want to do anything but sleep in here. It wasn't a place to live or laugh or share a life. It was simply a place to exist.

He closed the door slightly to give them some privacy without impropriety, walked back to the bed, and sat on the edge. He placed her foot on his thigh.

"What are you doing?" she asked in a thick voice as though drawn from a dream.

"Taking off your shoes." He dropped the shoe to the floor and ran the pad of his thumb over the ball of her foot. "I can't believe you wore shoes the whole time you were taking care of Jimmy. No one would have noticed if you were a little comfortable."

"It would have been highly improper."

"Meredith, out here children run around barefoot all the time."

"But I'm not a child."

He went to work on the second shoe. No, she wasn't a child. With the moonlight spilling across her features, she resembled a goddess and her reading had been a siren's song. He placed her other shoe on the floor, then knelt beside the head of the bed. He removed the ribbon from her hair and used his fingers to comb out the fiery tresses, fanning them over the pillow. Then he removed her spectacles.

"I can't see without my spectacles."

"You're fixin' to close your eyes."

"Are you going to kiss me?"

"Nope, you're gonna sleep." He set her spectacles on the bedside table that was bare of lace scarves or flowers.

She sighed dreamily. "I'd rather have a kiss."

"Would you?"

Her lips formed a sleepy smile. "They're better than sleeping."

"One kiss," he whispered as he settled his mouth over hers. She rolled slightly, and he felt her breast make contact with his chest. Dear Lord, but she was sweet.

He kissed her tenderly, slowly, knowing the kiss would take them nowhere, wishing like hell that it could. How could anyone not have seen the potential she carried for love? How could anyone have not taken her from the orphanage and given her a home and a family? How could he continue to keep Jimmy from truly being her son when the only thing she wanted was a family? Yet, she deserved more than a partial family. He wanted her to have a whole family, to know all the love a family could share.

Lifting his mouth from hers, he gazed upon her contented features. She smiled softly.

"You have as many kisses as you do smiles." She touched her fingers to his lips. "But I think that was my favorite."

"I'm glad you liked it, but you need to get some sleep.

I don't want you getting sick.''

"But Jimmy—''

He grazed his finger over the dusting of freckles. "I'll stay with Jimmy. You need anything before I go?''

Her fingers fumbled with the buttons on her bodice. "It's hot in here.''

Guiltily he glanced toward the door and wondered how soundly Mrs. Bennett slept. Meredith's fingers were too tired to do the task, but he was afraid his weren't tired enough to stop when they ought to. He brushed her fingers away and slowly undid the buttons. Her creamy white skin came into view, and he took a deep breath to steady his fingers.

He eased her bodice aside until he could see the lace of her chemise kissing the curves of her breasts. Sweet Lord, she was small and delicate. His mother didn't have a flower in her garden that could match Meredith's delicate features.

He trailed his finger along the rolling hills of her flesh and touched the luscious valley between. "Meredith, where do I kiss you in your dream?''

He shifted his gaze to her face. She was too tired to blink, but she was watching him through half-lowered lashes.

It was wrong, he knew it was wrong, but he seemed powerless to control his actions. After freeing the buttons of her chemise, he slipped his finger beneath the lace and eased it down. "Do I kiss you here?'' he rasped as he lowered his mouth to her bared breast.

Gasping, she threaded her fingers through his hair. His intentions had been honorable, to leave a chaste kiss, but her pale pink nipple hardened and tempted him as nothing had in his life. His tongue tasted and laved the small pebble while his hand gently kneaded her soft flesh. She arched her back, and he suckled the innocent offering.

"Such sweet dreams,'' she murmured.

With regret, he eased her chemise into place. Reaching

across the bed, he grabbed one side of the quilt she lay on and brought it over her.

"I've got to go, Meredith. Otherwise, I'm gonna crawl into bed with you and do something so damn improper it's gonna make your toes curl."

She slipped her hands down to his cheeks. "Stay."

"Lord, woman, you don't know what you do to a man. I can't stay."

Her hands fell away, her eyes drifted closed, and he heard the tiniest little snore. She'd been so close to slumber, she probably wasn't even aware of all he'd done. He didn't know if that was a blessing or a curse. He tucked the quilt around her. Smiling, he kissed her cheek. "Sweet dreams, Red."

Meredith awoke with the memory of dreams so vivid she thought she could feel whisker burns on her breasts. She pressed her palm to her chest, but didn't dare look. She was only half dressed and instead of being beneath the covers, she'd brought the top quilt over to form a cocoon.

She eased out of bed and worked diligently to make herself presentable before she walked down the hall to Jimmy's room.

The curtains were drawn back from the raised windows, allowing the early morning sunlight and a cool breeze to play within the room. Jimmy was sleeping peacefully. Quietly, she walked across the room and pressed her palm to his forehead. He felt cool. He opened his eyes and smiled at her before rolling over and going back to sleep.

It was only then that she dared look at Lee. He was sprawled in a chair much too small for his large frame. One leg was stretched straight out, the other bent at the knee. His arms were hanging over the sides of the chair, his hands nearly grazing the floor. His hair was disheveled. He was in need of a shave. Slowly he opened his eyes, and his gaze locked with hers. Then he smiled, and she thought he'd never looked more handsome.

"Jimmy's fever broke around dawn," he said as he sat straighter in the chair. Yawning, he lifted his arms over his head and stretched. He grinned. "How'd you sleep?"

She clasped her hands before her. "Fine."

"Did you have sweet dreams?"

She lowered her gaze. "Lee, I don't remember going to bed."

"I'm not surprised. You wore yourself out caring for Jimmy. You fell asleep in this chair, and I carried you to your bed."

She walked around the bed and came to stand beside him, still averting her gaze. "I was partly disrobed when I awoke," she whispered.

He stood. "I tried to make you comfortable."

"I appreciate that, but I feel it may have been improper."

He wrapped his arms around her. When she would have bolted, he drew her nearer. "Nothing improper happened last night," he said in a low voice.

She chastised herself for feeling disappointed. Hercules Daltry had his pick of the women of Paradise Plains. She was a fool to even contemplate that he'd settle for the ugly duckling when he could easily capture a swan.

"When I make love to a woman, I like for her to be awake." He skimmed his lips along her neck. "But I was damn tempted, Meredith."

His eyes held no teasing glint, but were warm, sincere, and filled with a longing she'd never expected to see directed her way.

"The next time I carry you to bed, I won't leave you there alone."

Chapter
Seventeen

Quietly Meredith opened the schoolhouse door. She didn't want to disturb Lee or the children during one of the few times that he had them inside where children were supposed to learn. She tiptoed across the entryway, peered into the room, and almost shrieked.

The desk was supposed to be in the center of the dais. Lee had shoved it to the side. He was leaning back in his chair so its front legs were in the air and the back of the chair rested against the windowsill. He'd propped his feet on the desk and crossed his arms over his chest. The sun filtered in through the window and caressed his shoulders. He was angled away from his class so any child who wanted could have been sleeping or daydreaming. Oddly, none were. He watched a tiny girl write a sentence on the blackboard.

Judging from her height, she couldn't have been any older than six. Her letters were squiggly, her spelling atrocious as she wrote, "It wil brak if it falz."

When she finished making a period almost as tall as the letters, she peered at Lee. He smiled. "Very good, Becky."

Very good? If Meredith had entertained doubts before as to his qualifications to teach, he'd just proven himself to her. The man couldn't even spell. How could he teach children?

She didn't want to destroy the fragile bond that had developed between them, knew he would lose all credibility if she took him to task in front of his students, so she balled her fists and stayed rooted to the spot.

He motioned Becky over and drew her onto his lap. Turning slightly, he addressed the class. "Can everyone read that sentence?"

Heads bobbed up and down.

"Would anyone write any of those words different?"

Hands shot into the air.

"All right, Becky, call on someone."

"Atlas."

"Atlas, come up here and write the words you'd use underneath Becky's."

Paper in hand, Atlas walked to the blackboard and wrote "will" beneath "wil," "break" beneath "brak," and "falls" beneath "falz." Then he returned to his desk.

"Can everyone read Atlas's words?" Lee asked. A few heads nodded. "What we have here are words that like to trick people," Lee said as he eased Becky onto the desk, dropped the front legs of the chair to the floor, and stood.

Meredith was astonished to hear him explain that "L" was a lonely letter and liked company so it often traveled in pairs and "S" was jealous of "Z" so sometimes it sounded like "Z" which was why "Z" wasn't used in many words. "S" was always stealing its place.

Then he wrote "E-A-T" on the blackboard.

"Does anyone know what this word is? Allie?"

"Eat."

Lee rubbed his jaw as though thinking a tough problem through. "Now if this word is 'eet,' why isn't this word 'breek'? Anybody know?" He shook his head. "Me, neither. But Allie is right and so is Atlas. That's why readin' and writin' is so dadgum hard to learn." He circled the "E" and "A" in both words. "These two letters together are just like women. They don't know their own minds."

Meredith gasped, and Lee's laughing gaze shot to the back of the classroom. "Why, Miss Lewis, you should have made yourself known."

She tapped the watch above her breast. "It's after four, sir. Class should be dismissed promptly at four."

"Then I guess you're here for Jimmy and not for me." The children giggled, and Meredith felt her face turn red. "All right, you young'uns, head home. Monday, we'll see if we can find some other words that like to trick us."

The children scrambled out of their desks and rushed past Meredith. Jimmy stopped at her side. "Can I go with Atlas to see if the dentist is pulling any teeth this afternoon? Please?"

She grimaced. "I suppose, but be back to the boarding-house in time for supper."

"Yes, ma'am." He rushed to catch up with Atlas.

Walking through the classroom, Meredith studied Lee's grinning face. "You knew I was there all along, didn't you?"

"Only toward the end."

"I assure you, Mr. Daltry, I know my own mind."

"I'm sure you do, Red." The grin eased off his face. "All right, go ahead and tell me what I did wrong."

"Why would you think you did something wrong?"

"I don't think I did something wrong. You think I did something wrong. I know because you're wearing that 'he doesn't know how to teach' look."

She tilted her chin. "Very well, then." She stomped to

the blackboard, picked up a piece of chalk, and circled Becky's sentence. "She prints her letters."

"I'm impressed, Meredith. A lot of people would have missed that."

She tapped the chalk against the board. "You are not supposed to teach children to print. You are supposed to teach them cursive writing using *The Spencerian Key to Practical Penmanship*. The emphasis, Mr. Daltry, should be on developing a beautiful, flowing penmanship."

"Meredith, I can write the most beautiful letters you'll ever see, but I can't—" Stopping, he placed his hand on an open book resting on his desk, his fingers touching the words. "I can't see how writing fancy letters helps teach a child to read."

"Reading and writing are two separate aspects of teaching."

"But they shouldn't be." He snatched the chalk from her fingers and wrote an elaborate G on the blackboard, with all the flourishes and filigrees required of the Spencerian method. Then he shoved an open book into her hands.

"Now, you show me where I'm gonna find a letter that looks like that"—he pointed toward the blackboard—"in that book."

She started to blink her eyes.

"Meredith, children come here on the first day of school, and their minds are like this blackboard with nothing on it. They don't know how to make letters, they don't know how to read. It just seemed to me that if I first taught them the letters they'd be reading, it'd be easier for them. If I teach them how to print the word and then ask them to read a sentence in a book that has the word in it, they'll know the word when they see it. But if I first teach them to write the word with a bunch of curls and fancy lines, how will they recognize it when they see it in the book?"

Her eyes began to blink faster. "But, Lee, it's the standard method to teach children to write cursive, not to print."

"That doesn't mean it's right."

"But it's always been done this way. Printing is simply not allowed in the classroom."

He tunneled his fingers through his hair. "I'm right on this, Meredith. I know I am. It's like the cattle—"

"There you go again applying everything to ranching. You can't do that."

He placed his hands on her shoulders. "Hear me out on this, Meredith. For years we've been driving cattle north in herds. It's the way my father did it. It's the way my grandfather did it. Now, railroads are coming through. Instead of trailing cattle for three months, we can drive them for a week, put them on a cattle car, and ship them north. Should we not put our cattle on a train simply because no one has done it before us?"

"The railroads, the trains, are new. They're an advancement—"

"So is my way of teaching. That doesn't make it wrong. Meredith, why teach a child how to write a letter he'll never use, a letter he'll never read unless someone else writes him a letter? It makes no sense."

He dropped his hands from her shoulders. "You're a teacher. You have a teaching certificate. Explain to me, make me understand why I should teach a child how to write one kind of letter and how to read another, and don't tell me because it's the way it's done. Tell me why."

Silence hovered around them. She licked her lips. "They need to know how to write cursive letters."

"I'll teach them how to make the fancy letters once they've mastered the letters in the books I'm asking them to read. Meredith, look at this sentence. Becky wrote this sentence without any help."

She opened her mouth, and he held up a hand. "I know some of the words are misspelled, but she knows her letters, and she can read, Meredith. Most of my first-year students can. I've only had them for two months, but they can read simple words and sentences, and they can write."

"But, Lee—"

"Meredith, I may be wrong about roping the wooden cattle and sitting outside in the breeze to read from a primer, but I'm right about this. I know I am, and I think you know it."

She laid the book on the desk. "You do plan to teach them cursive writing?"

"Yes, ma'am."

"So, in effect you're teaching them how to print letters that eventually they'll never use."

He smiled. "They'll use them when they read, but not when they write—eventually."

Nodding, she ran her finger along the edge of his desk. "Your method may have some merit, but I'll have to give it more thought. It goes against everything I was taught."

"But you don't think it's a dumb way to teach?"

"No, actually, it does seem to make a great deal of sense."

He grinned broadly. "My practical approach to teaching?"

She sighed, finding it difficult not to return his smile. "Your practical approach. Actually, Lee, I didn't come here to upbraid you on your teaching methods. I wanted to know if you'd like to have dinner with us tonight. Mrs. Bennett has left to visit her son for the evening. It would just be you, Jimmy, and me."

"Can you cook?" he asked.

"Certainly."

*   *   *

"She cain't cook," Jimmy whispered to Lee.

He rubbed his jaw. "Maybe it'll taste better than it smells."

"I don't think I'll be able to stand having it close enough to my nose to find out. Miz Bennett always does the cooking. I need to thank her proper when she gets back."

Meredith lifted the lid on the pot and slumped her shoulders. "I just don't understand. Persy gave me the recipe for your favorite meal, but this hardly looks edible."

"It stinks, too," Jimmy said.

Lee scowled at him and scraped his chair across the floor. He walked behind her and gazed into the pot. Dear Lord, he loved her but not that much, not enough to eat that. "Did Persy tell you the secret?"

"The secret?" she asked, hope filling her eyes.

"Yep. You put the lid back on and go for a long walk, leaving it to cook for a while. When you come back, it'll be ready."

"You're teasing me."

"No, I'm surprised she didn't tell you. Why don't you run and grab a shawl, and we'll go for a walk. Jimmy can stay here and watch it, make sure nothing happens to it. When we get back, it should be done."

"Are you sure?"

He shrugged. "That's the way Persy does it. She and I go for walks all the time while her stew is cooking."

"Well, all right." She untied her apron and set it over the chair. "I'll be right back."

As soon as she left the room, Lee grabbed Jimmy's arm. "All right, I'm gonna take her for a long, long walk. As soon as we leave, you run next door to the Buc and tell Rosy we got something worse than a muddy creek over here. Show her what Meredith is cooking. Tell her we need something that looks like it, but don't taste like it, and I'll settle up with her later. Soon as her food is here, move the lamp from the table to the window. Understand?''

Jimmy nodded just as Meredith walked back in. ''Jimmy, we won't be long, but you can go ahead and start studying your lessons while we're gone.''

''Yes, ma'am.''

Lee placed his hand on the small of Meredith's back and winked at Jimmy over his shoulder. He opened the door and escorted Meredith into the dimming twilight. He prayed she wouldn't see Jimmy hightailing it to the Buc in the early evening haze.

''Why don't we walk toward the school?'' Lee suggested as he wrapped his hand around Meredith's.

She peered up at him. ''Actually, I'm glad you asked me to take a walk.''

He stopped and put his arms around her, drawing her against his body. ''Yeah, me, too.''

He dipped his head down, and she pressed her palms against his chest. ''We need to talk about Jimmy.''

''Later.''

''Now.''

''Let me give you a little kiss first.''

She shook her head. ''If we start to kiss, we're going to forget that we need to discuss Jimmy.''

''That should tell you something right there,'' he said as he lowered his head again.

She pulled back, crossing her arms beneath her breasts. ''We have to consider our priorities, put our own wants aside, and put Jimmy first.''

He tunneled his fingers through his hair. ''Meaning?''

''We both said we want to be Jimmy's parent, but we're not treating Jimmy like he's our son because we don't know whose son he'll eventually become. He needs stability, he needs to know where he belongs.''

''He's where he belongs right now.''

Meredith felt her heart flutter. ''You mean with me?''

"No, I mean with us."

She sighed. "How can I explain this? You have a family. You know who your mother and father are. They're always there for you. We're not always there for Jimmy. Sometimes you're there, sometimes I'm there. I know what it feels like not to have someone who's always there. We just need to decide who should adopt Jimmy so he feels wanted."

"I think Jimmy feels wanted. Tonight feels like a family."

"I know, Lee. That's what made me realize how unfair we've been to Jimmy. We feel like a family, but we're not. He still calls you Mr. Daltry and me Miss Lewis. When we finish eating, you'll ride home, and Jimmy and I will climb the stairs to our borrowed rooms."

"Hell, Meredith. This is the kind of stuff I have to go to my thinking place and think about. I can't make a decision like this while I'm taking a walk."

"But you'll think about it? And we'll make a decision soon?"

"Yeah, we'll make a decision soon." Actually, he'd already made his decision. Sunday, he planned to take her to their thinking place. It seemed the appropriate place to ask her to marry him. He wanted to do it when her toes were bared, and he could watch them curl when he kissed her. He wanted to be in the sunshine so he could see her cheeks turn red. He imagined her eyes would blink faster than a hummingbird's wings, and he didn't want his heart's longings whispered in the dark where he couldn't appreciate her reaction. "Now, let me show you what I wanted to show you at the schoolhouse."

He took her hand, and they walked toward the building at the edge of town. They strolled to the back of the schoolhouse and stopped.

"What did you want to show me?" she asked as she

peered through the darkening twilight, looking for something out of the ordinary.

"What it feels like to be kissed behind the schoolhouse," he said as his arms went around her.

"Lee Dalt—"

His mouth swooped down to capture hers with no prelude to tenderness, just an insatiable hunger. He groaned deep within his throat and splayed his fingers across her back, pressing her hips against his.

Meredith felt her soft curves flatten against his chest. She wrapped her arms around his neck, relishing the urgency of his kiss as though she alone could satisfy his appetite. Her shawl slipped off her shoulders, and she was grateful the cool evening air was closer to her skin for she felt as though the summer sun had invaded her body. Briefly she wondered if she was coming down with Jimmy's fever, but she felt too blissfully alive to be ill.

His mouth traveled along her throat. Moaning, she tilted her head back to give him easier access to her throat. "We need to get back." Her voice sounded as though it came from far away.

"Yeah, I guess Jimmy will be waiting," he said as he rained kisses over her face, then dipped down to tease the sensitive spot below her ear.

"And supper."

"Hope so."

"What?"

He lifted his face. "Nothing."

They strolled leisurely back to the boardinghouse and walked into the kitchen. Jimmy looked up from his books, a grin spreading across his face.

Meredith walked to the stove and lifted the lid on the pot. "I don't believe it."

Lee looked over her shoulder. "Looks good enough to eat. Smells good, too."

"I wonder why Persy didn't tell me the secret," she said as she spooned the stew into bowls.

"I'll be sure and get after her about it." Lee took the bowl from her and set it on the table. Jimmy closed his books and hopped up to get his bowl. Then Meredith joined them at the table.

After the meal, Jimmy sat at one end of the table with Meredith and Lee on either side of him. He studied the word until he was nearly cross-eyed. "I don't know."

"You should know," Meredith said. "It's the same word you read on the other page."

"It's too dadgum long. I can't remember what the beginning sounds like by the time I get to the end."

"Because you're not trying."

"I am too trying."

"If you were trying," Meredith said slowly, enunciating each word carefully, "you'd be able to read. Reading is simply a matter of knowing the sounds of the letters, how those letters form words to make sentences that create thoughts."

"It doesn't sound so simple to me," Lee said.

Meredith snapped her gaze to Lee's. "This isn't your classroom. I don't want to hear about lonely letters and words that do magic tricks. There is no magic to reading. It's simply a matter of learning the rules and applying them."

Leaning back, Lee crossed his arms over his chest. "You're right."

"Of course I am. Now, Jimmy, try again."

Jimmy returned to the beginning of the sentence where the words were smaller, words he could sound out. He hoped the larger word would just come to him by the time he got to it, but it didn't. He struggled with the letters, sounding the vowels, wishing he didn't feel so dumb. He bowed his head. "I can't do it. I'm too dumb."

"Want me to show you how easy it is to read, Jimmy?"
Lee asked.

"I reckon," he said with defeat clearly evident in his
voice, surrender mirrored in his eyes.

Lee sorted through Meredith's stack of books, carefully
setting each book aside until he found the one he wanted.
He showed it to Jimmy. "*Great Expectations*. I started
reading it a couple of months ago. I almost finished last
night."

As he opened the book to the final pages, Meredith
leaned over the table.

"You're on the last page?" she asked.

"No, the page before."

"And you didn't finish reading it?"

"It was late, and I was tired."

"But it would have only taken you a couple of minutes
to finish it. How could you put the book aside when you
were so near the end?"

"Like I said. It was late, and I was tired."

Hunching over the book, he placed his large finger beneath the tiny word and studied the words stretching out
before him like an endless plain. " 'The fres . . . freshness
of her bee . . . uty . . . was . . . indeed gone, but its in . . .
dee . . . scrib . . . indescribable . . . maj . . . majesty and its
inde . . . indescribable charm . . . remained.' "

With reverence, he closed the book and slowly lifted his
gaze to Meredith's face. He didn't think she could have
looked more shocked if he'd just sprouted horns and a
pointed tail—or more disappointed. He looked over at
Jimmy.

"Sometimes in a herd of horses, there's one that can't
gallop as fast, but that doesn't mean he can't run. It just
means he has to work harder to get where they're going.
He'll get there last, but the important thing is that he got
there. You can learn to read, Jimmy. Your reading might

not sound as pretty as Miss Lewis's, but in my classroom, you'll be the only one that knows. Do you understand?''

Jimmy nodded. ''That's why you never read in class— 'cuz you're no good at it.''

''That's right, and that's why I never call on anyone who doesn't raise their hand. Now, I want to talk to you about something else.''

He shifted in his chair, digging his elbows into his thighs, focusing his attention solely on Jimmy. ''Someday, I hope to have a son like you. For whatever reasons your father left, not one of them had anything to do with you. I know that because you're the kind of son that a father would be proud of. I wish I could be your father, but the truth is, Jimmy, I don't think I'd make a very good father for you. Miss Lewis and I were talking earlier when we were out walking, and we agreed that she would make the better parent. So in the morning, she's gonna go see Sheriff Sampson and sign those papers that'll make you her son.''

''Why can't you both adopt me?''

''We'd have to get married and that just wouldn't work . . . not now.'' He stood and put his hand on Jimmy's shoulder. ''So, I'll see you Monday morning, and we'll have a picnic at school to celebrate your new name.''

He forced himself to look at Meredith. Her soft lips were parted slightly, her brow deeply furrowed, her eyes still blinking. ''I enjoyed the meal, Meredith. Thank you for inviting me.'' He walked across the kitchen, plucked his hat off the peg on the wall, and jammed it low over his brow before pushing open the door and stepping into the night.

Meredith heard his whistle, shoved herself away from the table, and rushed through the door. Reaching him before Pegasus did, she touched his arm, and he looked down on her.

''That's the kindest thing I've ever seen. Pretending—''

"I wasn't pretending, Meredith. I'm the slow horse. Always have been. The teacher didn't burn my hand because I was bored. She burned it because I couldn't read. When you're trying as hard as you can and nobody appreciates it, you stop trying. Jimmy's still trying. He was left alone for over a month and kept coming to school when no one made him. Why do you think he did that if he didn't want to learn? Not everything is easy for everyone, but the boy's trying. If I ever see him with that defeated look on his face again, I'll come back for him, and the hounds of hell won't stop me from taking him."

He mounted his horse, and she watched him ride away until he was no more than a shadow that eventually melted into the blackness of night.

The tear trailed slowly down Meredith's cheek until it touched the pillow like so many others before it. How could a grown man struggle over reading words that a child could have mastered?

The confident smiles, the legendary charm of Hercules Daltry, had disappeared at that kitchen table. He'd shown her and Jimmy the man he truly was, and she'd seen within his eyes how difficult that had been. To reveal his weakness when all around him considered him strong; to reveal his vulnerability when all thought he was invincible.

Even she had begun to see him as something apart from mortal man.

She heard the tap against her window, followed shortly by another. Sitting up in bed, she wiped the tears from her eyes and reached for her spectacles on the bedside table. Throwing the covers back, she tiptoed to the window.

Lee stood in the yard, tossing small pebbles against her window. She opened the window slightly. "What are you doing?"

"Need to talk to you."

"Wait there."

She closed the window and retrieved her wrapper off the bed, pulling it on as she padded down the stairs. Quietly she opened the front door and went outside.

He swept his hat from his head, and she was reminded of the first night they'd spoken at the schoolhouse. He'd been somber then as well.

"How's Jimmy?" he asked.

"He's fine."

"Do you think he understood all I was trying to say this evening?"

"I believe so."

"I don't want him thinking I didn't want him."

"He doesn't think that. Before he went to bed, he told me he thought you must care for him a great deal to do what you did this evening."

He nodded. "You know what's really sad?"

She shook her head, a hundred answers springing to her mind, certain not one of them was what he was looking for.

"I love books. I used to sit in a chair and just turn the pages, looking at all the words I couldn't read, impatiently waiting for the day when they'd take me on journeys I never even dreamed of. The day was a long time coming."

"That's why you're teaching your students to print."

"It probably wouldn't have made a difference in my case, but it sure didn't make it any easier to learn to read when the letters I was writing didn't look anything like the letters I was reading." He shifted his stance as though shifting his thoughts. "I, uh, I've been out to my thinking place. It's not the same anymore. Can't seem to do any real thinking." He gave her a crooked grin. "I just kept thinking about your toes."

She placed one bare foot on top of the other.

He reached into his pocket, pulled out an envelope, and

extended it toward her. She took it. "What's this?"

"Money for passage back East for you and Jimmy. We owe it to you for taking your teaching position. Don't know why I didn't think to give it to you before except sometimes, I'm . . . slow-witted."

She crushed the envelope to her chest; he crushed the hat in his hand.

"Meredith, I want you to know that I've enjoyed your company these past weeks. I wish things had worked out differently, but I think if you keep smiling like you've been lately, and if you take the ribbon out of your hair once in a while, you'll find another man who'd like to spend the rest of his life with you and give you the family you want."

He placed the battered hat on his head at a lopsided angle, which made him appear endearingly vulnerable. "Sorry it couldn't have been me. Sorry I took up your time when someone else could have been courting you. You take care now."

"I will."

"And have Jimmy write me from time to time."

"I will."

He mounted Pegasus, then drew the horse near the porch. "Bye, Red."

Watching them gallop into the night, she no longer thought they could fly.

Chapter Eighteen

"Are you ready?" Meredith asked.

Dressed in his Sunday best, Jimmy nodded. "Yes, ma'am."

Meredith met Sheriff Sampson's gaze. "We're ready."

"Well, then, little lady, just sign here on this piece of paper, and Jimmy Stellar will legally become your son."

Smiling, Meredith squeezed Jimmy's hand, then picked up the pen and dipped it in the inkwell. In the distance she heard a horse whinny. She walked to the window of the sheriff's office and saw Lee standing beside Pegasus in front of the mercantile. With his hat in his hand, he stared at the boardinghouse. She touched her fingers to the glass as though that would enable her to touch him as she should have last night, as she'd wanted to. Then he turned and walked into the mercantile.

Her hand shook as she looked at Jimmy who was looking at her, waiting. She had a feeling he wasn't waiting for her to sign the papers. The pen slipped from her fingers.

"I think I love him, Jimmy," she whispered.

He smiled. "Yes, ma'am. I think I love him, too."

She grabbed his hand and rushed out of the sheriff's office.

"You planning on reading all them books?" Hank asked.

Lee shifted the stack of books in his arms. "Nope, I'm gonna put them on a shelf in my classroom so the children can take them home one at a time to read. Let me know when my next order arrives, will you?"

"Sure thing."

Lee walked toward the door. Suddenly Meredith burst through. She rammed into him, bounced off, and landed on her backside. The books tumbled out of his arms and scattered over her and the floor.

Kneeling, he began picking the books off her. "Good Lord, Meredith, you sure enjoy watching books sail through the air, don't you? Are you all right?"

She braced her palms on either side of his handsome face. "Marry us."

The books he'd gathered fell to the floor. "What?"

"Marry me and Jimmy." She shook her head. "Or marry me and be a father to Jimmy."

He sat on the floor and cradled her cheek with his palm, a deep sadness filling his eyes. "Ah, Meredith."

"I don't care if reading comes hard for you, I truly don't."

"It's more than that."

The enthusiasm fell from her face. "Is it because I'm plain?" she asked quietly.

Gently he stroked her cheek with his thumb. "You could never be plain in my eyes, Meredith."

He looked past her, into the dusty street that was visible beyond the open door. Meredith didn't know if he wanted to bolt, or if he was trying to find the words to explain what he found lacking in her person. She removed her hands from his cheeks, ignored the stinging behind her eyes, and folded her hands in her lap. "It's all right. I understand."

His gaze came back to hers. "No, Red, you don't. You've been right from the beginning. I've got no business teaching, but the true reason is far worse than any you've ever given me." He took a deep breath. "I never graduated from school."

Her eyes began to blink.

"I was seventeen the last time I took the all-day comprehensive exam. When the teacher told me I didn't pass, I walked out of the classroom and I didn't go back. I told myself I kept failing because I didn't go to school all year. I helped Pa during roundup and sorting time. I drove the cattle to Abilene, Kansas, but so did C.J. He passed the exam when he was fourteen. Eventually, I had to face the truth. I just wasn't smart enough."

Lee couldn't stand the defeat rolling across her face, claiming victory over her heart, or the way her fluttering eyelashes caused the tears to splash onto the lenses of her spectacles. He drew her against his chest and bent his head so his lips were close to her ear. "I'm so sorry, Red," he said in a strangled voice, trying to hold his own tears at bay.

She sniffed. "I don't care. I don't care if you can't read. I don't care if you never passed the exam. I wouldn't care if you'd never even gone to school, if you used 'ain't' instead of 'isn't.' "

She lifted her head away from his chest and held his gaze. "You can read constellations when all I can see is stars; you teach children how to enjoy learning when all I do is teach them how letters form words and words make sentences to weave stories. I can read fast and well, but you bring the books to life. I think we complement each other."

"I'm always giving you compliments, but marriage is more than that."

She gave him a quivering smile. "I meant I think we go well together. My strengths outbalance your weaknesses; your strengths override the weaknesses I have." She lowered her gaze and studied her clasped hands. "And I love you dearly."

He touched his finger beneath her chin and lifted her gaze to his. He was wearing the tender smile she loved.

"Say that again."

"I love you. I love your smiles. I love that you care enough about the children to teach them more than reading, writing, and ciphering. I love that you have the strength to reveal your weakness when it matters the most. Last night, you gave Jimmy everything, knowing it would leave nothing for you."

He wiped the tears trailing down her cheeks. "I hate the way your spectacles make your tears look so damn big."

"Then you'd be wise to marry me. Otherwise, I promise to spend the rest of my life with tears in my eyes, and I'll run around town searching you out just so you can see them."

"So will you marry us, Mr. Daltry?" Jimmy asked.

Lee gazed into the beaming face of youth. "Reckon I have to. I've seen the woman's toes."

Meredith gasped, and Lee effectively cut off her planned tirade with a kiss.

A week later, Lee drew the horse and buggy to a halt, shifted his body, took Meredith into his arms, and kissed her the way he'd wanted to kiss her when the circuit preacher had pronounced them man and wife. Beneath the roof of the gazebo, with his family looking on, he'd kissed her tentatively, and she'd responded shyly.

Now, he kissed her like a man starved for the taste of

her. Which he was. He'd seen her little since she'd proposed. He welcomed her back into his life, sweeping his tongue along the velvet cavern of her mouth, retreating so she could explore his mouth. He groaned. Lord, he loved it when she came to him.

Drawing back, he cradled her face between his hands. "We made a mistake, Meredith."

Doubt surfaced in her eyes, and he smiled warmly. "We should have gotten married in town so everyone could have appreciated what a beautiful bride you are."

Her cheeks flared a brilliant hue, and she lowered her lashes. "I liked the wedding we had with just your family around us." She lifted her gaze. "I've never been surrounded by family before, and I was afraid I'd lose them in the crowd."

He chuckled. "My family's kinda hard to lose." His face grew serious, and he caressed her cheeks with the callused pads of his thumbs. "I've got nothing against the good people of Paradise Plains, but you know getting married the way we did—so fast, at my house with only my family there—most are gonna think I've already given you a baby."

He didn't think it was possible for her cheeks to burn any redder, but they did. Her eyes began blinking. He smiled tenderly. "If you want to hold off a month or so on having a wedding night, I'll understand."

She dropped her gaze to her gloved hands folded so primly in her lap. "But we got married quickly so Jimmy's adoption papers would reflect both our names, and he'd have a sense of belonging to a mother and a father. Then we left him with your family so we'd be alone tonight."

"I know. I'll still kiss and hold you, but I don't want gossip circling around you."

Slowly she tugged off a glove and laid it over her lap. Then she removed the other one and placed it neatly on top of its mate. She pressed her palms on either side of his face, threading her fingers through the curling hair at his temples, then settled her gaze on his. "Every night, I dream about touching you." Her fingers started to tremble. "I dream about touching more than your face. I don't want to wait. This evening, I want to be your wife in every way, and I want to give you children as soon as I can, even if it causes a scandal."

He grinned broadly. "I sure am glad to hear you say that. Pa told me I needed to be considerate of your feelings on this matter and not cause tongues to wag if it wasn't what you wanted."

Meredith smiled. "Your grandmother told me not to worry about wagging tongues. She said she could stop them with a look."

Laughing, Lee draped his arm around her, drawing her into the crook of his shoulder. "Yeah, I bet she could at that. Well, then, Mrs. Daltry, let's make this marriage official." He flicked the reins, and the buggy lurched forward.

"Where are we going?" she asked.

"To our thinking place."

Although Meredith was married to a rancher, a cowboy, a man accustomed to sleeping beneath the stars, she hadn't expected him to want to spend his wedding night outside where every creature, large and small, could gape at the newly wedded couple.

But she loved him too much to disappoint him. If he wanted to camp out at his thinking place, she'd accommodate him. It wasn't how she had envisioned her wedding night, but she was determined not to let her distress surface.

She'd seen so little of Lee or Jimmy during the week. As soon as school let out, they headed for the Daltry Ranch. Each time she invited them to come by the boardinghouse and have supper first, they refused. She hid her disappointment because she realized they were rapidly becoming father and son, building a bond stronger than a little slip of paper ever could. She didn't resent the time they spent together—she only wished it included her. Even though Lee's mother and sisters had kept her occupied making the wedding arrangements, she'd missed Lee and Jimmy terribly.

A familiar clearing came into view, and Meredith heard the rushing river, the tranquillity easing through her soul.

"Wait there," Lee said as he halted the buggy and climbed out.

Lifting her into his arms, he carried her to the river and stopped at the muddy bank. "You told me once that you liked this place. Did you mean it?"

"I think it's my favorite place in the whole world."

"You know after I brought you here, it was never the same for me. I came back a time or two, but it always felt empty. This evening, with you in my arms, it feels right again."

"Is that why you want to spend our wedding night here?"

"This has always been a special place for me. I want it to be a special place for us."

She swallowed her uncertainty about making love with little more than a canopy of leaves serving as a shelter. "We will make it special."

"Do you know that I've never heard you say the word home? You lived in an orphanage, you lived in Mrs. Bennett's boardinghouse, but I've never heard you say you were going home. I want to give you a home, Meredith. I want us to spend our wedding night here because this is where we'll make our home. Our children will play by the riverbank. We'll grow old skipping rocks, dangling our feet in the river, and watching the water flow by."

"You're going to build a house here?"

He smiled tenderly. "Already have."

He turned away from the river, and Meredith saw a small white clapboard house peering at her through the trees.

"Me and Jimmy built it this week with a lot of help from Pa, C.J., Atlas, and the ranch hands. That's why we couldn't eat supper with you. Hurt like the devil to see the disappointment in your eyes every time we said no, but I promise I'll make it up to you."

Wrapping her arms around his neck, she buried her face against his shoulder. "Oh, Lee." She was powerless to stop the tears trailing down her cheeks.

"Just tell me when you want to go home," he said quietly.

She lifted her head from his shoulder, cupped his face between her hands, and kissed him. Gratitude, love, and appreciation swelled from her heart and carried over into her kiss. She'd never been so bold in her kisses, had never wanted to give anything as badly as she wanted to give him reassurance that his actions were truly appreciated. She drew back, wanting to become lost in his eyes, but finding she was lost in her own tears. She loosened her hold on him and swiped her tears away before smiling. "I want to go home."

He carried her over the ground where their children would play and stepped onto the porch.

"We can clear trees away if you want a garden. We can make all sorts of changes. We just built this house because it was simple and quick, but Pa will change it so it's whatever you want it to be."

Bending his knees so he could reach the handle, he pushed open the door to reveal a bare living area with a stone hearth at the far end. "You can order the furniture you want this week. I brought the furniture from my bedroom at home so we wouldn't have to sleep on the floor tonight." His blue eyes darkened. "Kiss me, Meredith."

She pressed her mouth to his, totally unprepared for the

power of the kiss, filled with passion and promises, he gave her in return. She felt physically weak, emotionally strong. She tightened her hold on him as he stepped over the threshold of their home.

"I love you, Red. Welcome home."

While Lee tended the horse, Meredith folded down the quilt on their bed. Their bedroom was on one side of the house, Jimmy's was on the other. In a few days, they'd bring Jimmy home and truly become a family, but for now, she and Lee needed time alone to become man and wife.

She ran her hand along the sheets that covered the mattress where Lee had slept as a boy, had slept as a man. Where tonight, he would sleep as a husband. She could smell his unique scent ingrained in the mattress and pillows. She wondered how her presence would alter that scent.

She walked around the room, touching his oak dresser, his wardrobe, things that had belonged to him, and now belonged to them.

Stopping before the cheval mirror, she could hardly believe her eyes. The ivory lace of her wedding gown brought out the highlights of her hair. She'd left it loose, to drape over one shoulder. Lightly she ran her fingers over her hair. She hardly looked like herself. She thought if she removed her spectacles so her eyes didn't look so large, she might almost look pretty.

Shifting her gaze, she saw Lee's reflection in the mirror as he stood in the doorway. He closed the door, shrugged out of his brown jacket, and tossed it onto a nearby chair without taking his gaze off hers in the mirror. He removed his tie and his vest and loosened the buttons around his throat. He walked to the bedside table and lowered the flame in the lamp. "Come here, Red."

Taking a quaking breath, she clasped her hands to still their trembling and walked stiffly to him. Her gaze darted to the bed, then settled on his blue eyes. If she never moved her gaze from his, she thought she might be able to survive the night.

"Nervous?" he asked.

She nodded briskly, her eyes blinking.

"Me, too."

"Why are you nervous?"

"Never slept with a schoolmarm before."

"Oh, Lee." She laughed nervously and pressed her forehead against his chest.

He wrapped his arms around her. "It's gonna be better than blackberries. I promise."

She listened to the steady pounding of his heart, felt the warmth of his flesh beneath his shirt, inhaled the scent of bay rum, mingled with leather. "I don't know what to do." she whispered hoarsely.

"Dear Lord, Meredith, don't tell me no man has ever made love to you before?"

She snapped her head back and met his laughing gaze. He knew good and well no man had ever before made love to her. "Are you going to tease me all night?"

His eyes darkened as his grin grew serious. "No, I'm gonna make love to you all night."

He lowered his mouth to hers, and she learned the man had yet another kind of kiss, different from any he'd given her before. This kiss touched her deeply, drew her up on her toes, and caused her arms to circle his neck so she wouldn't melt to the floor. Even when he moved his mouth away from hers, she knew the kiss hadn't ended, that it was just beginning.

Taking one of her hands away from his neck, he kissed the tip of each finger before placing a kiss to the heart of her palm. "Unbutton my shirt," he said in a voice that sounded strangely unsteady.

She lowered her heels to the floor and her hands to his

chest, slipping a button through its opening. As her fingers freed his buttons, so he eased his shirt out of his trousers. The tiny crevice she created gave her a glimpse of the dense mat of light brown hair covering his chest. When her fingers finished their task, he rolled his shoulders and his shirt fell to the floor, revealing a chest that had been molded to perfection by years of working a ranch.

"You said you touched me in your dream. Where?" Lee asked.

She pressed her palm against the center of his chest. "Here." She placed her other hand beside it. "Here." She rolled her hands up his chest and over his shoulders. He shuddered. "Are you cold?" she asked.

"I'm anything but cold, Red."

He drew her against him, continuing the kiss he'd begun earlier. She became lost in the sensations, the eagerness of his mouth, the warmth of his flesh. She grazed her hands along his chest, relishing the soft hair curling over her fingers.

As he eased her gown away from her back and off her shoulders, she leaned into him, deepening the kiss, trying to divert her attention away from the realization that her gown was about to join his shirt on the floor.

She became absorbed in the kiss as her clothes melted away until her bared breasts were pressed against his chest, her bare thighs against his trousers.

Breaking away from the kiss, his breathing labored, he placed his hands on her arms and held her away from him. His eyes slowly roamed from the top of her head to the tips of her curling toes. "Dear Lord, but you're lovely," he said in a low, reverent voice.

Standing before him with nothing to shield his eyes from the sight of her body, she was surprised to find that she did feel lovely.

Kneeling, he buried his face within the lush valley between her breasts. He nudged the side of her breast. "No freckles. I get to kiss you where the sun doesn't."

As he rained light kisses over the soft, pliant mounds, she felt as though she were in the heavens, and he were a god delivering the stars at nightfall for earthly creatures to enjoy. His lips took a loving sojourn over her body, along her ribs, across her stomach, leaving tiny, twinkling diamonds of light in his wake. His mouth moved lower, nestling between her thighs, as his hands cupped her buttocks and held her steady.

Then he kissed her, a deep thorough kiss as though he were kissing her mouth. She felt as though she were a star shooting across the sky.

Her knees weakened, and she threaded her fingers through his thick hair. "Lee, this has to be improper."

"Nothing between us is improper, Meredith. You're my wife. Don't you like this?"

"I just wasn't expecting it."

He kissed the hollow at her hip. "Does it make you feel beautiful?"

Her fingers tightened. "It makes me feel . . . treasured."

He gave her an endearing grin. "I'll settle for that." His lips again traveled along her flesh as he rose to his feet and towered over her. "I want you to feel beautiful, Meredith. I want to take you to the heavens, put you alongside the constellations. When you leave my arms, I want you to know how lovely you are."

His mouth swooped down to capture hers. She felt the movements of his hands, his knuckles grazing her stomach, as he worked to unbutton his trousers.

Pressing her hands over his, she withdrew from the kiss. "No," she whispered.

Questioningly his eyes met hers. She took a shaking breath. "I want to do it."

Smiling tenderly, he trailed his fingers along her collarbone, leaving hers to finish the task his had begun. Slowly she worked the buttons through their holes until her task was completed.

"I want to see you," she whispered as she stepped back, surprised at her audacity, grateful he was her husband, knowing it wasn't improper to want to gaze upon his beautiful body as he'd gazed upon hers, wondering if someday she'd want to kiss him as intimately as he'd kissed her.

Slowly he peeled his trousers down, revealing muscle and flesh that looked as though it had been carved from granite. Meredith sank onto the bed, folding her hands in her lap. Her eyes slowly traveled the glorious, sculpted length of him. "You're gorgeous. More so than I even dreamed."

He knelt before her. "Then why do you look disappointed?"

"I'm not disappointed. It's just that you look like a Greek god, and I feel like a mortal woman."

Taking her hand, he pressed a kiss to her palm. "Mortal women are the best. Why do you think the gods always descended from Mount Olympus to sire their offspring? Perfection is boring." He held up his scarred palm. "I'm not perfect."

"You are to me." She took his hand and trailed kisses over his palm. "Am I very different from what you expected?"

"No, I imagined you just as you are every night while I slept. Only in my dreams, when I touched you, I couldn't feel the warmth of your flesh." He cradled her breast with his palm.

"I couldn't feel your softness." His fingers gently molded and reshaped the mound.

"I couldn't feel your excitement." He grazed his thumb over her erect nipple.

''I couldn't taste you.'' Settling his mouth over her breast, he suckled gently.

Meredith dropped her head back and moaned.

''And I couldn't hear your sounds of pleasure,'' he said as he gazed into the depths of her eyes. He reached for her spectacles, and she stilled his hands with her own.

''What are you doing?''

''I think you'll enjoy this more, be more comfortable if we take these off.''

''But you'll just be a blur.''

''You'll probably close your eyes anyway.''

She ran her hand along his chest. ''Then give me a smile to take with me.''

''I love you, Meredith.'' He bestowed upon her a smile, infinitely tender, a smile that reiterated what his lips had just spoken.

She closed her eyes, holding within her heart the memory of his smile. He removed her spectacles, and she heard him set them on the bedside table. Then, he slipped his arms beneath her knees and eased her onto the bed. She felt the bed dip beneath his weight as he joined her, laying his body next to hers.

''I love you,'' she whispered.

His groan was deep, feral as he kissed her with all the force that surrounded Mount Olympus. His scarred palm cradled her breast, kneading it gently. His tongue swirled around her nipple, teasing, taunting. She combed her fingers through his hair, pressing him closer, wanting him so close that there would no longer be a him and a her, but a them. He suckled the taut peak that had formed with his ministrations, and Meredith felt the sparks of desire shoot out from her core.

He kissed her forehead, kissed her toes, and every hill and valley in between. She'd never felt so cherished as his hands and mouth touched her in ways she imagined, touched her in ways she never knew existed. No matter where he touched her, her entire body responded.

He was the heavens, and she but a glimmer of light growing in intensity as the sensations rippled along her flesh, traveled deeply through her heart.

He eased up until she felt his breath fanning her neck. "Touch me, Red. Don't be afraid to touch me. Touch me the way you did in your dream."

She opened her eyes. He was little more than a shadow in the dim light, but her heart could see him as clearly as if he'd been surrounded by a halo of radiance. She pressed her palm against his chest. "My dreams were nothing like this, Lee. I didn't know about all this."

"Then, I'll teach you," he said in a husky voice as he took her hand in his and guided it slowly over his flesh.

She marveled at the different textures of his body. The callused palms, the smooth skin of his back, the soft hair covering his chest. She smiled at the way his muscles rippled and corded. She reveled in the throaty groans her actions caused. He moved his hand away from hers.

"Just keep exploring, Red, until you've explored all you want to explore. I've got my own exploring to do."

His mouth covered hers as his hand whispered across her stomach, carrying its secrets to the sensitive valley between her thighs. Gasping, she arched against him as his fingers revealed secrets like a flower slowly unfurling its petals.

Gently he eased her thighs apart. He trailed his mouth along her throat, nibbling at the sensitive spot below her ear. He took her lobe between his lips and tugged lightly. Then he pressed his mouth to her ear. "It may hurt, Meredith."

"I love you," she whispered.

He lifted himself above her. Her body welcomed him home with only the slightest of resistance. She felt the pressure, a sharp pain that disappeared almost as quickly as it surfaced, and then there was nothing but the sensation of Lee, filling her, rocking against her.

She wrapped her hand around his neck and brought his mouth down to hers, kissing him deeply as her body responded to his movements.

The world receded until there was nothing but the man she loved and the heavens beckoning to her.

His thrusts quickened, and she moaned, pressing her head against the pillow, exposing the slender column of her throat. He trailed his hot, moist mouth along her flesh. She felt the stars burning brightly through her body.

Then he carried her to the heavens, and she knew at last what it was to be a beautiful swan as her body exploded into a thousand tingling, brilliant stars.

Clinging to him, she felt his last powerful thrusts as his body arched over hers, taut as Cupid's bow. He shuddered and groaned, then stilled. His body spent, his love circled around her as he gently pressed his lips to the hollow at her throat.

"The reality is definitely better than the dreams," he said as he breathed deeply. "Are you all right?"

Smiling, she threaded her fingers through the mat of hair on his chest, feeling the rapid, steady pounding of his heart. "I felt like a constellation thrown into the heavens."

Easing off her, he sat on the edge of the bed. Meredith felt the loss, physically and emotionally. She wasn't ready to give up the feel of his body over hers.

He placed her spectacles on her nose and kissed her lightly on the mouth. Then he stood, and she watched the play of his muscles as he drew his trousers on.

"Where are you going?" she asked.

"You'll see." He pulled a quilt off the end of the bed and wrapped it around her.

"What are you doing?" she asked.

Smiling, he lifted her into his arms. "You'll see."

He carried her out of the house to the riverbank and sat beneath a tree, cradling her in his lap. "Do you see the stars, Meredith?"

The black velvet stretched out before them, minuscule diamonds sparkling.

"Yes."

"Not one shines more brightly in my eyes than you do. I've spent a lot of time lately trying to find one that I could name after you, but none of them do your beauty any justice. Do you know now how beautiful I find you?"

Tears gathering in her eyes, she nodded. "You made me feel beautiful, Lee."

He kissed her, deeply, thoroughly. The stars left the heavens and sparkled within her body. His hand slipped within the blanket and cradled her breast.

Toying with the curls at the nape of his neck, she pressed a kiss to his throat. He groaned, and she laughed as the vibrations tickled her lips. Then she slowly moved her hands and mouth over his chest as he had moved over hers earlier, using her mouth, her tongue, to tease and titillate.

"I think I just said good-bye to my thinking place," he said in a raspy voice.

"Oh?" She asked innocently as she felt a shudder run the length of his body.

"Yeah, I think this just became our loving place."

Gathering her into his arms, he stood and carried her home.

Epilogue

August 20, 1879

Beneath the covers, Meredith stretched lazily, unaccustomed to waking up without Lee's body draped over hers.

She eased out of bed, slipped into her wrapper, and padded across the hardwood floor to the walnut dresser Lee's father had given her as a belated wedding present. Kneeling, she pulled open the bottom drawer, pushed her undergarments aside, and removed a brown-wrapped parcel.

Lee's birthday present.

She didn't know why he was apprehensive about this day. A birthday was a time for celebration. Yet, he had held her last night as though he were afraid she'd leave him just because he was going to be a year older. Smiling, she wondered if she should tell him that the only thing that would change with the passage of time was her love for him. It would deepen with the years, never diminish.

Walking from her bedroom, she crossed the living room and peered in Jimmy's room. She felt her contentment and happiness increase at the sight of her son sprawled across his bed, sleeping deeply. She was grateful she hadn't conceived a child right after she and Lee were married. With Jimmy, they'd needed time to become a family.

Leaving the house, she strolled to the thick copse of trees by the riverbank. As dawn eased over the horizon, her husband sat on the tree branch and tossed rocks into the flowing water. The love she felt for him swelled within her heart.

When the final day of the school year arrived, he asked her to administer the comprehensive exams. Since he'd never passed the exam, he didn't feel qualified to sit in judgment of the students' efforts.

Six people arrived at eight o'clock that morning. Meredith sat behind the desk and watched as they labored over the written exam.

All but one stopped at noon to eat a meal.

By late afternoon, all but one had finished the exam.

When twilight began to filter in through the windows, she lit the lamp on her desk. Then she lit another lamp and placed it on the desk of the one person who remained.

Tunneling his fingers through his hair, he lifted his weary gaze to hers. "Shouldn't you be calling time?"

"Are you finished?" she asked.

"No."

"Then it's not time to quit, is it?"

"No other teacher gave me this much time before. I don't want any special favors, Mrs. Daltry, just because I'm your husband."

She smiled warmly. "You never had me for a teacher. I don't believe in closing the gate until the last horse has come home. I'll keep it open as long as it takes him to get where the other horses are."

She spun on her heel and walked back to the desk.

"I love you, Meredith."

She sat at the desk, opened a book, and couldn't read a

single word for the tears welling in her eyes. It was sometime later before he tentatively laid the test booklet before
her.

"You gonna grade it tonight?"

Apprehension was clearly etched in his features. She
knew the waiting would be torturous for him and tried to
keep her own worries from surfacing in her voice. "I might
as well. I've already graded the others."

Nodding, he stuffed his hands into his pockets and
rocked back on his heels. "Did Allie pass?"

"Yes, and Hal."

"I'm not surprised. They do so much together, it's only
fittin' they should graduate at the same time." He continued
to rock. "Jimmy'll pass next year."

"I feel like he will. He's made a lot of progress with his
reading. I'm glad you encouraged him to wait."

"I didn't want him to feel like he was a failure if he
didn't pass." He pointed toward his booklet. "Reckon
you'd best get to grading it if you're gonna do it tonight."

"As soon as you go outside."

"Why don't I just sit—"

"You've been inside this building for twelve hours, Lee.
Go breathe some fresh air, ride Pegasus, do something."

"What if I didn't pass?"

"What if you didn't? I won't stop loving you. I've told
you for months now there was no reason for you to sit for
the exam."

"But I wanted to," he said with stubborn determination.

She slapped her hands down on the desk. "And you did.
Now go outside so I can grade it."

Reluctantly he lumbered out of the building. Meredith
folded back the first page of the test, picked up her grading
pencil with shaking fingers, and started to mark the questions he'd answered wrong.

Much later, she stepped into the warm night air and took

a deep breath. Lee was pacing back and forth, wearing a trodden path between the schoolhouse and the oak tree.

She walked to him, wrapped her arms around him, lifted up on her toes, and kissed him. His hold on her tightened as he drew his mouth away from hers and pressed his forehead against the top of her head. "Damn, I didn't pass."

"Yes, you did."

He pulled back, his eyes searching hers in the darkness for the truth. "I did pass?"

With tears in her eyes, she nodded. "It wasn't a perfect score, but it was a passing score."

He released a victorious cry, picked her up, and twirled her around. "I did it, Meredith! After all these years, I finally did it!" His laughter filled the night air.

Now his diploma hung in a large wooden frame on the wall overlooking their bed.

She ambled through the dew-drenched grass and stepped onto the bough of the tree. With a smile, Lee extended his hand toward her and helped her settle onto the branch so her bare feet were dangling in the water.

"Morning, Sunshine," he said, just before he kissed her.

"You should have stayed in bed," she said in a seductive voice as he trailed his mouth along her throat. "I didn't know older men could kiss so well."

He chuckled low in his throat, his eyes taking on a deeper hue of blue. "I promise to make it up to you tonight."

Accepting his promise with a smile, she set the package on his lap. "Here."

"What's this?"

"Your birthday present."

He grinned. "I was afraid you wouldn't remember."

Her eyes widened. "How could I forget? It's been the only topic of conversation with your family for the past month. I'm beginning to think your family is obsessed with birthdays.''

"You don't know the half of it, Meredith.''

"And maybe I don't want to know." She nudged his arm. "Open your present.''

He pulled on the string holding the paper in place, then folded the paper back to reveal a dime novel. "*High Stakes Gambler*," he said as he trailed his fingers over the cover.

"I thought it might be fun reading for you. I hear Buck Buchanan is a very popular author.''

"Yeah, I remember C.J. talking about a book written by Buchanan that he'd read.''

"I know the gifts aren't supposed to be store bought.'' She lifted her shoulder slightly. "But I have no talent for making anything.''

Lee gave her a devilish grin. "You're very talented at making love.''

He wished the sun had risen higher in the sky so he could fully appreciate the redness accentuating her cheeks at this moment.

"Then maybe I'll give you a little homemade gift later tonight,'' she teased.

"I have a gift for you, too," he said as he reached into his pocket, pulled out a small box, and handed it to her.

"But it's not my birthday.''

"I know, but giving you a gift is like giving me a gift. Open it.''

She lifted the lid on the box and stared at the key nestled inside. She knew the key. Lee took it out of his pocket every night and set it on the bedside table.

"It's the key to the schoolhouse," she whispered. Her brow furrowing, she looked at him. "Why are you giving it to me?''

"Because in two weeks, Mrs. Daltry, you're gonna be teaching the children of Paradise Plains.''

Clutching the key in her hand, she pressed it to her breast. "You're sacrificing your teaching position for me?"

"It's no sacrifice, Meredith. From the beginning, I knew I'd only be teaching for a year."

"Why didn't you tell me that?"

Heaving a deep sigh, he gazed out over the river. "I wasn't allowed to tell anyone outside the family. If I told anyone, I'd forfeit the prize."

"The prize?"

He threaded his fingers through hers. "My grandmother likes to give unusual gifts."

"Yes, I know they have to be homemade."

He shook his head. "Nah, these are different. When a child in this family reaches his twentieth birthday, she assigns him a labor and gives him one year to complete it. At the end of that year, if he's met with success, she gives him a prize."

Meredith blinked her eyes. "And your labor?"

"To be the schoolmarm for one year."

Her eyes were blinking so fast he wondered if they stayed open long enough at any given second for her to see out of them.

"She took *my* position and gave it to you as a birthday present?"

"In a manner of speaking."

"Why?"

He shrugged. "She likened my labor to getting the golden apples from the Hesperides. I had to shoulder the responsibility of teaching in order to acquire the apples of wisdom, to learn I wasn't as dumb as I thought."

Her eyes finally stopped blinking, and she shook her head. "If we have any children at all, Hercules Daltry, we are having girls. I'm not going to let that grandmother of yours—"

"The girls are given a labor, too."

''Are you serious?''

''Yep. Come October, Grandma will announce Persy's labor.''

''Do you have any idea what it might be?''

''Nope.''

''And everyone accepts her challenge without knowing what the prize will be?''

''Yep, but I do know this. No matter what prize Grandma gives me tonight, it won't be nearly as valuable as the prize I've already received.''

''Which is what?''

''You,'' he whispered as his mouth claimed hers.

After sharing Lee's birthday dinner with the family, Meredith and Lee had slipped away to the family room for a few moments of privacy while everyone else helped Persy clear away the dishes. Nestled between Lee's thighs, Meredith squirmed on the hard wood of the window seat.

''Will you be still?'' he ordered.

''You keep putting your hands and mouth where you shouldn't, and your family might walk in at any minute. Besides, we need to sit properly now. I can't hear any more noise coming from the dining room.''

Wrapping his arms around her, he held her firmly against his chest. ''But I like it when we're sitting like this, and I'm certain this is what Pa had in mind when he designed the thing. We fit perfectly.'' He nibbled on her ear. ''Want to go fishing this evening?''

Meredith giggled, and Lee tightened his hold on her. He loved the sound of her joy.

''I think we already have a full agenda for the evening if you keep your promise and I keep mine. Maybe we should see if Jimmy wants to spend the night here.''

''I've already taken care of that.''

She placed her hands over his. "I always knew you were an intelligent man."

The door to the front parlor opened, and Venus swept into the room, wearing an emerald-green gown that accentuated her blond hair and fair features.

As Meredith scrambled over Lee's legs, she was grateful Venus had come into the room first because she knew her sister by marriage would be too preoccupied with positioning herself on the settee to notice what was happening in the window seat.

Meredith shoved Lee's legs off the bench seat before sitting primly on the edge of the seat, her hands folded neatly in her lap. She fought against Lee's tugs, but eventually succumbed to his charming smile and nestled against his side. If she'd just stop looking at the man, she'd win a few of these tugs-of-war, but the truth was, she didn't want to win.

Venus eased onto the settee, allowing her skirts to billow around her. Then she pouted. "Honestly, Lee, it's becomin' such a chore to come up with a gift you'll appreciate for your birthday. I swear, I'm beginnin' to think you've gone blind. You haven't even noticed my new gown, or the way I fixed my hair just for you."

"I'm sorry, Venus. I guess these days I only have eyes for Meredith, but that's as it should be, don't you think?"

Venus rearranged her skirts and sighed deeply. "I suppose."

Persy walked into the room. "I'm sorry it took us so long to clean up. I guess I shouldn't have prepared so many dishes."

"They were all wonderful, Persy," Lee assured her.

"Are you apprehensive about your upcoming birthday?" Meredith asked.

Persy smiled softly. "I try not to be. I don't really think my labor will be too earth-shattering."

"Any idea what it might be?"

"I only know what it won't be. It won't have anything to do with cooking because Grandma tends to pick something you're not skilled at doing. And it won't take me away from Paradise Plains. Otherwise, everyone around here would starve."

C.J. escorted Minerva into the room and eased her down into her padded rocking chair. Smiling, he glanced over at Meredith and winked, then leaned against the wall, his arms crossed over his chest as though he were serving as a sentinel. "Lee, I meant to ask you at dinner if you'd mind if I used Pegasus as stud for Grandma's white mare."

Lee grinned. "So you're living up to your namesake and doing some matchmaking, huh?"

C.J. returned the grin. "Only where horses are concerned."

The remaining members of the Daltry clan filed into the room and took their respective places. Jimmy crossed the room and dropped beside Meredith's feet. He'd filled out over the summer, eating Persy's meals and helping Lee work the range. Meredith ruffled his blond hair.

"It's hard to believe a year has passed," Minerva said as she rocked gently in her chair. "Tell me, Hercules, do you intend to extend your labor, to continue to teach the children of Paradise Plains?"

"No, ma'am, I gave Meredith the key to the schoolhouse this morning."

Minerva smiled. "Well, Meredith, it appears my grandson has given you back your dream."

"He fulfilled my dreams long before today," she said, squeezing Lee's hand. Against her will, she had developed an affection for Lee's grandmother and no longer resented the woman for taking her teaching position. In her wisdom, Minerva had known Lee needed the position more than Meredith did, in ways Meredith didn't. Meredith knew that regardless of what Lee had said this morning, regardless of what prize Minerva bestowed upon her grandson, his true reward hung on the wall above their bed.

Jimmy shifted around and stared at Lee. "You're not gonna be the schoolmarm anymore?"

"No, your mother's gonna be the teacher."

"What are you gonna be doing?"

Lee cleared his throat and shifted his backside on the hardwood bench. "I got something else planned."

"What?" Jimmy asked.

"I got some studying to do."

"How come you're studying if you're done with school?"

Lee looked at Meredith. "I'm figuring on getting a teaching certificate."

He had expected her to start blinking her eyes. Instead, she smiled. "And where are you going to teach?"

"I figured to teach at least some of the time with you. I think it's crazy for one teacher to try and teach twenty students who all know different things. I figure you can take the fast learners, and I'll take the slow."

She quirked a brow. "You honestly think my students are going to sit in my classroom and pay attention while your students are out roping cows?"

He smiled. "Your students can join us for special lessons."

"We'll discuss this later after you get your certificate."

"What if I don't earn it?"

She squeezed his hand. "Then we'll work something else out because I think you're right. More than one teacher is needed in a schoolroom."

The love reflected in her eyes was almost enough to make Lee forget every member of his family was sitting in that room. It was certainly enough to make him regret that every member of his family was sitting in the room. Where was their loving place when they needed it? Too dadgum far away. He stood, tugging on Meredith's hand. "Well, we're gonna head on home now."

"Lee, don't you even care what your prize is?" Allie asked incredulously.

Lee dropped onto the bench seat, slipped his arm around Meredith, and drew her against him. "Well, Allie, I thought I'd already gotten my prize." He kissed Meredith quickly on the lips. It wasn't satisfying, but it would have to do until they could get away. "I don't think Grandma can top Meredith or Jimmy."

Glancing over at his father who was sitting on the sofa, Lee smiled. "Funny how these work out, huh, Pa?"

Odie wrapped his massive arm around Jane's shoulder and nestled her against his side. "Yeah, they always seem to work out for the best somehow."

Smiling, Jane patted his thigh. "I will admit, Lee's labor had me a bit concerned, but now that he's successfully completed it, I find the suspense is killing me. What is his prize, Minerva?"

"I fear my prize will pale in comparison to the prizes he already feels he's received," Minerva said. She turned her wizened gray eyes to her eldest grandson. "But, I am extremely proud of all you have accomplished this year, Hercules. Your prize will be a library for Paradise Plains, built in your name and your honor."

Lee smiled. "Filled with books?"

Minerva returned his smile. "Filled with books."

"I'll help you organize the books, Lee," Atlas said. "If it's gonna be a building filled with books, you're gonna need something better than alphabetizing by title or author."

"I'd be obliged, Bub. I know there's nothing in this world you can't organize."

Lee stood and walked over to his grandmother. Kneeling,

he wrapped his arms around her. "Thanks, Grandma. I've always loved books."

She patted his back and whispered, "I know. Before you were old enough to read, you were always looking in books, pretending you could read. It just took me a while to figure out why you stopped taking books from my library. It fills my heart with joy to see you borrowing them again."

Lee returned to Meredith's side and slipped his arm around her shoulder. C.J. was the first to release a whoop and clap his hands. The others in the room followed his example with shrill whistles and applause.

When the cheering died down, Odie got up from the sofa and walked to a table. He slipped his spectacles onto his nose and unrolled some crackling parchment. "Come here, daughter, and I'll show you what I had in mind for the library."

Meredith waited for one of Lee's sisters to join his father, but none of them moved a muscle. Lee squeezed her shoulder. She glanced at him, and he tilted his head in his father's direction. She looked at Lee's father. With kind, deep blue eyes, he watched her. He smiled, and she felt as though he were a reflection of her husband years down the road.

"Come along, daughter. The library will honor your husband. I think you should have a say in how it looks."

For as long as she could remember, Meredith had yearned for someone to call her daughter. Still, she hadn't expected the endearment to flood her eyes with tears. She forced a quivering smile. "Yes, yes, I want to see what it'll look like."

Gripping Lee's hand, giving him no choice but to come with her, she walked to the table. Once there, Lee stepped behind her, wrapped his arms around her, and held her in his strong embrace.

"I thought something along the lines of the gazebo,"

Odie explained. "Something like a Greek temple, but larger and grander. And with walls, of course. What do you think?"

Meredith glanced around the room filled with family. She tilted her head back and met her husband's blue gaze. His hold tightened as he bestowed upon her the smile she loved most of all.

"I think," she said softly, "that I'm the one who received the prize."

If you enjoyed this book, take advantage of this special offer. Subscribe now and...

Get a Historical

No Obligation

If you enjoy reading the very best in historical romantic fiction...romances that set back the hands of time to those by-gone days with strong virile heros and passionate heroines ...then you'll want to subscribe to the True Value Historical Romance Home Subscription Service. Now that you have read one of the best historical romances around today, we're sure you'll want more of the same fiery passion, intimate romance and historical settings that set these books apart from all others.

Each month the editors of True Value select the four *very best* novels from America's leading publishers of romantic fiction. We have made arrangements for you to preview them in your home *Free* for 10 days. And with the first four books you

receive, we'll send you a FREE book as our introductory gift. No Obligation!

FREE HOME DELIVERY

We will send you the four best and newest historical romances as soon as they are published to preview FREE for 10 days (in many cases you may even get them before they arrive in the book stores). If for any reason you decide not to keep them, just return them and owe nothing. But if you like them as much as we think you will, you'll pay just $4.00 each and save at *least* $.50 each off the cover price. (Your savings are *guaranteed* to be at least $2.00 each month.) There is NO postage and handling—or other hidden charges. There are no minimum number of books to buy and you may cancel at any time.

FREE

Romance

(a $4.50 value)

Send in the Coupon Below

To get your FREE historical romance and start saving, fill out the coupon below and mail it today. As soon as we receive it we'll send you your FREE Book along with your first month's selections.
